The
Haunting
of Cambria

The Haunting of Cambria

Richard Taylor

TOR®

A TOM DOHERTY ASSOCIATES BOOK

NEW YORK

THE HAUNTING OF CAMBRIA

Copyright © 2007 by Richard Taylor

This book is printed on acid-free paper.

A Tor Book
Published by Tom Doherty Associates, LLC
175 Fifth Avenue
New York, NY 10010

www.tor.com

Tor® is a registered trademark of Tom Doherty Associates, LLC.

Library of Congress Cataloging-in-Publication Data

Taylor, Richard, 1949 Feb. 22–
    The haunting of Cambria / Richard Taylor.—1st ed.
        p. cm.
    "A Tom Doherty Associates Book."
    ISBN-13: 978-0-7653-1705-6
    ISBN-10: 0-7653-1705-2
    1. married people—Fiction. 2. Cambria (Calif.)—Fiction. 3. Bed and breakfast accommodations—Fiction. I. Title.
    PS3620.A9655H38 2007
    813'.54—dc22

                                                            2007008359

First Edition: July 2007

Printed in the United States of America

0   9   8   7   6   5   4   3   2   1

for M L T
...a long time coming, old man, but here

ACKNOWLEDGMENTS

FIRST, my thanks to Peter Miller, Lisa Silverman, and all of the folks at PMA Literary and Film Management for their hard work in placing this book, and to my editor at Tor, Natalia Aponte, who championed it.

I also want to express my appreciation for early readers/editors Bill Goergens, Keith Walker, Paula Pezzato, Lucy Moreno, Tom Wing, Leon Plato, Rory Aylward, Donna Player, Tom Merino, Cathy Dufty, Jim Sweeney, Mike Mortara, and Jason Cooper.

Also, I mustn't forget to thank fellow writers Pierce Gardner, Peter Delacorte, Miguel Tejada-Flores, Jay Bonansinga, and Christopher Moore for their assistance and sage advice, as well as former editor, and now agent, Stephen Hanselman.

And last, but never least, thank you Jackie Ward, my first draft editor, for helping me to reach the finish line. I could never have gotten there without you.

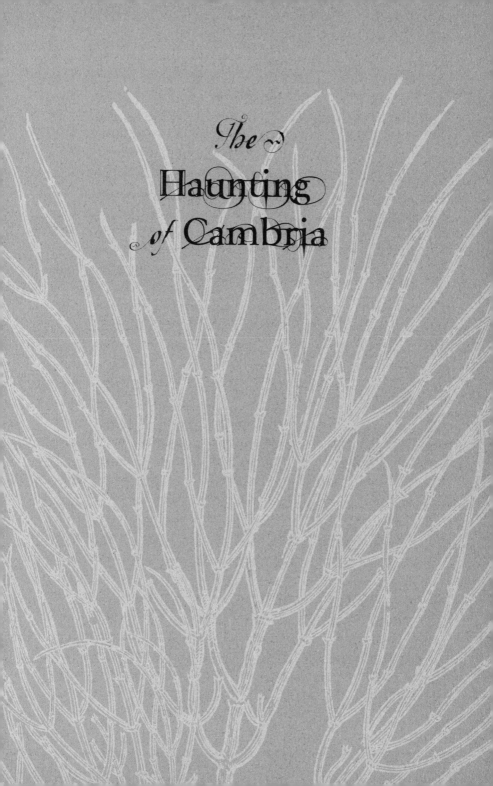

The
Haunting
of Cambria

one

LILY died the day we signed the escrow papers for the bed-and-breakfast.

It was late October and one of those wonderful Cambria days. Fog raced across the treetops and wrapped around their trunks like cloaks of mist. Yet it wasn't cold. The sun was glorious as it flickered from every facet of the sea. Cambria is special in this way, fog and sunshine sharing the day like loving siblings.

We were realizing Lily's dream of living in the tiny seaside California town. It wasn't my dream. Truth is, I had no dream, and stole hers like a pickpocket. I wanted to write, but about what I didn't know. Nonfiction, as it turned out. I wrote nonfiction because it was about something from outside me. Lily, on the other hand, had wanted to live in Cambria and become one of its quaint denizens since her parents brought her to the place when she was a child.

I took her to Moonstone Gardens for lunch after we left the escrow office. We ate salads and relished our dessert of lemon ice cream and raspberries. Lily talked of Monroe House, as our recent purchase was called, a ramshackle two-story Victorian dating from the turn of the century—the century before last. It had been run as a bed-and-breakfast before our entrance into its aura, and a badly managed one at that. It was located half a block off Burton Way in the East Village—Cambria is divided into villages, east and west, god knows why—and had failed because it was obscured by curio shops and restaurants. Lily had a plan to correct this deficiency, of course. Lily was filled with plans. It's the curse of those destined to die.

"We'll place a sign on Main Street," Lily said between spoonfuls of yellow ice cream and red raspberries. "Just like The Brambles. You know, an in-your-face kind of sign."

The Brambles was Cambria's most famous establishment, a four-star restaurant that early on, as Cambria began to transform itself from a sleepy little mining and logging community into a tourist attraction, had put the town on the map. The restaurant was a converted house, as many of Cambria's more established businesses were, with a sign at the corner of Main and Burton that left no doubt where it was located.

"They might not let you put a sign there," I suggested.

"They let The Brambles do it," Lily retorted.

"The Brambles is famous. Monroe House isn't."

"We'll make it famous!"

"Lily, I'm just saying, it might take a little convincing for us to be allowed to put up a sign like The Brambles's, that's all."

"Do you like the wallpaper in the lobby?" That was the way with Lily. Opposition was either overwhelmed or ignored, and changing the subject was a tactical maneuver. She knew I didn't like the wallpaper in the lobby—knew, in fact, that I didn't like wallpaper at all. It's anachronistic. The lobby wallpaper in Monroe House was a dark, dingy representation of flowers I couldn't identify. It had been put up by the previous owners recently, another miscalculation on the way to accumulative failure.

"It's awful," I responded.

"It has character."

"So do punch-drunk fighters," I said.

"Even so, I think we need to have wallpaper throughout the place."

"Sure. It's your hotel."

Technically, it was our place. Community property. But the money to purchase Monroe House came from Lily's trust fund, a small inheritance left by Lily's grandfather that barely covered the cost of the bed-and-breakfast. It was ours; it was hers.

"It's yours, too!" she protested.

"Fine. Will this town give me a variance for slot machines?"

"Wallpaper," she insisted.

"I demand veto power. Otherwise, you decorate the place by yourself."

"But something brighter."

Yes, something brighter. That was Lily. Something brighter.

We met in Los Angeles. I was born there thirty-four years ago. She had taken a job doing ad layouts at the magazine where I wrote and sometimes edited. She was a star the day she walked through the door, and unlike many beautiful women, and some not so beautiful, Lily had handled the knuckle-callused attempts of her male coworkers to get her into bed with grace and wit.

I was living with someone then and, ever the loyalist, didn't realize it was over until she arranged to have me walk in on her making nice with another guy. Had I been a drinking man, I would have dove into a bottle and not surfaced for a month. My way of handling hurt is to clam up, to withdraw inside and replace sentences with grunts and groans. Lily noticed this, somehow, as no one else had. She made an effort to cheer me up, a crusade that did not utilize her body or her femininity. She made me laugh. She was a great physical comedian. She had wit, as I mentioned earlier. And she was an empath who finally said, "Geez, Parker, who wants a woman who arranges for you to walk in on her with another man?"

At that moment I realized several things. One, everyone at the magazine knew about the incident, probably because Nancy wanted them to know about it, and she worked in distribution.

Two, the only one in the place with any guts had just put her professional relationship with me on the line. And three, really, who *would* want a woman who arranged to hurt you and break up with you at the same time? Had I been a drinking man, I would have ordered a Coke.

A week later I asked Lily out. She said no.

"Seeing someone?" I asked.

"Not you," she replied, not unkindly.

Two weeks later I said, "You know, I'm really not a bad guy, no matter what Nancy says."

"I don't know what Nancy says," Lily replied. "She's too busy rutting. But I still won't go out with you."

"Why not?"

"You're the only person at this magazine I like." Lily logic. There it was.

So the campaign began. Flowers failed early on. I tried humor. I left notes on her desk, e-mail in her computer mailbox, and grinned repeatedly and without masculine grace from across the room whenever I could. I stood by and watched her with disapproval as she briefly dated a guy from accounting. I made myself annoying, an achievement of little repute, true, but there it was.

"Is there some way I can make you desist?" she asked one day at the coffee hutch.

"I'm sure I don't know what you mean," retorted I.

"You're making me anxious."

"You mean, you have a nervous condition?"

"No, apparently I have you."

"Then let me buy you dinner."

"No. And you've used the last of the half-and-half."

I have an endearing trait. I don't give up. If it were not for my disarming smile and dismissing shrug, cops would have hauled me off long ago and placed me where I could annoy no one. But

I was always charming in these little pursuits, witty whenever wit struck like lightning and was available for theft.

I left notes wrapped in origami. Paper fish with a joke inside, birds with wit droppings. I clipped cartoons, drew several of my own, and sent them all to Lily's desk. Depictions of twosomes in awkward, sweet, cute, or just bawdy situations suggesting the bliss, clumsiness, adorability, or rapture that might await us.

"Okay," she said one day in May, and with an exasperation that tingled my heart, "I'll go out with you. But dutch, and for lunch only."

So we went to lunch. She chose the place. Plastic blinds and plastic tabletops. Paper napkins. Too much light and too little atmosphere. And the house wine was iced tea.

"I thought you liked me," I said, leading with my chin, another endearing trait.

"Lunch," she replied. "We're having it. So don't push it, buster."

Buster. What an adorable little word. Women used to use that word back when the world expected them to say things like, "Straighten up and fly right," or "Keep your hands to yourself." My hands were to myself; I had them inches away from hers.

"No," I said in uncharacteristic earnestness, "I mean it. I thought you liked me."

"I'm not staying in Los Angeles, Parker."

"Well hell, of course not," I said. "No one plans to stay in Los Angeles anymore. The Beach Boys left. So did The Mamas and the Papas, and aren't The Doors buried somewhere in Paris?"

"Jim Morrison."

"Same thing."

"I'm not staying here. I'm just sorting a few things out, and doing it here, and then I'm leaving."

"Yeah, so?"

"So I'm not getting involved with anyone who is staying in Los Angeles."

Ah, she liked me even more than I thought.

"Lily, what makes you think I want to stay in Los Angeles or give a rat's ass"— I said *rat's ass* because it made me sound more manly than *rodent's heinie*—"about staying in Los Angeles?"

"You have a career."

"I have a job."

"You have a condo."

"It's an apartment with pretension. It has a fireplace and a mortgage. It means nothing." For the briefest of moments I thought she might be jealous of the condo, as if to say, *I'm just an apartment kind of girl, while you, you're a condo man. We come from two different classes, Parker, and that would always stand between us.*

"In a few months I'm going to receive a small inheritance, Parker," she said earnestly, "and then I'm going to a small town to live. I'm going to open a bed-and-breakfast there. It's my dream. It's what I want to do. I couldn't expect someone to set aside their dreams for mine."

But of course at this point Lily didn't know I had no dreams, no ambitions, nothing really except the aforementioned condo that my previous significant other had insisted I buy. But of course none of this was meaningful because I wasn't asking Lily to marry me, or even to become my lover. (Well, okay, so maybe I might have asked that, if I thought I could get away with it.) No, I was just interested in the girl herself and wanted to spend time with her. I told her so.

"Well, you see, Parker, that's the problem. You know how you can tell sometimes how things will work out?" Actually, I didn't. I almost never saw how things were going to work out. "I can just tell that if you and I, if we . . . It's just better if things never get that far."

A beautiful woman telling a man that things should never get that far is like pouring gasoline on a three-alarm fire.

"Lily, I don't care about staying in this city, or any other city, really. I don't care about anything. Everything's a joke to me . . . except you. You are not a joke, so I guess I do care about you."

Lily blushed then, and so did I.

I don't remember much after that. At some point I took her to my condo—maybe this was hours later, or minutes, I forget—and she said to me, "I'm not that kind of girl." Lily was a fan of old movies, did I mention? Anyhow, she said it, and I replied, "Okay then, just what kind of girl are you?"

"I'm the sort of girl who must feel a deep commitment before she gives herself to a man."

"And do you feel that commitment?"

Lily thought about the answer for a time. Then she circled her arms around me, drew me to her, and caressed my mouth with her lips.

We became lovers. I won't go into the details, even though they're implanted in my mind like road markers. But I will say this, and it's not about sex, really, but about love. The door to the bedroom in the condo was at one end of the room, where I'd placed the bed. I had lain in it many times and seen various women walk down the hall from the bathroom. Some of the women wore clothes, some didn't. Some aroused me greatly, some didn't. They were all women who for some reason or another I had brought home and romanced. On one particular occasion I watched Lily. It was not the first, or the tenth, or maybe even the twentieth time she had walked down that hall toward me naked as a free-range animal.

I had grown to know every inch of her, every shape and line, every contour and quiver. Lily's eyebrows were sexier than the entire body of any woman I had ever known. I was mesmerized by the beauty of her, the absolute, exquisite—painful, even—beauty of her. On this occasion she was rubbing her tummy with her hand, looking down at something I couldn't see, a blemish too small to be identified by a man from ten feet away. Then she looked up and saw the expression on my face—it must have been something akin to awe—and she laughed. It wasn't an unkind laugh, triumphant or arrogant. She laughed out of joy, that someone would love her so much that the very sight of her would fill him with happiness and wonder. When she reached the bed, she playfully tousled my hair and slipped beneath the sheets. "You've got it bad, kid," she said.

Yes, I had it bad.

So did she.

WE kept our office romance a secret, at first. Then about ten minutes after we entered the place after our first tryst a buddy, Joe Peralta, said, "You're nailing Lily, am I right?" So it was obvious that we were in love, obvious too that Joe had better watch his mouth when he was talking about my girl. Later that night, at Lily's place (variety is the spice of life), Lily reported the same phenomenon. One of her girlfriends said, "You're getting some from Theo Parker." People can see things even when they're hidden.

With the secret out, we became brazen about it. We took lunches together, so to speak. We sneaked away for a brief rendezvous now and again. We spent every idle moment together, and so I learned something about Lily, and she me.

Her parents were dead, divorced when she was ten, father killed in an industrial accident when she was twelve, mother dead of leukemia when she was sixteen. There was a grandmother; someone Lily had mixed emotions about. Lily had been named for her, though Lily was assigned the diminutive early on, leaving the full name, Lillith, to the matron of the family. There was money. Lily didn't say how much, and I didn't care enough to ask. There had been boarding schools, Choate, Harvard, and then an arranged job where the luckless girl ran into me. Lily had seventeen cousins, all on her mother's side of the family; she was Lillith's only heir.

My story was simple. Father a machinist who retired to the same town where he worked for forty years, Harbor City, a bedroom community (parking lot is more accurate) of Los Angeles, where he drank himself to death in three years of aimless inactivity. Mother a home health worker (she cared for invalids and the aged) who made the money that sent me to private schools my entire life. I was not grateful for this until some years after her ruined, worn-out body was buried at Green Hills Memorial Park, a hundred yards and down the slope from her husband. My brother Danny was a lieutenant colonel—a "light colonel"—in the Army (I used to make the obvious jokes, "Colonel Light—less filling, fights harder!") and my sister Kate had four boys, three of them addicted to what are called in polite society controlled substances. Strangely, the fourth might yet be saved, because he's gay—he has outside interests.

If you see a disparity here between my background and Lily's, yes, we didn't share the same dimples. I made sure she understood this, even though my salary at the magazine was easily three times hers. (I was nearly a decade older, a decade farther through the workplace pipeline, and I occasionally went out and had a drink with the boss, who thought I was funny.) Lily didn't care that her private schools looked down on my private schools, that she graduated from Harvard with honors and I graduated from UCLA with validated parking, or that some people, her grandmother surely, would think I was a gold digger.

I was a gold digger. Lily was pure gold to me.

Lily cared about two things. One, me, Theo Parker. The second, a moment in time that had become a dream. Once, before her parents separated, when it seemed they would be in love forever, and a family forever, they took her on a vacation to a place called Cambria. They spent the weekend in a bed-and-breakfast, and it was a singular moment in her life, never duplicated, never approached again. They were happy in this tiny village along the magnificent Central California coast, where sea mist and sunshine dance about as if in love. Surely, it was the town that made their happiness possible, and its absence that destined each of them to regret.

As a young adult Lily returned to Cambria again and again. She stayed near where the old bed-and-breakfast had been (it was long since gone, the victim of a fire) and walked the streets of the simple village and its wondrous beach where once moonstones were culled. Her grandfather had established a small trust fund for her and it was enough, barely, for her to buy and restore an old bed-and-breakfast like the one she stayed in when she was a little girl. This was Lily's dream, and Lily was mine.

"What would you do there?" she asked me.

"I'll work as your counter man. Front!"

"There won't be any bellboys, Theo." I was Parker no more, but Theo, alas.

"Then I'll brew coffee in the morning. I'll make the pastry run. I'll cook—"

She laughed.

"No, I won't cook."

"Right, you won't cook."

"I'll change the linen. I'll trim the hedges. I'll do anything, just to be with you."

"It's a big step down, sweetheart. I'd be stealing you from your life of success—"

"Success? I'm successful?"

"Yes. Didn't you know?"

Come to think of it, it hadn't occurred to me, but I was successful. I owed money on a Mercedes. I had a condo on Wilshire

Boulevard near Westwood. I owed money on that, too. Yes, successful.

"I don't care about that," I told her. We were in bed together, naked and honest and without a thread to hide behind. "I'll give it all up and follow you."

"I can't let you do that," she told me gently, sweetly, concerned more for me than for herself. "I won't let you do that."

"Then you'll have to marry me," I said, "so I'll be management."

That night, as Lily lay sleeping across my body, her breath rushing like the sea to my neck and drawing back, I could think of no other future but in her arms. How fortunate I was to have found this woman. I knew that long after our bodies were no longer young or hers beautiful, long after every pulse but that of life had left us, we would still be together and I would still hear the sea in her breath and see the sky in her eyes.

Fools. We are all fools.

WHEN Lily turned twenty-five she inherited seven hundred thousand dollars, enough to buy Monroe House from a bank and to set about converting it into the bed and breakfast of her dreams. We were married on the drive north out of Los Angeles. I had placed the condo on the market, traded the Mercedes in for a swift little Mazda Miata and no debt. Escrow was scheduled to close that very day. Lily was delirious with happiness. She wore shorts and a sweater, and I the same, male version. We were leaving the corporate world behind.

After signing the escrow papers, I took her for lunch to Moonstone Gardens, a hidden little bistro on the Coast Highway at the northern tip of Cambria with a vast and locally famous view of the Pacific. We sat in the gardens themselves, not upstairs where the jazz combo played at night, and enjoyed the mist as it swirled past us, first at treetop level, and then lower, racing past our table. The fog was getting thicker.

"Let's take a run up into Big Sur," Lily suggested.

"Maybe as far as the Piedras Blancas lighthouse," I agreed. We had just driven 250 miles, gotten married, signed contracts ad nauseam, and eaten a meal with a bottle of wine. And we had reservations at an inn on Moonstone Beach where I hoped for Lily and sleep.

We drove north, past Mr. Hearst's little castle. The road was two lanes, one north, one south, and danced around dunes and bluffs. The fog grew thicker, became a shawl thrown across everything. Lily loosened her seatbelt and put her feet up on the dash.

"Put your seatbelt back on," I told her, even as I looked at her lovely legs.

I never saw the SUV coming the opposite way as it drifted across the center line and slammed into the Miata, killing Lily and sending me into a six-week coma.

two

"You killed my granddaughter," Lillith said to me when I woke up. It was not the first time I had awakened since the accident, nor was she the first person I saw since Lily was cast out of the world from a vehicle whose steering wheel was in my hands. But it might have been. I drifted on a sea of drugs, slipping across an unknown dateline almost as lost as when I was in a coma.

Lillith was in her late sixties, and there was an uneasy resemblance between the woman who remained, a decaying sculpture of a person, and the Lily I remembered. The same eyes. The same lips. Lillith had inherited the rest of her features from other ancestors, cheeks and brow, the disturbing set of her chin, the shape of her head. She looked down at my broken body as if the accident had not done enough. I should have been killed. I was not in disagreement with her.

"Mea culpa," I said after a moment, surprised at how broken and hoarse my voice sounded.

"What? I didn't hear you," Lillith replied.

"I said yes, I killed your granddaughter and I deserve to die."

Well, there, I'd said it. We were in agreement. There was nothing more to say. Or do. Unless of course, she had secreted some instrument of murder into the hospital hidden in her handbag and was prepared to use it now. I hoped for it. I had killed Lily. Her body had been torn nearly in half while my eyes were on her legs and not the road. Oh, the official report said the driver of the SUV had fallen asleep and his vehicle crossed the highway and struck the Miata head on. I was not at fault. But that was just official jargon. Lily was dead, and I killed her.

Lillith stared at me for a long while. We had finally agreed on something. I had killed her granddaugher, and I deserved to die. She had disliked me from the first moment we met, politicked with Lily to drop me like the blue collar scum I was. When that failed, she withdrew her affection from Lily and disinherited her. Again, there was a lot of money at stake, and again, I never asked how much because I didn't care.

"You'll never get a dime of her money," Lillith said.

"Hire someone to kill me," I said in my raspy voice. "Better yet, do it yourself."

"Fuck you," Lillith said, probably the first time she had ever used that word in her life, and maybe the last. She pivoted and left then. She would hire no one to kill me. Nor would she use a gun or a knife or a garrote to do the deed herself because deep down, far below knowledge of etiquette and form, Lillith knew I loved Lily more than life and leaving me in the world without her was far more sadistic than murder. And for me, far more painful.

I won't go into detail about what happened to my body. Suffice to say, when the SUV hit the left front of the Miata it made the little convertible spin. The SUV's second strike killed Lily, and later the SUV's rear tires rolled across her already dying body, which had been thrown from the car. I, however, was strapped in and protected initially by an airbag that saved my neck from being broken. Six weeks later I awoke in a hospital in San Luis Obispo, in traction, unable to see out of one eye. Later I discovered that I was blind in that eye only temporarily owing to a recent operation to reattach a retina. My hair was growing back in—they'd had to shave my head for the initial cranial procedure. I had double vision for a while, a not unusual response to eyes not being in sync for some weeks, and the headaches continue periodically to this day. When I finally stood up for the first time, the doctors discovered that my left leg was an inch shorter than my right.

I couldn't walk, of course. Really, I didn't want to. I wanted to die.

My sister Kate made the trek up from Torrance five times, over as many weeks, twice bringing several of the drug addicts with her. It was duty. I cried, and she was embarrassed because no one in my family had ever seen me cry before. One of my nephews smiled for an instant. I don't blame him.

Several of my friends from the office visited once, and one twice, and my ex-girlfriend, too, so she might spread the word of my ruin to her pals, no doubt. The truth was, friends and faux friends alike weren't very interesting to me. I wasn't amused by the happenings back at the magazine, as I had left it to be with the woman I loved, and now she was gone. And so on.

Most of the time I stared out of the window in my room. There was an artificial lake out there, several hundred breast-strokes across, and in my mind I dove deep into it, so deep sunlight was lost to me and I was swimming near the center of the earth, swimming away from what I'd done.

And Lily, damn it, Lily didn't visit me in my dreams or stand at the end of my bed and tell me it would be okay and that she had gone to a better place, or even join the cast of my nightmares. It was because I had robbed her of her life, taken the one dream she had ever possessed, and deprived her of it. I tried to think of her as I'd known her, a beautiful young woman of twenty-five whose bed I'd shared and whose dreams I'd stolen because I had none of my own.

Four weeks after I came out of the coma I was transferred to a rehab facility in Santa Barbara. Once there, no one came into my room and said, "Get out of that bed, mister. You're going to rehab!" No. Two guys whose names I never bothered to learn came each day and took me to a gym where two women, again whose names I never bothered to learn, made me do things that caused my body to function again. Not quite as it had. No, I was never to be the graceful Theo Parker of my past. I was given a cane. It didn't have a silver wolf 's-head grip or solid oak staff beneath it, but it did support my weight on one side. I began to walk. A woman in a white pantsuit gave me a schedule and came in each day to remind me to meet it, so I walked.

An attorney threatened to sue the insurance company of the dead SUV driver—he had worn no seatbelt, and when the airbag blew he was bulleting across the cab heading for the passenger widow, which he pierced with uncanny precision. Against my attorney's advice I accepted the insurance company's offer, a sum near to what Lily inherited the day I killed her. I really didn't care.

A week or so before they released me, I met with an outpatient counselor who wanted to make sure I had someone at home to keep an eye on me. I lied and said, "Of course. No problem. Sure-sure. Fine-fine."

And then one day they released me. The shorts and T-shirt I had worn the day of the accident were inappropriate now, and ruined as well. Somehow my baggage, and Lily's, which had been strapped to the rack on the trunk of the Miata, had been lost. An aid society gave me the essentials to wear, used slacks and a shirt and a jacket with a zipper that broke as I used it the first time. No one else talked to me about where I was to go. It was assumed I would go somewhere and do something, as human beings do, but I had no such plans.

The desk called a taxi for me after I stood in the receiving lobby for half an hour, unable to come to a resolution where I should go, or what I should do. I got into the taxi, and the driver asked, "Where to?"

Where to? What did I have? The condo had closed escrow and belonged to someone else now. Unexpectedly, I had not been offered my old job back at the magazine, not that I cared. They'd hired a replacement, a young woman just out of Yale, and she was sensational. What did I have?

"Home," I said. "Cambria. Do you know where Cambria is?"

As it turned out, he did. He took me to a train station. I took another taxi from San Luis Obispo into Cambria and Monroe House.

I HAD had four hundred and seventy some-odd dollars and change in my pocket when the accident happened, and the hospital had kept it in the hospital safe with my wallet and the escrow papers Lily and I had just signed. I paid the cab driver with a portion of it and stood in front of Monroe House for some moments, leaning on the bland plastic and aluminum cane. It was hard to see why this odd two-story structure had brought joy to Lily. It was impossible for me to see it.

During my six weeks of coma and four months of rehabilitation the court had appointed an attorney to represent the interests of Theo and Lily Parker, and those interests included Monroe House. Someone had been hired to look after the place, to make sure it was locked up, clean it or have it cleaned periodically. I knew the name of the woman who was hired for this task but couldn't recall it. I knew she had a telephone number and an address for somewhere in Cambria, although that information was elusive, too. Most importantly, I knew she had the key to the front door, which I did not.

So I sat on the steps, lowering myself to the uppermost slat with a grunt, and bridged my knees with the cane. It was after three in the afternoon by this time, the day cool and filled with fog. It didn't seem so romantic now, Cambria's famous fog. Oh Lily, what light you brought into the world!

I assessed Monroe House, twisting painfully (and with some satisfaction from the pain) to take it in. A porch embraced the structure on three sides. The front door was particularly wide and filled with cut glass and backed, from the inside, with a lace curtain. Overhead and out of my line of sight (but remembered quite well from that first day we visited the place together, some weeks before Lily's death), were gables, each window a view from a bedroom. Beyond the rooms was a hall, similar rooms on the back side (which actually had a better view, of a wooded creek), a staircase that descended to a parlor on one side, and a kitchen and dining room on the other. There were other rooms in the back that Lily thought she would make handicap accessible. All told, eight bedrooms, nine if the master suite was counted. We would have taken the master suite.

Originally, of course, Monroe House had been a private dwelling of only four bedrooms, a parlor on the first floor, and a study on the second. It had been expanded extensively by a succession of failing hoteliers.

I was prepared to sit there all day and all night, in truth prepared to sit and die a slow and justifiably painful death on the porch, but a young woman intervened. She came to the gate in the picket fence (added by the most recent failed owners, for sake of character) and was startled to find me sitting on the uppermost step.

"Oh!" she said, dropping the bicycle she was leading.

I said nothing in return because frankly, I didn't give a damn if the earth opened up and she fell into it, bicycle and all.

"I'm sorry, but this is private property," she said after a moment to compose herself. The old-fashioned swayback bicycle lay at her feet. Clearly she thought I was a wayward tourist, like so many who flock to the romantic little town, who had somehow wandered onto the front steps of Monroe House.

"I own it," I said, with less than convincing tone because in my mind it was Lily's house, and Lily's dream.

"You're Mr. Parker?"

"I'm Parker. You can forget the mister. Who are you?"

"Eleanor Glacy. I'm the court-appointed . . . uhm, caretaker."

Eleanor "Uhm" Glacy was a woman of possibly twenty-three, tall and plain and lean. Her chest had not even a blister of a figure—I remember once when I was ten, my mother said to a neighbor lady, "There goes poor Joanne Hart. God gave her nipples and little else!" My mother could have been speaking of Eleanor Glacy.

But, to be fair, Eleanor had sharp, intelligent eyes, rather pretty brown hair held back with barrettes, of all things, and a long, lean face that would grow prettier with age. No sagging. Her voice was her best feature. It had a pure, clear, harmonic female sound.

"You're the caretaker," I replied finally.

"Yes sir."

"I'm not a 'sir' either. I'm not your employer."

"It's your house, isn't it?"

"It's yours, if you want it. Although I guess I'll be staying the night. Is it in any shape for someone to spend the night?"

"Certainly." She lifted the bicycle by its handlebars. "It's fully outfitted," she said. "I've had a cleaning person out twice a week to dust and bring it up to standards. It's been empty a long while."

Just my kind of place.

"Caretaking. I thought that was your job."

"Actually I'm a property manager, Mr. Parker—"

"Just Parker."

"There are a lot of summer rentals in Cambria, seasonal rentals, really, and someone has to manage them, so . . . that's what I really do."

"Oh."

"When I'm not working at the bookstore."

She smiled self-deprecatingly, as if in truth she was none of these things, but merely a day laborer grabbing work catch as catch can.

"You have a bookstore, too?"

"Oh, no, I just work at . . . Tiller's Books, in the West Village. Part time. If you spend any time in Cambria, Mr. Parker—"

"Just Park—"

"Any time at all, Parker, you'll soon learn that everyone has two jobs, some three. It's the only way people can get by. Small economy, you see."

She leaned the bicycle against the picket fence, then offered her hand to help me from my perch on the top step. I looked at it and she self-consciously withdrew her hand.

"No, you don't understand," I told her. "I was waiting for two hands."

With both hands she pulled me to my feet and we entered Lily's dream.

It was dark and dank. Yes, dank. The absence of sunshine makes for moisture. Eleanor opened shades, invited sunshine in, but it resisted. There was a small hotel-like desk, the parlor where rolls and coffee were once served and which was converted into a dining room in the mornings, when the place was operating. I stood just inside the door as Eleanor did the things one does to make a place presentable.

There was that awful wallpaper with flowers from the planet Vulcan. I could just see Spock looking at them and growing wistful for his home planet, in a logical kind of way, of course.

"Cozy," I noted.

"It could be made cozy, with the right touch."

The touch of Lily's hand, cold now, I thought.

"You live in this town all your life?" I asked her.

"Moved here from Fresno last year."

"What do you know about Monroe House?"

"It hasn't been the most . . . successful of businesses," Eleanor told me with understatement. She stood behind the desk as if seeking a defensible position, I thought, or maybe she was just hiding herself. "Location is a factor," she continued. "Monroe House is off the main drag. Although that land over there, just beyond the side door, is part of the parcel and could be made into something . . . romantic. Put a gazebo there, possibly, plant a garden."

Those had been Lily's plans, too.

"The place smells," I said.

"That's just must. The windows haven't been opened in a long time."

I climbed the stairs to the second floor. Eleanor followed me, but at a distance and with a caution that told me she knew about the accident and Lily's death. Dear god, the whole mess had turned me into an old man.

I looked into each room. Victorian furniture. Lace curtains. Lovely. Awful.

And then the master bedroom, where Lily and I were to live our lives, our secret and truly intimate lives.

"What's this?" I asked, my voice suddenly hoarse.

Eleanor stepped around me and saw the garment. It was a negligee lain across the comforter of the bed as if in invitation, a promise of nights to come.

"Who put this here!" I screamed.

Eleanor didn't know.

It was Lily's negligee bought for our marriage night.

three

ELEANOR stepped around me. There was spittle on my lips, I felt it, and a throbbing in my brain that was twice as powerful as my recurring headaches. She found the two suitcases on the opposite side of the bed. I recognized them immediately. They were our suitcases, which I had secured to the back of the Miata with bungee cords moments before we left Los Angeles half a year ago. How had they found their way here?

Eleanor set them on the bed, beside the negligee, first Lily's bag, then mine. Someone had dusted them over the past months. There was the vestige of a bug whose fortune had been changed by the speeding Miata, possibly in Ventura before Lily and I stopped to be married, or before or after the crawl through Santa Barbara traffic.

How had they arrived here?

I closed my eyes and thought back six months. I was young and Lily was alive. We were having lunch at Moonstone Gardens. We were laughing, drinking the house wine, two just-married people who had also just become property owners. That was at Lily's insistence, too, that we should marry before Monroe House was bought, so that it would be our dream together, realized the same day.

How had these bags arrived here? Someone had removed them from the car, carried them up those stairs just outside this room, opened Lily's bag and removed her negligee. . . .

When we left Moonstone Gardens that day, had the bags

still been strapped to the car? I tried to recall, reached out to envision lovely Lily in her knit top and shorts, me in walking shorts and tennis shirt, arm-in-arm strolling down the tree-lined parking lot to our car. I hadn't looked, although it was in plain sight, the back of the two-seater convertible where our bags should have been.

No, I couldn't recall it. It was memory gone forever.

But I did remember that Lily had excused herself to the ladies' room while I basked in the misty sunshine. How much time passed between Lily's going and coming? Five minutes. Ten? Fifteen? Did men count the time women used in bath-rooms, for all the various mysterious reasons they retreated to them? Could she have driven the Miata to Monroe House, lugged the bags up the stairs, opened hers and laid out the neg-ligee as a gesture of her love for me and of her intentions for that night, and driven back to the Gardens unmissed? Had she cancelled our reservations for the inn on Moonstone Beach so we could sleep in our very own dream house that night?

"Maybe the highway patrol found the bags that day. . . ." Eleanor suggested dully.

"And laid out the negligee as a little joke?" I replied harshly.

"Oh," Eleanor said. "How stupid of me."

"Lily did this," I said.

"Your wife?"

My look told her just how stupid she was. Eleanor looked away.

"We had just been married. It was to be a surprise."

"Oh, dear god, how sad."

"God is not dear, Eleanor. God kills." But of course, it had been my hand on the steering wheel, my acquiescence to Lily's request to drive north, toward Big Sur, to the lighthouse at Piedras Blancas where the road snakes through the Garden of Eden. My fingerprints were on those bags, and Lily's, not God's.

"Take them!" I barked.

"What?"

"Take them! Now! Get them out of here!"

"And do what with them?"

"I don't care. Burn them! Give them away! Throw them down a ravine! But get these bags out of here! Now!"

Eleanor took both bags in hand and headed for the door.

"That, too!" I ordered. I meant the negligee. I didn't want to touch it. I didn't want to see it ever again.

Eleanor lowered the bags to the Persian carpet, reached past me and snatched Lily's negligee in one hand. As her fingers tightened around it, I saw Lily wearing it lying on the bed, laughing as my eyes took her in. Laughing in joy that I had it so bad for her that her body and her soul and her voice and her thoughts sent trills of yearning though me.

I half expected Eleanor to return once she'd dragged the two bags and Lily's garment to the first floor and out the door, but she didn't. After an hour I closed the door to the master suite and went downstairs, where I found the smallest room in the house and collapsed across its double bed. I was crying, I was surprised to discover, something I had not done in months.

I DON'T know how much time had passed when finally I woke up to find Eleanor Glacy sitting in a Victorian chair located at the foot of the bed, legs crossed, long skirt draped to her ankles, arms bisecting her flat bosom, staring at me.

"Go away," I mumbled.

"You're sleeping in my bed," she said.

I sat up on hearing that. Her bed?

"Mr. Parker," she began.

"Just Parker."

"Right, Parker, I want to show you some documents, just so you know that everything I've done is legal and correct."

There must have been some vestige of the old me left, because I made a joke. "I doubt you can document that."

"I mean regarding my residence in Monroe House."

"You live here?"

"For two months, yes. I've been paying rent. It also allows me to keep a close watch on the place, coordinate maintenance and repair, that sort of thing."

I held out my hand. She placed a sheath of documents there. I looked through them. With the court's authority the attorney it delegated had set up an account with the local bank. Into this account Eleanor Glacy had deposited a sum of four hundred dollars, two hundred for each month that she had occupied this, the smallest, least accommodating room of an otherwise empty bed-and-breakfast equipped with far more spacious and comfortable accommodations.

"How much does one of these rooms go for? For a night, I mean."

Eleanor flushed. "Well, if the facility were serving breakfast and the customary wine and cheese in the afternoon, and changed the sheets regularly, maybe . . . a hundred and fifty dollars a night. Maybe two hundred."

"And yet you find two hundred dollars a month sufficient?"

"I wash the sheets myself. I clean the room. I—"

"No one questioned the amount of rent money you were paying?"

"I'm the property manager, Mr. Parker—"

"Just Parker," I said.

"Oh, shut up! I'm the property manager and I determined the amount. I can compensate you for any shortfall. I'll have my bags packed and be moved out before . . . well, when I can find a place to move to."

"At two hundred dollars a month, you mean? Is there a place in Cambria you can rent for two hundred dollars a month?"

Eleanor flushed redder. Of course there wasn't. But I sensed that I—or more appropriately, Lily—had gotten her money's worth.

"Forget it," I said.

Eleanor noticed that I had drooled on her pillow while I slept.

"Let's call it even," I suggested.

"Let's not," Eleanor said, standing abruptly. "I can stay with friends until . . . well, until I find a place to rent."

I was startled when she stood up, and I jerked back reflexively, dropping the folder of paperwork. Eleanor instinctively knelt down and fanned all the papers into the folder. She quickly organized everything back the way it was originally, multiple documents on the bottom, quarter-page receipts at the top. I watched the back of her head as she worked, studied the neat part of her hair, marveled that anyone could be this young and this alone, here in Lily's house.

"Eleanor, please forgive me," I said with what sounded to me like real contrition. "I'm sure you're an honest person. I didn't take into account the other services your occupancy of Monroe House provided. Please accept my complete apology."

It's also true I didn't know where the bodies were buried yet, and I didn't want the one person who did to quit before she told me where they were. Okay, there it is, sometimes I'm a heel.

But then it hit me. A part of me cared. A part of me cared enough to apologize to a strange woman to keep her from quitting. Was I actually taking proprietary rights to Monroe House? I looked around the room, the tiny Victorian "cozy" box with godawful lace curtains and a wing chair right out of a Charles Laughton movie.

Other thoughts came to mind. Lily. Death. My hands on the wheel.

No.

"I'll stay," Eleanor reported.

I mumbled, "Uh-huh."

"Do you intend to open for business anytime soon?" she asked, apparently mollified.

"I have no plans," I replied. "Yet."

"Are you hungry?"

I was, in fact.

She had stocked the kitchen for her own use, and she made me a ham sandwich with a glass of milk, then watched me eat it from across a large table, her lean arms and elbows supporting her questioning face.

"Not too much mustard?"

"No."

"You know, Monroe House can't compete with the other bed-and-breakfasts in town. And certainly not with the inns out on Moonstone Beach. But with the right repairs and restorations, it could—"

"What are my chances of selling it?"

Eleanor twiddled her fingers on the tabletop, tied them together, pulled them apart. She was a nail-biter, I noted, fingernails chewed to the quick. The skin on her hands was rough and red.

"As is?" she asked.

"Without a nickel invested."

"None," she replied without having to think about it.

"What if I made the repairs," I suggested, "maybe replaced the wallpaper and the curtains?"

"Some of the furniture, too. It's recent, but it's heavy and grim."

"Okay," I said, "replace some of the furniture, too. Could I sell it then?"

Eleanor thought about it for a time, then asked, "How much have you invested already?"

I told her Lily had paid cash for the place six months before.

"Cash?" she asked, incredulous.

"What can I say? My late wife was a dreamer. She wanted to own it."

"How much?"

I told her.

Eleanor was so startled at the amount she shoved her chair back from the table, but she restrained herself from standing.

"Not good?" I asked.

"Not good. Even with all the repairs." She thought for a moment. "You could donate it to a charity at full sale value, but I'm not a tax person, so—"

"I'm screwed."

"Would you like another sandwich?" she asked as a token of consolation.

"No," I replied, "the smell of cooked bacon has turned my appetite."

But again, I surprised myself. By caring whether Monroe House fell into a sinkhole and was lost forever, taking with it every dollar I possessed.

Except I had the insurance money from the accident in some bank account or another. I had that, and Monroe House. And I apparently cared about something.

It startled Eleanor when I took the room opposite hers. It was identical to hers, mirrored, with another wing chair and another double bed. It was far from the master suite, where the expectations of our wedding night, Lily's and mine, haunted the place, and would me, forever.

"You can lock your door," I suggested to Eleanor.

"I can take care of myself," she replied after I explained to her that I couldn't stay on the second floor, and why.

I had no clothes to change into, but Eleanor found some

things left by previous guests. They included every manner of male clothing, all washed and stored away months or years before. I showered, decided against jockey shorts or underwear of any kind—wearing somebody else's underwear, washed or, for that matter, nuked, just didn't appeal to me—chose pajamas instead and crawled beneath the covers and comforter of the double bed. I turned off the faux Tiffany lamp on the bedside table and was surprised by the absolute darkness, both inside and outside. Cambria contributed little to the light pollution of the world. After a time my eyes adjusted, and I saw the chest of drawers across the room, the wing chair, the bedposts.

I heard Eleanor preparing for bed across the hall. Her bed squeaked as she slid into it—it was apparently not as quiet as mine—and I even heard the lamp snap off.

I wished for Lily to come to me, but she didn't, and soon sleep washed over me like a wave swallows a wayward ship.

It was three o'clock when I heard the noise.

four

I don't know that the noise awakened me. Possibly it did. Or possibly I was in a sleep cycle that beckoned my mind close to the surface of consciousness. But I did hear the second sound, and it was of Eleanor opening her door.

I had found a robe the previous evening to go along with my inherited pajamas. I slid this on in the dark, easily found my way to the door, and opened it. Before the door swung open I saw the yellow beam of Eleanor's flashlight sweep beneath the crack below it.

She turned toward me when I opened the door, startled only for an instant, then resumed her natural expression—a kind of indifferent stare—and looked where the flashlight beam took her.

"What is it?" I asked.

"You don't hear it?"

"Hear what?"

There was nothing but silence.

"Then maybe I'm going nuts after all," she said.

Then I heard it. It was the most baleful, awful wail I had ever heard in my life—not a cry, really, but something far worse, a noise akin to the sound of something dying, and not. Something indescribable.

"What is it?" I asked. The words caught in my throat, squeaked through my larynx like air through the mouth of a balloon.

She looked at me with an expression that told me what she

thought of the question, and me. I deserved it. I reached out for the light switch. I flipped it. Nothing.

"Where are the lights?"

"Out," Eleanor said.

"I thought there had to be a storm or something for the power to go out?"

"It's not the power," Eleanor replied evenly. "Whenever the sound comes, there are no lights. I don't know why."

The wail grew louder. I was overwhelmed with fear, irrational as fear is in the face of nothing.

"It's an animal, a hurt animal," I said.

"It's been hurt for the two months I've slept here, Mr. Parker."

No, not a hurt animal.

"God, it sounds awful, doesn't it?"

Eleanor nodded her head. Yes, it sounded awful.

"Where does it come from?"

"Everywhere. Nowhere."

"You're not saying it's a ghost, for chrissakes," I said.

"I'm not suggesting anything."

"Give me that!" I said, taking the flashlight from her hand. I thought twice about it, but led her out into the hall, then the foyer. The wail got no louder. I flipped a light switch. Nothing. Then another. Nothing. The lobby lights. Nothing. A lamp. No. The porch light. No response. Outside, the rare and distant lights of a sleeping small town could be seen. Obviously, Cambria still had power, the few streetlamps still glowed; mists still danced about them like ghosts in the sky.

I stepped back from the front door, releasing the lace curtain that I'd pulled aside to look out.

"How often does this happen?" I asked Eleanor.

"Not every night," she said softly. "Several times a week, though."

"For two months?"

"For the two months I've been here."

The wail echoed through the dark house once again, and I thought I recognized it. Oh God, please don't let me be right, I thought.

"Lily!" I shouted and bolted for the stairs.

"Parker, don't go up there!" Eleanor called. She followed me as quickly as she could, but I was pulled forward by a primal force, the thought that my Lily's spirit had been drawn to this damn house and wandered it, wailing her sorrow at having lost her dream, and her husband, to outrageous fate.

I reached the top of the landing as the wail bellowed again. I turned and made for the master suite, flashlight beam dancing in front of me like a crazy firefly. I turned the knob to the suite and allowed it to swing open.

It was as we had left it that afternoon, not a wrinkle in the bedspread, not a chair out of place, but cold, colder than the rest of the house by far, cold enough to make breath seem to be fog rushing from our mouths.

Eleanor stopped behind me, placed a hand on my shoulder so that each of us was sure the other was there, and real.

"It's not coming from in here," Eleanor said.

"No."

"But there is that other thing. It gets so cold in here, so . . . unusually cold."

"Lily . . ." I said. Who else could it be but Lily, so lost that she had returned to the one place on earth she loved?

"You don't know it's her," Eleanor said.

The lights came on downstairs.

"It's over now," Eleanor whispered. "For tonight."

I flipped the wall switch and electric light bathed the room. It was no longer cold. Or, at least, no colder than any other part of Monroe House.

🕊

I T was 3:40 a.m. Eleanor placed a kettle on the stove in the kitchen. I sat at one end of the table, too stunned to say anything. I still had her flashlight in my hand and rose to return it to her. It was then I noticed that Eleanor was wearing a nightgown. In the haste of the event she had forgotten to put on a robe. I could see through the nightgown, and I didn't want to see through the nightgown, so I removed my robe and placed it over her shoulders. "Here," I said, "you'll catch cold."

She misunderstood the gesture as an expression of caring and pulled the robe on with a thankful smile, cinching it closed around her.

"Tea or coffee?" she asked. Domestic girl, this Eleanor.

"Heroin," I replied.

"None in the sugar jar, I'm afraid. I do have some marijuana."

I thought she was kidding, but a quick look up at her expression proved otherwise.

"Eleanor, you are full of surprises. But no. Coffee for me. That'll be enough."

I was taking the whole thing well because I no longer believed it. While it was happening, while the house was dark for reasons not logical, and a wailing sound echoed that could never have originated in a living larynx, I believed the worst thing possible. Could Lily have returned from death to haunt this house?

"It seems as if it never happened," I said.

"I read once where the human mind can't accept what it thinks is impossible. Well, at least most can't. Fantastic events are dismissed moments after they happen because we're just not equipped to accept them."

"You believe we're haunted?"

"Yes."

"I think it's bad plumbing," I said.

"And the lights going out?"

"Bad wiring," I replied with male certainty.

"Bad plumbing and bad wiring, that's what we just experienced?"

I laughed. "Or a plot to drive the price down so Monroe House can be bought for a fraction of its real worth. Are you plotting against me, Eleanor?"

For a fraction of a second she took the question seriously, then set instant coffee before me with a clink. "Cream? Sugar?"

"And bourbon. Do we have any bourbon?"

" 'We' have no bourbon. 'I' have brandy."

"That'll do."

She found a bottle of brandy high up in a cupboard and set it before me. She took a tea bag from a tin, dropped it in steaming water and placed the cup beside mine, sitting in the chair beside me. Since this morning we had become friendly enough to sit beside one another.

"Why is this place called Monroe House, anyway?" I asked.

"The man who built it, James Monroe. No, not the president. This Monroe was a botanist who moved his family to Cambria in the late eighteen-hundreds and built this house. The estate was much bigger then, twelve acres." It was an acre parcel now with the house on one side.

"What happened to him?"

Eleanor shrugged. "I don't know. But I do know his family didn't live here long, because by 1905 Monroe House was a boardinghouse for the mining trade. Later it became a speakeasy, then a boardinghouse again, and then the first of many bed-and-breakfasts."

"Monroe House sounds pompous," I commented.

"It's your place, Parker. Call it what you will."

"Parker House," I suggested. "We could serve rolls."

"Not a bit pompous," she replied, sipping hot tea with a feminine slurp.

I assessed Eleanor Glacy, this female Ichabod Crane beside me whose clear gray eyes looked back at me with such honesty that I was disarmed. She smiled, understanding the moment, as women do, when men see them as they really are. I was still in love with Lily and mourning her, yes, certainly, probably forever, but it didn't keep me from assessing women, even unattractive ones.

"Eleanor," I said after a moment, rushing in my mind to find something to ask, "you stayed here two months with that . . . occurrence happening almost every night? Why didn't you run away?"

"The rent was cheap," she said with the practicality of women who keep faded clothes to wear when no one can see them. "And it didn't all happen at once. It came on gradually, the worst of it over the past few weeks."

I said nothing while thoughts ran through my mind, wondering just how desperate for a place to stay a person would have to be to accept a *haunting*—well, she certainly thought the place was haunted, even if I knew that it couldn't be, or told myself that it wasn't.

Eleanor filled the silence. "You refuse to let anyone call you by your first name. Why is that?"

"Because it's a lousy name."

"Theodore," Eleanor said gently, savoring the syllables, allowing them to roll softly off her tongue. "Theodore. It's in the court papers. It's not a bad name."

"My family called me Theo, because of my mother."

"She didn't like the name she gave you?"

I considered not telling her the story, but what the hell. It's a good story, and unfortunately, it's true.

"My father was an alcoholic. My mother was pregnant with

me. He had his paycheck. She wanted it, so . . . she told him he could name me anything he wanted if he signed his paycheck over to her. He obliged, and three months later named me Theodore Roosevelt Parker."

"I guess Rosey was out of the question. As a name, I mean."

"You are a cruel woman, Eleanor."

"What about Ted?" she asked.

"No one thought of it," I replied. "It's true. We were an unimaginative family."

Eleanor's expression said she didn't believe this at all. "But Theo is kind of cool. Theo Parker, Attorney at Law. Theo Parker, the DA. What is it you do, anyway?"

"I write articles on carburetors."

"Carburetors? Not fuel injection?"

"That was another guy. I'm attracted to anachronisms."

Eleanor laughed, then allowed her eyes to stroll around the room. "Welcome home, Parker."

At the doors to our rooms, Eleanor removed the robe and handed it to me, as I returned her flashlight, forgotten earlier. Being a guy I couldn't stop my eyes from trailing down to her nightgown, and for the first time Eleanor realized she was as good as naked. She turned bright red, shoved the robe at me and said, "Good night, Parker!" Her door slammed in my face.

Safely returned to my bed, I was overwhelmed with a sense of well-being, as if I knew that what had happened couldn't have happened, that there had to be a reasonable explanation for everything. I fell asleep quickly, around 4:30, and for the first time since her death Lily visited me in my dream. She wore the shorts and knit shirt she died in, but they were as fresh and clean as the morning she put them on. Her hair was a glorious auburn, her arms and legs golden from the sun, with not a blemish, not a stain of blood anywhere on her. She sat beside me on the bed and in my dream I felt it settle a little beneath her weight. She stroked my arm until I awoke in the dream and looked at her.

"It wasn't your fault, Theo," she said.

"It was my fault."

"No, the other driver fell asleep. You've got to stop blaming yourself."

"Lily, I miss you."

"I've learned a secret, Theo. It's the secret that keeps people going, that gives life meaning, and it's this. To love once is to love always. You will love me all your life, and every time you think of me, I'll be there."

"Lily, I miss you," I told her.

"It wasn't meant to be, Theo. Your fate turns and moves elsewhere now. Forgive yourself. Learn to laugh again."

She stood and moved toward the door.

"Lily, it's not you, is it? You don't haunt this place?"

But she disappeared and a dog woke me up at seven, barking outside the yard.

five

PEOPLE rise early in the country and in small towns, so I was prepared to find Monroe House vacant when I left my room. There was that box of old clothes to choose from, khakis and jogging shorts and sweatshirts, ink-stained or food-stained or just stained, but washed clean and stored away by someone long gone. I chose a pair of pants that were threadbare at the knees, a bland shirt that a farmer might have worn, and two nearly matching tennis shoes and equally disparate socks, one white, one off-white. The shower in the room was fully outfitted with soap and towels, so there was no problem there. When I closed my bedroom door and stepped into the light of day I was as new a man as I had been in more than six months.

Lily had come to me last night and forgiven me for killing her.

I rapped on Eleanor's door, and when she didn't answer, I opened it and leaned in. The bed was made, house shoes were at parade rest beside the bed and Eleanor was nowhere to be seen. I checked my wristwatch. It was 8:20. Clearly she was gone, out doing what property managers do in Cambria early in the morning.

I chanced a look from her window, and in turning to leave rifled her closet. The truth is, I'm a snoop, and I was curious what a woman of somewhat diminished capacity in the looks department had hanging in her closet. There was, alas, little. Several dresses, a half dozen pants, some slacks, blouses that were as lean as her chest and shoulders and equally bland. I felt a sudden pity for Eleanor Glacy, because she had not found a man, and as all men secretly believe, I was certain this was the ultimate desire of every woman. I rarely suspect I'm a horse's ass, but on this occasion the thought occurred to me that I am.

I left her closet door askew and closed the door to her room behind me.

I heard a telephone ringing and followed its sound to the parlor, where a rolltop desk revealed a phone. Before I could answer it, I heard, "You've reached Eleanor Glacy Property Management. To bypass this lengthy list of available short-term or vacation rentals, press zero now." Someone pressed zero. "Hi, Eleanor. Just letting you know that Sally's wedding rehearsal has been postponed after all, so you're not needed for this afternoon. She's taking the shift. The new Janice Cromwell book hasn't come in, either."

The bookstore where Eleanor worked part-time apparently thought of her as an asset of secondary quality too.

I went into the kitchen to fix something to eat—I would reimburse Eleanor for the food later, I thought, if I remembered—and found a note beneath a sugar dispenser on the kitchen table.

Parker—

I have to check on a house over on Moonstone Beach, but if you can wait until 9:00 we can have breakfast together. I want to talk about last night.

—Eleanor

A chill ran up my spine. Had this female beanstalk—is there such a thing?—set her sights on me? I was still quite a catch, I thought, assessing myself. True, now I had one leg shorter than the other, or to look at the glass as half full rather than half empty, one leg *longer* than the other. I had no job, of course, nor any prospects for one, but I owned a failed business and was preparing to pour what money I did have into it. It was also true that I had killed the love of my life as we drove, and my eyes were not on the road, but on her lovely legs, which were carrion just minutes later. . . .

Stop it!

I had a Rorschach mind, and it sometimes amused itself with these little intellectual ditties. Sometimes they led where they should not go.

Still, I wondered if Eleanor were beginning to see something in me I didn't want seen. I imagined for the briefest moment Eleanor in my arms, each of our lips seeking the contours of the other, my hands on her back, her breast pressed against mine . . . and my wondering if her chest were smaller than my chest.

"What are you thinking?" Eleanor asked as she entered the kitchen.

"I was wondering if you had any extra flesh hidden anywhere on your body, and if so, where," I said. Well, no, I really didn't say that. I said, "Nothing."

She held a bag of groceries in her hands. "Hungry?" she asked.

"Famished."

"Now there's a word you don't hear much anymore—*famished*," Eleanor commented, setting the bag down on the kitchen table. "I've noticed you're a little, what's the word—behind the times?"

"I'm verbal, you mean. I'm a writer."

"Yes, but you write about things people don't use much anymore. Carburetors, for instance." She pulled a carton of eggs from the bag, bacon, bread, butter.

"I was only being amusing," I told her.

"You should let me know when you're going to do that," she commented.

THE HAUNTING OF CAMBRIA 🕊 51

"Actually I wrote about all sorts of things. It was a hot-rod magazine, so there was plenty of opportunity to write about . . . obsolete equipment."

"Is that where you met Lily?"

I had almost forgotten about Lily. Ten, fifteen seconds there.

"Her family owns the magazine. Owns the publishing group. Owns a lot more, in fact."

"Then you're rich?"

"Me? Nah. Shabby in-law. Worse than divorced, now."

Eleanor began to cook. Omelets. She was clearly familiar with the inside of a kitchen, something lost on most women today in the same way most cats can't catch mice anymore. Cats have to be taught by their mothers, you know, and aren't taught much these days, so are just as repulsed by mice and as incapable of catching them as we are. But Eleanor knew mice, I could see.

"You cook," I said.

"Family of four sisters. Three are beautiful, smart and popular. They had to be fed."

"Mom didn't feed?"

"Only until she taught me. But breakfasts are nothing," Eleanor said. "Breakfasts are bush league. Even my sisters can cook breakfast, only usually they do it for dinner, with a salad and a red wine."

No salad, nor red wine here. She whipped us up cheese omelets with bacon. There were little green things on the top which I didn't mention because while I thought they might be garnish, I wasn't sure. I ate them. Capers, I found out later.

"You got a message from the bookstore," I told Eleanor. "Somebody's wedding rehearsal has been postponed, so somebody can work and you've got the day off."

"That bitch," Eleanor said. "Her sister is no more getting married than I am."

I placed my tongue between my teeth and bit down.

"She just uses these excuses to keep the schedule free. Her grandmother died twice, and I've met both her grandmothers. They're both still very much alive."

"And the bookstore owner doesn't get this?"

"Ed Tiller can't keep his eyes off her chest."

Ed Tiller would need a map and a compass to find Eleanor's chest, but I was still biting my tongue.

"Is the omelet okay?" Eleanor asked.

"Hhmm?"

"The omelet?"

"Oh, fine. I was just savoring it."

"Do you taste the dill?"

I nodded in polite deception. There was dill in this omelet? No, I couldn't taste it. All I knew was that it was delicious and different from any other omelet I'd ever eaten.

"I like to cook," Eleanor said matter-of-factly. "I could spend all day in the kitchen."

"Isn't this town known for its restaurants?" I asked. "I mean, I know there's The Brambles, and The Sow's Ear and Moonstone Gardens. Couldn't you . . . ?"

"No. They have chefs. I'm a cook."

"Oh." The distinction was lost on me.

"Anyway, I like to experiment, try new things. You can't do that and stick to a menu."

"You said there was something you wanted to talk to me about," I suggested, pulling the conversation away from break-fast.

Eleanor grew quiet a moment and just looked at me. Oh boy, here it comes, I thought. This is the beginning. I should let her down early. I'm not over Lily. I may never be over Lily. And we're just not . . . compatible. Yes, compatible. I like women who look like women, and clearly Eleanor is not the kind of girl who looks, well, womanly.

"I believe Monroe House is haunted," she said evenly, surprising me with the subject. "But not with your late wife. Lily was taken quickly, unexpectedly, it's true, but she wasn't—"

"Wasn't what?"

"She was loved, and she loved back. There's a peace that goes along with that. What haunts this house is . . . not peaceful."

"It's the plumbing," I said.

"No, it isn't, Parker."

"It's the electrical, then. Something shorts out. The power goes wacky. Maybe something, uhm, held in place when the power is on is released and . . ."

"Parker, a spirit haunts this house. I don't know why, or how it came to live here, but it's a living, evil thing." She was serious. *A living, evil thing.*

"You don't know that it's evil."

"Yes," Eleanor said. "I do."

"That sound we heard last night doesn't mean anything. It certainly wasn't evil."

"Over the two months I've lived here, I've more than heard things, Parker," she said.

"You have?"

"I've seen things, too."

"What kind of things?"

Eleanor buttered a piece of toast and plastered jam across it, making me wonder how she remained so thin. "I'm not going to tell you," she said finally. "I want you to see them for yourself."

"Oh, swell."

"Swell. There it is again; a word people don't use anymore."

"Yeah, like the name 'Eleanor' has been really popular since Mrs. Roosevelt died."

But Eleanor didn't mind my comment at all—it was as if I was unimportant to her. She rose from the table and took the dishes to the sink. "I'm not completely retro, Parker. I cooked, that means you wash. Afterward I'll show you a little of the town you live in now."

six

CAMBRIA is really a series of villages, strewn together like seeds fallen from a torn bag of grain. There's East Village, home of The Brambles and The Sow's Ear, two of the more famous restaurants in town. There's also Linn's, a new addition to the hamlet representing the Linn family's truly extraordinary success with the olalaberry and what can be made from it. Started as a farm's side business twenty-something years ago, Linn's now includes a restaurant in town opposite The Sow's Ear, plus a curio shop selling jams, pies, and other sweets. This area is really the old village where the township began. A copse of pines (I would hardly call it a forest) atop a knoll separates it from Highway 1, which slices through the countryside, sharp blade to dripping fruit.

Here in the East Village are the old graveyards, too, Santa Rosa Cemetery established for those of the Catholic faith and located on a hill overlooking the original village. A tiny chapel stands guard among the dead, where visitors are as welcome as anywhere else in town, which is to say, stroll right in and make yourself at home.

Down Bridge Street, a long and narrow road leading from the East Village where it began as one of the hamlet's original streets, and lined by brooding wood, is the Cambria Community Cemetery. Here everyone is welcome, dead or not. Recent changes now make it possible to drive through the graveyard and view gravestones that date back to the early nineteenth century. Names from the founding families of the township are found here. An old wood cargo wagon parked near the entrance to the hallowed ground reminds visitors what hearses used to be like, or at least, what served the purpose in a lurch.

Then there's West Village, down Main Street about a mile from East Village. There are many curio shops here, boutiques, real estate offices, coffee shops, businesses associated with business itself. In recent times it has begun to compete with the East Village in terms of restaurants. The Main Street Grill is as close as the township will allow to a fast food place. It serves the best burgers in town. Equidistant between the villages is the Cookie Crock, the town's only supermarket, located on a bluff (and to a certain degree, hidden by the bluff, as it's too modern a contraption for the quaint little town).

The Coast Highway and Main Street almost meet at the town's westernmost intersection. Across the Coast Highway is Moonstone Beach Drive. Two dozen inns face one of the most beautiful beaches in the world, where driftwood lies across sand frequented far more by seagulls than human feet, and where a boardwalk winds through terrain rough and gentle at turns, providing access to athletes and the disabled alike.

Then there are the neighborhoods themselves, each with a name and personality.

I knew all this, of course, because Lily had taken me to visit each of them by story long before I ever set foot in the tiny hamlet of Cambria. She knew it better than any of its natives, of course; there are none so devout as the converted. She loved Cambria far more than I ever could, more than I could even imagine anyone else loving it.

Eleanor didn't know this, of course. Nor did I try to dissuade her from driving me by every point of interest or from coaxing me to climb the hill to Santa Rosa Cemetery. From the hill overlooking the town the view was worth almost any climb, it was true, though Cambria is more an idea than an ideal. It was lovely anyhow.

"Do you believe in life after death?" Eleanor asked me.

Tender flesh, this. Lily was dust now, buried somewhere back east by her grandmother while I lay in a coma. I said nothing for a long while, then, "I believe almost anything is possible."

"That's like saying you believe everything," Eleanor retorted with a snort.

No bider of fools, this Eleanor.

"Okay. Here it is," I said. "We're born. It's painful. We grow, and it's painful. We love, and it's wonderful, but it's painful. We die, or someone near us dies, and it's painful. There. That's what I believe."

"You don't believe in anything, Parker," she said softly.

"Belief. That's painful, too."

We stood to the east of the church, where the family plots were distinguished by small stone encirclements or by rusting fences, some replaced by persons unknown long after anyone who knew these names had himself or herself become dust. "I love this place," Eleanor said. "I don't know why most people think cemeteries are hideous, or scary. They're beautiful."

"They contain dead people, for chrissakes, Eleanor," I mumbled.

"No, they're about love, Parker. Look here."

I looked there. A tree trunk carved of marble; the most beautifully decayed thing I had ever seen. Once there had been limbs to this trunk, and leaves, all carved from a single piece of marble. Now all that remained was the trunk itself. The date read 1847. There was an inscription. It was written in a foreign language I couldn't identify.

"One of the church historians translated it for me," Eleanor said. "I don't recall the exact words, but it's a poem written to a dead bride, brought from Switzerland with her husband, a mining engineer—there were once mercury mines in these hills, did you know?—and she was taken ill with some disease her immune system wasn't prepared for and died. He had the tree carved—a tree, Parker, an entire tree with limbs and branches and leaves shaped from marble—and wrote a poem that said their love for one another was just one leaf of one branch of one limb and as long as the tree survived, their love would survive, too."

I was never one for such sentiments. I would have made a joke, but none came to mind. "That seems to be all that's left, the trunk of the tree," I said.

"But it survives, Parker."

"The tree is marble, Eleanor," I pointed out.

"You're missing the point."

"The point is about marble, Eleanor," I retorted, "not about flesh."

Eleanor kneeled beside the marble tree. How many storms had ravaged it, and this hill, I wondered, since that day when the mining engineer laid his lovely bride to rest beneath its weight? Below, in the village of Cambria, horses and wagons had given way to bicycles and cars and yes, goddamn it, SUVs. Above, birds had given ground to airplanes, many of them traveling so high they were merely silver bullets traversing the sky.

Eleanor reached out a lean arm and ran fingers across the detail of the marble tree trunk. "This is what I believe, Parker," she said solemnly. "The love that makes these gestures doesn't die, can't die. I don't know where most of us go, heaven or hell or somewhere else, Valhalla maybe, or the Bardo, where souls wait to reincarnate. But I know they go somewhere. The joy of love between people just can't die."

I wondered about Eleanor, then, this isolated woman whose family had turned her into a servant and whose gaggle of friends made nary a sound, if they existed at all. She talked about love as it if were something she was intimate with, and yet I suspected she had experienced none of it.

"It's a magnificent gesture," I said softly, "this tree, and a sentiment to wrap our hopes in." *Like day-old fish,* I thought, but didn't say it.

Eleanor said nothing for a time, then, "The thing in your bed-and-breakfast, Parker, isn't like this. It's angry and it's become evil. It haunts Monroe House."

I drew her away from the marble tree. We had lunch at Linn's, on me of course, because I still had the cash and what the hell. Outside, as I waited for Eleanor to do whatever it is women do in bathrooms (you can't convince me it's the same thing men do, because we're in and we're out as quickly as possible), I stood outside the restaurant in my used clothes. Now they were clean, as I mentioned earlier, and they weren't wrinkled, but they were threadbare in places. There was a stain on the fly of my pants, a paint stain it appeared although I couldn't swear to it, and the shirt sleeves were a little short, but I had them buttoned anyway because it was breezy that day. Also, my shoes, while similar, didn't match, nor did the socks. Still, I was presentable, I thought, certainly in any small town.

I noticed a man looking at me. Sixty; bald; bushy eyebrows. He was waiting to go into Linn's (it was tourist season and there were lines at all the restaurants), and for some reason he couldn't seem to take his eyes off me. I realized he thought I was looking hungrily inside Linn's when in truth I had already been well fed (try the corn fries) and I was really looking inside hoping Eleanor had finished her bathroom ritual (involving incense, perhaps, and the sacrifice of a small bird?). In any case he gathered up his courage, walked up to me, shoved something into my shirt pocket, said, "God bless you," and returned to his place in line where he immediately disappeared inside for lunch.

I pulled the paper out, expecting a religious tract possibly or the phone number of the local Salvation Army. It was a five-dollar bill. I was considering the career possibilities of this event when Eleanor stepped out of the restaurant looking absolutely no different from when she left for the ladies' room. "What?" she asked, misinterpreting my expression of wonder at having been paid for nothing as a comment on her appearance. "Nothing," I said finally—if I mentioned the clothes thing she would insist that I actually buy some, and I was in no mood to go clothes shopping. "Let's go," I urged.

She had a house to check on just off Moonstone Beach. I sat in her pickup truck (not an SUV, but a sensible Ford Ranger, a stripped-down model not standing anywhere near the word *new*) while she went inside a nice little beach house that was for rent. She returned a moment later and leaned elbows down on the passenger window frame. The wind rustled her blouse and pants and did I imagine it, or was she wearing cologne? "They still haven't fixed the bathroom door," she reported, as if I knew anything about the bathroom door. "Care to take a walk?"

It was a glorious afternoon. We walked the boardwalk first, maneuvering past tourists with similar intentions. The boardwalk at Moonstone Beach is quickly becoming world famous, and rightly so. It twists and turns through open ground and out to craggy points, providing civilized access to land and rock that know no civilization. Moss clings to boulders and surf sweeps into and out of tidepools to the sound of a symphony of moving water. An hour passed as we idled without words, living in an exquisite moment.

Later we found our way to the state beach due south of the boardwalk, where driftwood provides places for bottoms to flatten and the sky and sea make every care in the world seem to blow away. We lingered for another hour, neither of us saying a word about the power of love, the thing in my house, or anything else. Instead we felt gusts of sea wind gently slapping our faces, saw the dance of light across the surface of the sea, and soared not unlike seagulls on thermals of experience.

When finally I suggested we leave, it was because the sea air, and time, had made me hungry again. Eleanor offered to make us a quick dinner. I accepted. One dish was something with potatoes and cream; another, steak simmered in onions and other things one picks wild and free from hilltops. It was wonderful.

Eleanor said little, just, "The sea air's made you sleepy." And it had. It was barely nine o'clock.

"Go on," she said, dismissing this tenderfoot whipped tired by sea air. "Go to bed. I'll get the dishes."

So I did as she told me. I trundled to my room, brushed my teeth, stripped naked and fell between the sheets of my bed, where sleep overtook me in a matter of seconds.

Hours passed that I wasn't aware of. In those hours Eleanor finished the dishes, went to her own room, showered, probably sacrificed another small bird or performed some other ritual in the bathroom men don't and never will know anything about, and went to bed. She read three chapters of a Stephen King book, turned out her light, and she too was overtaken by sleep, galloping up from behind like the headless horseman.

More hours slipped by.

Then the door to the master suite upstairs opened. Something came through that doorway. Man, woman, spirit, I don't know what it was, but its eyes glowed red and it moved with a speed that was frightening. It came down the stairs in a flash, circled the staircase, moved for my room, slammed open my bedroom door and moved on me so quickly it was all I could do to scream before its talonlike fingers wrapped about my throat.

seven

W AKE up!"
I thought I was awake. I thought I was being stran-
gled in my own bed. But I had been asleep. It had been a dream.
God, what a dream. Real. Tangible. Tactile, even.

I cleared my vision and saw Eleanor sitting beside me. Her
flashlight was standing on end, beam shooting toward the ceiling. *The electricity must be out again*, I thought with rare clarity
in the early morning haze between dreamland and wakefulness.
Eleanor's hands were on my shoulders, and she stared into my eyes
as if searching for a human being lost somewhere deep inside.

"I'm okay," I said.

"The hell you are."

"I'm awake. I'm fine. I just had a nightmare, that's all."

I didn't tell her what it was. I didn't want to put thoughts into
her head. She released me, settled back on the bedside where
she sat. "I heard your voice," she said. "You were screaming."

I was screaming. I remembered screaming. I remembered the
door slamming open, the thing in my dream rushing to me to
wrap its long fingers around my throat. The dream still existed.
It floated in the room like the halo of smoke after a fire, a ghost
of timber and tile, fabric and flesh.

Seeing my expression, Eleanor ordered, "Tell me about the
dream."

"No."

"Okay, let me guess. Was it the one where the thing comes

out of the master bedroom upstairs, eyes glowing blood red. It rushes down the stairs and breaks through your door and—"

"You've had the dream?"

"Only one of many, Parker. But this was the first one."

The first one. I considered that for a moment.

"Lights are out again?" I asked.

"Uh-huh," she replied.

"Ah."

We sat in the gloom for a minute more as the smoke retreated and my mind cleared. I heard the refrigerator compressor down in the kitchen kick in and knew that the power had been restored. I reached out and turned on my bedside lamp. The flashlight's puny beam was suddenly lost, shadow to sunlight. Eleanor switched it off.

I saw Eleanor's face more clearly now. She looked strained, pinched, and anxious. She wore a flannel nightgown that connected ankle with neck. She hadn't stopped to pull on a robe as she rushed to save me, not that she needed to. The nightgown was as impenetrable as the walls of Troy. Still, I wondered what she knew, what she had experienced in this house in the weeks and months before I arrived.

"Is this what you meant when you said you saw things?" I asked as we gained sanity from the bedside light.

She looked at me a long moment before replying, "No, that's not what I meant."

"Oh."

"I won't suggest things to you," she said. "You'll discover them for yourself."

Now here was a pleasing thought.

"Because I was thinking," I continued, "instead of a bed-and-breakfast, we could market this place as a haunted house. Spend the night, have a nightmare. Think of it as 'Haunt and Hammock.' Or 'Scare and Scones.'"

"Or maybe we should serve them dinner first," she suggested, "and afterward they can be scared shitless?"

"Now that was a rather tasteless remark, Eleanor."

"Come on!" she ordered, rising to her feet. "I'll make us some warm milk and we'll sleep through the night."

"Warm milk?" I hadn't heard of anyone drinking warm milk since I was a boy, and even then it was in a rerun of a thirty-year-old movie playing on TV.

"Works every time. No more nightmares," she asserted.

I shrugged my acceptance and threw the covers back, hopping out of bed. Eleanor froze. I followed her gaze down before I remembered I had crawled into bed naked, lacking underwear you may recall. Or, at least, underwear of my own. I looked up at Eleanor before she looked up at me. Then she turned bright red yet again and ran from the room.

Surely she had seen one before? Even if only in movies?

She was quiet for a time after I arrived in the kitchen wearing a refugee robe and house shoes. Her robe was equally practical, even if I could make out the flannel nightgown below the hem of the robe.

"Excuse me," she said as she poured warm milk into my mug.

"For what?"

"For looking."

"Think nothing of it, Eleanor. I can show it to you again, if you're interested."

"Theo Parker, don't you dare!"

"You know, Eleanor, for a person who likes to point out how out of step other people are, you seem to be a little awkward in your own time."

The milk steamed as it came to rest in her mug. She sat opposite me, brought the mug to her lips, winced, and blew on the milk's surface to cool it.

"I'm shy," she said.

"No, you're sexually repressed." It was this, or talk about what might linger in this house. Sex is a great comfort, you know, in more ways than are generally known. You can whistle while walking through a graveyard at midnight, but a good bawdy story works twice as well. Of course, it helps to have someone to listen.

"I am not sexually repressed," Eleanor said, more forcefully than was necessary.

"Either that," I said, "or . . . you're gay."

"I am not gay!" she said, her voice dripping with frustration. Frustration drips, doesn't it? Then she blushed. She must have recalled my leaping out of bed. "I don't think of sex as purely recreational in nature," she announced as if a host of microphones were arranged in front of her. This was a pronouncement to the world.

"You're a virgin," I said.

"I am not!" Eleanor spat at me, as if in response to an insult. "I've had plenty of opportunities to have relations with men. I could probably entice you to have sex right now."

"Well, Eleanor, I'm a man, which means I don't have to be enticed. So, you are a virgin."

She stared at me a long while, as if trying to concoct a slicing return, but finally said, "I'm saving myself. I'm celibate. Temporarily. Until the right man comes along."

"Really, Eleanor, this isn't any of my business."

"I don't think so!"

"I judge you only on how you conduct yourself, and thus far, you've conducted yourself with, uhm . . ." There was no way to get around this, even if the male chauvinist in me winced as I said it. "With bravery."

She looked up, surprised. "Bravery?"

"You've spent months in this house—which I still say has maybe bad wiring or plumbing problems—but in any case, you've stayed here, alone, with the noises and the nightmares and everything. I would be hard-pressed to equal that." Truth was, I would be back in LA talking long-distance with a real estate agent after the first night. Alone, I mean.

"I believe one shouldn't give in to their fears."

"Exactly," I confirmed.

"And the rent was cheap. First reports had you suicidal."

Now this was an interesting tack. Suicidal? Had I been suicidal? Well, maybe I had.

"Meaning?" I asked.

"Meaning long-term property management as the estate went through probate."

"If I offed myself?" I suggested.

"Yes, if you committed suicide."

I assessed Eleanor, sweet, innocent, virginal, shy Eleanor sleeping in the bedroom opposite mine for months and months and waiting for me to commit suicide. "So," I said, "you were gambling on the probability that I would kill myself, thus enriching your economic possibilities?"

"I didn't even know you then, Parker," she explained.

"But you know me now, so now you wouldn't want me to kill myself, right?"

"Right."

We both slurped warm milk.

"Hm," I said.

"I took you to see my favorite tree," she suggested.

"The marble tree?"

"Yes."

"Hm," I said.

"I take only friends to see my tree, Parker," Eleanor said earnestly. "And I talk about my spiritual feelings with people who are, or I think will become close friends."

I slurped milk again.

"How many other dreams are there?" I asked after a time.

"A number."

"Yes, a number, but how many, Eleanor?" She counted them on her fingers, up to ten, then moved into the teens. "And yet," I said as she continued counting, "nothing has happened to you, or harmed you in any way, isn't that correct?"

She stopped counting.

"Eleanor?"

"Sixteen," she whispered. "Maybe seventeen."

"Eleanor?"

She said nothing for a long while. She emptied the saucepan of warm milk into her mug, filling it maybe a third of the way. She sat down at the table again, held the mug between hands suspended on elbows that rested on the tabletop like bridge supports. Finally she said, "There's one dream that comes more often than others."

"What's the dream about?" I asked.

"I won't tell you," she said.

"Why not?"

"It's too . . . personal."

"Have you been hurt?"

The room was so quiet I thought I could almost hear the surf at Moonstone Beach, a quarter mile away. But it was probably the wind. Or something worse.

"Do you promise not to leer?" she asked. Tears welled in her eyes. I nodded. She stood, uncinched her robe, allowed it to drop to the chair. She reached down to the hem of her flannel night-gown and pulled it up. She stopped near the top of her thighs. There were four dark bruises there, deep bruises, finger and thumb bruises, two on each thigh, the kind men leave when they maneuver a woman's legs a certain way, for a certain purpose.

"I see them," I told her softly.

She dropped the gown.

"When these dreams happen, do you . . . ?"

Eleanor pulled her robe back on, cinched it, sat down again.

"It isn't pleasant," she responded softly before finishing the milk. "It ends before . . . anything happens. I wake up. Screaming, usually."

"Tell me the dream, Eleanor," I asked.

"No," she said.

I escorted her back to her room and helped her remove her robe. She looked at me with worry for a moment, but I smiled and gestured that it would be okay. She slid between the covers and I pulled them over her, up to her neck. Then I lay down beside her, above the covers. For a long time Eleanor's eyes were on me, but finally they closed.

Half of me wanted to believe these were not self-inflicted manifestations, that people live after death, because if they did Lily was alive somewhere, and someday, after I was dead, and Eleanor was dead, we would be alive too.

Meanwhile, nothing would harm Eleanor again. Not while she slept under my roof.

eight

WHEN I awoke the next morning, Eleanor had already vacated the bed. I heard the shower spray from the bathroom. I crawled from beneath my covers—and my inherited robe, which had proven too light for the job, by the way—pulled the robe on and leaned against the door frame to the bathroom.

"Sleep okay?" I asked.

"Like the dead," Eleanor answered. Not the phrase I would have chosen. "You?"

"Good."

"I'll make you some breakfast," she told me, "as compensation for being my hero . . ." I imagined a smile flitting across her lips. "But then I have to work at the bookstore this morning. You can borrow the pickup if you want."

"Eleanor, when these things began happening, you . . . had someone check out the wiring, and the plumbing, didn't you?" I asked.

The shower spray slowed to a trickle. Water is a precious commodity in Cambria, and the most expensive of its utilities. All the showers are of the slow-flow variety and can be shut off at the head between lathering. There was a quiet moment as she scrubbed herself, I imagined, before, "You still don't—"

"No, I believe you, Eleanor. I believe myself. But if we're to bring some help in to get rid of this . . . infestation, then we've got to prove we've covered all the bases."

The shower spray struck again, for a moment only. I imagined she was spraying her body free of soap. "I use an electrician, Tim Coake. He has a shop off Main Street in the East Village."

"What about the plumbing?"

"Oh, for god's sakes, the plumbing, Parker!"

"All the bases, Eleanor."

"Alice Champlain."

"You used a female plumber?"

"Parker!" she protested.

"Okay, Alice Champlain."

"I'll give you her number if I can get out of here without putting on a show for you."

"I'll be in the kitchen," I told her. Actually, I would be in the shower first, but being a man and lacking Druidic ritual, I doubted she would beat me to the kitchen. As it turned out, she did, wearing a different robe from the previous night and with her hair damp but combed. She smelled of vanilla, which is an odor I've always been fond of.

"Scrambled eggs okay?"

"You're going to make a man a fine wife someday," I told her. And I meant it when I said it. And I regretted saying it a second later.

"Parker, you are the worst kind of male chauvinist," she barked over her shoulder, scrambling eggs at the stove. "The kind that hasn't a clue he's a chauvinist."

"You said you liked cooking," I said, defending myself.

"Soft or hard?"

"What?"

"The eggs."

"Soft, but not runny."

She shoved a plate of soft scrambled eggs and sausage before me a moment later. Two minutes after that, she sat down opposite with eggs sunny-side and more sausage. Toast was piled on a plate at the center of the table.

"It was a . . . nice gesture, what you did last night," she said, the food before her and me and no other task needing taking care of.

"Aw, shucks, ma'am."

"Parker, I trust you. I want you to know that. Lily had herself a good man."

Uh-oh. That issue again. I took a bite of the eggs. "If you don't mind, I will borrow your pickup this morning. I'll talk with Tim Coake and Brünhilde—"

"Alice Champlain. She's a good plumber and a nice person, Parker. Don't you prejudge her, or hurt her feelings."

"I won't. I promise," I told her. "Eleanor, what you said about trusting me. It would help a lot if you talked about . . . what's happened here."

She chewed. She swallowed. She chewed and she swallowed. Then she said, "I'm not like most other women, Parker." This I already knew. "I . . . have a hard time letting people in. I have a hard time talking about things."

"Okay." It was enough for me.

"But maybe, someday, I can let you see things. About my life and who I am. Maybe then I can let go. . . ."

I drove her to Tiller's Bookstore, which was on the second floor of a small building on Main Street in the West Village. Tiller's, Eleanor told me, featured local writers. Maybe someday I would have a book featured there. Somehow I doubted it. Eleanor wore slacks and a pretty blouse with frills at the neck and shoes one doesn't ordinarily kick horse manure with. She looked nice in a lean, Katharine Hepburn's skinnier great-granddaughter sort of way.

The female plumber was out on a call, but Tim Coake was in. He was rewiring a lamp, of all things. It was made of driftwood, the lamp, and looked as old as, well, old driftwood. I introduced myself as the owner of Monroe House. Tim looked doubtful. On this morning I was wearing somewhat less presentable pants than the day before. They were clean, of course, but stained in a way that suggested the owner was really trying to make a statement about stains in general, and his own in particular. The shirt was lacking half a collar. It had been torn or ripped off, and someone had seen fit to sew the two pieces of cloth back together to form a kind of prosthesis collar. Who was I to challenge the wisdom of this unknown but obviously skilled individual? My tennis shoes almost matched, as before, but alas today the socks did not, being varying shades of brown.

"You own Monroe House?" Tim asked.

"Scout's honor," I replied, making a three-fingered gesture. Never having been a scout, or for that matter having any honor, the whole thing was a bluff.

"You don't look like you own much of anything," Tim said. Good, honest, straightforward man, Tim Coake, who was fifty if not older, sandy-haired and slightly stoop-shouldered, which I would have pointed out to him but I am not the sort of man Tim is.

"I understand you have the account," I prompted.

"What account?"

"The Monroe House account," I said. "For electrical."

"Oh, well, if you mean Eleanor Glacy brings me in every now and then to fix things, sure, I have that account." Tim was amused by my pretension. I was amused by it myself, but not nearly as amused as I was by his breath, which was eighty proof and recently replenished.

"Ah," I said. "Ugh!" I meant.

"The wiring is old. I rewired the back porch last fall. That was just after that couple bought it and the damn fools got themselves killed up by Piedras Blancas lighthouse." He paused a moment, and I thought he had realized who I was and was about to apologize, but no. "Or one did, anyway," he continued. "I guess that makes you the survivor."

I thought about this for a moment and tried to decide whether it was better to knock Tim Coake on his rummy ass, or proceed as planned. I proceeded.

"What else can you tell me about the wiring?" I asked.

"It's old," he replied.

"I mean, beyond that."

"What 'beyond that'? It's old. It needs a complete rewiring job, but I told old Olive Oyl that at the time." Tim Coake was the first person I had met in Cambria I wanted to drop, one punch directly to the chin and down he would go. I restrained myself. In part because I'm not a violent man. In part because there was always the chance that it would be my butt hard-landing on Tim Coake's floor.

"Could the wiring be responsible for . . ." Responsible for what? Finger bruises on a maiden's legs? Dreams of things with glowing eyes rushing downstairs and taloned fingers closing about your throat? The voice, the noise, that terrible noise in the middle of the night?

"Responsible for what?"

"Uhm—noises, for instance?"

"Mr.—?"

"Parker."

"Mr. Parker," he began, and I allowed him to call me Mr. Parker because I did not like this man at all, "everyone," he said, "everyone who has lived in this community for more than three months knows Monroe House is strange. It may be haunted; I don't know. It may be pixilated. I don't know that either. But I can assure you, nothing in the wiring causes either of those things. It's not the wiring, Mr. Parker, unless we're talking about the wiring in your head!"

Coake took a pint of rye from his hip pocket and emptied a

good portion of it into his mouth. He seemed to stagger a little. I looked at my watch. It read 10:37. It wasn't even noon yet, and Coake was plastered to high hell.

"I just may come back here and kick your ass!" I told him. I was not going to strike a man diminished by alcohol.

He burst out laughing. Dignity demanded that I leave.

ALICE Champlain was not what I expected at all. My expectations—I am a male chauvinist lout barely evolved from Homo Nineteenfiftyus, I admit—said Alice would be equipped with everything she would need to be a man except the single thing that would have finished the feat. She was in fact a diminutive woman of no more than five feet in height, with naturally sandy blond hair, pretty eyes, a petite figure, and the girl-next-door presentation with male strangers.

"What can I do you for?" she said with a smile, extending her hand. I took it, marveled at how small it was, not callused at that, and shook it.

"The name's Parker," I said. "I own Monroe House."

Well, there it was again; the clothes I wore were a disincentive to belief. How could anyone who dressed as I did, yada, yada, yada . . .

"You do a lot of the work on the place yourself?" Alice asked. Well, of course that would have been the logical explanation from the beginning. Old clothes to work in. Why hadn't I thought of that?

"Yeah," I responded nonchalantly. "Look, Alice, I understand you do plumbing work for us?"

"Eleanor calls me out sometimes. The pipes are pretty old, Mr. Parker—"

"Just Parker."

"You really need to replumb the entire place. The previous owners put a lot of money into making the appearance presentable—"

Presentable. Now there's a word that almost fit. Presentable on the Planet Vulcan, maybe.

"—but the plumbing is old. It's only a matter of time until a line bursts, even with our mild winters."

"Alice, could the plumbing be the source for—"

"No," Alice responded deadpan.

"No?"

"Everyone knows about that house, Mr. Parker. Everyone knows it goes bust as a bed-and-breakfast because of what lives in it, or at least visits from time to time."

"And the plumbing couldn't—"

"No."

"Did Eleanor tell you—"

"No."

"No?"

"Eleanor's a nice person, Mr. Parker. And generally speaking, people like her around here. But she's strange and she's not—" She had to think about this a moment. "She's not popular. So it's unlikely she would tell me things, because we're not friends. We don't socialize."

"Oh."

"Not saying anything against her."

"No," I said, "of course not. You don't socialize with her because she's strange, or because—"

"She's awkward around people, that's all. I never thought to invite her down to Morro Bay for a movie, or somewhere. I just never thought of it."

ELEANOR's shift ended at two. I went up to Tiller's Bookstore to pick her up. Tiller was a man of about my age, with about half again my weight. It was clear he was very impressed with a woman of twenty-five or so, Eleanor's replacement, Sally, whose wedding rehearsal had been postponed several days before, thereby depriving Eleanor of work. Sally had a shapely figure, though I've seen better. She also had a lovely face, although it was the beauty of youth and not the sort that would abide into old age. At thirty-five Sally would have to resort to low-cut blouses to arouse attention from men, and later, well, that was problematical.

As I ascended the steps Eleanor threw me a little wave and smiled. She was talking with a customer. After he bought a trade paperback she took me to the counter, introduced me to Tiller and Sally, who seemed not to be put off by my choice in clothes at all. Sally was in fact far more attentive than necessary, which I could tell by observing Eleanor had happened before with other male customers Eleanor had found attractive. I ignored Sally, focused all my attention on Eleanor, and left with my hand on her elbow, possessive.

And what the hell, I drove her to Morro Bay, twenty or so miles south of Cambria, and we took in a movie.

nine

WE drove back in time for dinner at The Sow's Ear, in the East Village. It was Eleanor's favorite restaurant in Cambria, and I saw why immediately. Built in a space totally inappropriate for a restaurant, narrow and with a low ceiling, it had been converted into the perfect, quiet little bistro, with American arts and crafts furniture. Its specialties included bread, white and dark, baked in terra cotta flowerpots and served with butter as flavorful as the local countryside. We took a table near the big fireplace, which was ablaze with a growling fire. She ordered tea, I coffee, and we talked about the movie for a time.

Eleanor looked surprisingly lovely in this light, her face animated and filled with happiness bordering on joy. I had put that smile there, I knew, because I'd thought to take her to a movie in Morro Bay. She still wore her work clothes from that morning, but they were far more appropriate than my clothes, which continued to garner glances from those sitting nearby.

"You need new clothes," Eleanor said, stating the obvious.

"I'm eccentric," I replied. "People like eccentrics."

"I'll bet you looked good in suits," she said.

"Of course," I replied. "I was a regular cutie."

"Parker, stop it, I'm serious," Eleanor said, even though the grin written across her face said that she wasn't, not completely. "You're a good-looking man, you know."

"Now it's my turn to say stop it, Eleanor." I waved with faux dismissal.

"No, really. You're a handsome man. I don't mean anything by it." No, of course she didn't. "You have this . . . Cary Grantish quality."

"Oh, I do not!" I protested.

"Good face. Ears maybe a little too large. Mouth too big, too, but just barely, although it flaps too much, if you know what I mean."

"So I've been told."

"Good physique, too. I can testify to that!" She didn't blush, which surprised me.

"Eleanor, surely you must know," I said seriously, "must know I'm still getting over Lily and I couldn't, wouldn't even consider—"

"We're friends, Parker," Eleanor said immediately. "I know that."

Her gaze remained locked on my eyes, her smile a friend's gesture, her shoulders flat and back straight, the posture of certainty and self-confidence.

"We are," I said, "friends."

"I guess I can tell my friend he's handsome," she said. She meant it. I was a good-looking man, in her eyes.

"Thank you, Eleanor."

"But you need some new clothes."

Well, yeah.

I HAD the chicken-fried steak with country gravy, Eleanor the sauteed calamari, with shared bread pudding for dessert, all Sow's Ear specialties. We both thought dinner was wonderful. By this time I had forgotten the name of the movie we'd seen, or who was in it, or what it was about. Eleanor had become thoughtful, staring out at Main Street and noting the occasional passersby. I knew what was on her mind. We were returning to Monroe House. Soon.

"You know, there's that room opposite the master suite. It has two double beds," she suggested.

"That's fine," I mumbled.

"What are you going to do, Parker?" she asked. "Not tonight, but ultimately?"

What was I going to do? Eleanor could move out and at a whim. In fact, I wondered why she hadn't already. I was stuck with the place with few if any options other than reopen it. Which of course meant scaring the ghosts out, or whatever they were.

"Maybe I'll hire an exorcist," I said. I had already told her about the plumber and the electrician's comments—Monroe House had a long history of unexplained behavior.

"Every ghost story is a mystery," she said, taking the last sip of her cooling tea. "I learned that in creative writing class. Whatever is happening in Monroe House is occurring for a reason. The creature has a history. If we find it, maybe we can force it to leave."

I said nothing about the "we." "Okay."

"There's no shortage of historians in town," she suggested. "Maybe we should start talking to some of them."

We found Monroe House particularly dark and uninviting that night. Eleanor dressed for bed in her room, then rendezvoused with me in the room upstairs and opposite the master suite. She was shy about entering a room with a man waiting for her, even if that man was her friend, as she'd decided I was. When finally she came through the doorway she wore a third robe I had never seen.

"I'll leave and you can get in bed," I suggested. "Then I'll come back and you can turn the light off while I get—"

She dropped the robe. She was wearing a nightgown similar to the one I'd first seen her in, short, full, somewhat see-through.

She was a little nervous and didn't dally, slipping between the covers immediately.

"Okay," I said, "turn off the light."

"Oh, for god's sakes, Parker, you're wearing pajamas." And of course I was. I slipped off the robe and placed myself between the sheets. I reached over and turned out the lights.

We talked for some time in the darkness, words stepping stones between encroaching shadows. About news of the day. A recipe she wanted to try. Why I became a writer, short subjects all. Then, after a period of silence I thought might be a threshold for sleep, she said, "It's as if the place breathes." The darkness of the room, of the house, the darkness of the world around us seemed to breathe in and out, as if we were lying in the belly of a—

"You're spooking yourself," I told her. I didn't mention me.

"No, really, it is," she continued. "I used to lie awake at night and listen to the sounds the house makes only at night."

"All buildings have noises, old ones particularly."

"Yes, and this one sounds like it's breathing."

"Maybe it's not the house you're hearing," I said.

But Eleanor said nothing more, and soon I heard her sleep breathing pattern, deep and measured. I remained awake for some minutes, not hearing anything, really, certainly not the house. Then I was led to a dark pool and dove in, stroking deep toward its limitless bottom.

WHEN I woke, Lily was standing in the door, smiling at me. She wore the shorts and blouse from the day she died. I thought I was dreaming, but she gestured no, and motioned for me to follow her.

Outside, on the landing, I said, "Lily, you're a dream."

She turned, placed both of her lovely hands on my back and drew me into a kiss that lasted for almost as long as we were married. Oh, Lily's lips tasted as only hers could taste, their contours and ridges sweet and familiar territory for me to rediscover. I felt her breasts flatten against me, felt her sun-warmed legs beside mine even through the pajama bottoms.

"Lily, you're dead," I said.

"There is no death," she replied. "There is only now. We possess the 'now,' Theo. It belongs to us."

I followed Lily down the stairs, my eyes taking in her exquisite back, the long, muscled, feminine legs, the bottom that had sat as if in a bicycle seat in the palms of my hands more than once, the fragile, almost indiscernible twist of her body at the waist as each foot found the stair beneath it.

She led me into my bedroom. She removed the blouse, then the shorts. She undressed me, not allowing me to speak even a word. Then I had Lily back, had her in my arms and in my heart, lust and love and human treasure expressed in an act older than language, and a million times more complex. It seemed to last forever. When we were done she rose from the bed and looked at me with such enduring love that tears welled in my eyes.

It seemed to take forever for Eleanor's scream to pierce the fog as Lily drifted away. I rose naked from the mattress, found my pajama bottoms at the foot of the bed and rushed out the door and up the stairs.

I found Eleanor thrashing about in bed as if a man were on top of her and he was raping her. But there was no one.

"Eleanor, wake up!" I shouted. "Wake up! It's a dream!"

She continued to scream. I leaped onto the bed, just to wake her, to bring her to consciousness. I straddled her. Eleanor's gown had been ripped and was pulled up. She was nearly naked. She awoke and saw me there, on top of her, bare-chested. Eleanor lashed out with all of her strength, knocking me from the bed, shouting, "No! No! Get away from me, you bastard! Get away!"

I stood as she turned on the lamp beside the bed, swaddled herself in covers and cowered at the far edge of the mattress, staring at me as if she had never seen me before, never truly seen me. I was her rapist, a betrayer of a deep trust. "Get out!" she screamed.

"I didn't do this," I said gently, and then left.

I returned to my room where I found the sheets. I tore them from the bed and placed them in the hamper. I cleaned myself up. It was nearly dawn. I dressed, layered clothing against the cold, and went outside to the porch swing.

A dog barked, far away. Had this been fifty years ago, I would have seen milk trucks driving their routes, delivering bread, butter, and milk, of course, but that America was gone. The local paper, *The Cambrian,* is a weekly and mailed, not delivered, so this refugee found himself alone without hope of seeing even a paperboy, sitting on a swing on the porch of an insane bed-and-breakfast, if such a thing can exist.

After a few minutes there were several vehicles moving on the street, passenger cars and trucks, the ubiquitous SUVs.

I heard the door unlatch, then the screen door swing open. Eleanor stood there dressed like a logger, including a hat with flaps. She had changed nightgowns—this one hung down to her ankles beneath the heavy coat. Eleanor clutched the coat around her and squatted in front of me, legs together in ladylike fashion, house shoes half deserted with her heels in the air.

"I'm sorry," she said. "I know you didn't . . . try to rape me."

"Tell me the dream, Eleanor."

She said nothing for a time, before, "He's a big man. I don't see his face. Not clearly, anyway. He tears my nightgown— except it's never torn when I wake up, that's just in the dream. He shoves my legs apart, but I scream and wake up and he's gone."

"The bruises," I said.

"Yes, the bruises," she repeated. "The bruises. They're real, Parker."

"Could be psychosomatic," I suggested.

She started to shiver. "Y-y-yes," she agreed.

"But your nightgown was torn this time," I said.

"I thought you . . . I thought you did it. Trying to wake me up, or . . ."

I shook my head no.

"Then . . . then I don't know," she said.

I stood and took my friend into my arms. I held her for a long moment before she began to cry. I might have cried, too, but it was damn cold this morning and I opted to lead her off the porch and inside, where I learned the heavy logging jacket belonged to the hall closet. We retreated to the kitchen.

I made hot water, my specialty, and she had tea while I drank Taster's Choice with cream and Nutrasweet. I removed several layers of clothes. Time passed.

"I guess it doesn't work," she said after a few minutes.

"What do you mean?"

"Our sleeping in the same room. It happened anyway. The dream happened anyway."

I explained to her about Lily, everything, everything but the act itself. I did mention the soiled sheets.

"Soiled by who?" she asked.

"Me," I replied. "Only me. She wasn't there, Eleanor. She's dead."

"Then it was a dream?"

"A very lucid dream. I followed her out of our bedroom, Eleanor, back to my own room where I thought Lily and I made love."

Eleanor thought about that a long moment. "Whatever's in this house enticed you out of our bedroom so it could get to me," she said with a shiver.

"Maybe," I replied. "Maybe it wants both of us. Maybe it just finds me a more compliant accomplice."

"I don't understand," she said.

"You're a maiden, aren't you?" I asked. "A virgin?"

She nodded. Such words need not be spoken.

"The ghost wants to be your first."

ten

IT was well after nine before we actually did anything. The repetitions of tea and coffee were comforting, and the rising sun, which glared through the east window of the kitchen, was comforting, too. And there was the issue itself, which demanded time to be thought about, to be considered.

"A priest?" Eleanor suggested.

"You mean an exorcism?"

"Yes."

"Not Catholic," I said.

"The house?"

"No, me. You?"

"No. Not much of anything, actually. My family's pretty flexible when it comes to religion."

"Parapsychology department at the university," I suggested. I called and discovered that the local California university system had no budgetary excess to throw away on parapsychology departments.

"How about famous psychics?" Eleanor proposed. I called that show about contacting the dead, but couldn't get past screeners who asked more questions than was necessary, for reasons that seemed suspicious to me. Eleanor called that show's competitor, with much the same result.

We drank more tea, more coffee.

"Well, one thing's for sure," I said during a lull in the middle of a lull, "and that's you've spent your last night at Monroe House."

"No," Eleanor said. "I'm not leaving."

"Of course you're leaving."

"No," she said.

"Eleanor, after what happened to you—"

"It was a dream, Parker."

"Your nightie was torn."

"Nightgown," she corrected. "Nightie is what we call them when we want to excite men. And furthermore, you'll be with me to protect me."

"That didn't exactly work last time."

"So you'll be forewarned the next time," she asserted.

"Eleanor," I said evenly, trying not to reveal my frustration and anger, "something tried to tear your clothes off and maybe hurt you, too."

"Something tried to hurt me, Parker, I admit that," Eleanor said. "As for tearing my clothes off, I'm beginning to think it was psychosomatic . . . I think maybe you have this thing for skinny women and in your haste and confusion to come to my aid you, you . . ."

"Tore your clothes off?" I said, astounded.

But she was smiling. Because it was a good joke. And because secretly it pleased her to think it could be true.

"You're not staying in this house tonight," I said firmly.

"Now there you're right. I have a wedding go to. In Fresno." She stood up, washed her cup and saucer (No, I didn't have a saucer, I'm a real man, for god's sakes), and put them in the dish drainer.

"Fresno?" I asked.

"My brother Dougie's getting married tomorrow. The rehearsal and dinner are tonight. I'm a bridesmaid."

"You're a bridesmaid at your brother's wedding? Isn't that . . . countertraditional?"

"Dougie's fiancée has three brothers. Ushers, every one of them."

"And you have three sisters?" It was to be a trade, four brothers for four sisters.

"Now you get it. Parker," she began, her voice going from informational in tone to intimacy, "I have a favor to ask."

Uh-oh. I was about to get drafted.

"All of my sisters have dates. . . ."

"Doesn't anyone in your family believe in marriage?"

"And I would really appreciate it if you could come along. Not as my date, mind you—they think I'm a lesbian anyway—"

"They think you're a lesbian?"

"Long story," she retorted, "and a funny one. I'll tell it to you sometime. But if you could escort me, as a friend, well then, I wouldn't be so alone."

I wouldn't be so alone. This girl was going to wring every ounce of pity out of me yet.

"I wouldn't have to do anything?"

"Just sit in a pew, eat some cake later, talk, something I know you like to do."

"I don't have any clothes," I told her. Aha! Checkmate! I was home free.

Eleanor darted from the room and returned a moment later with my blue suit. She had apparently opened my suitcase, the suitcase Lily had packed the day we were married, the day we bought this dreadful house, the day her flesh was so traumatized by rolling rubber that she was cast out of this world . . . and removed the suit.

I stood up and left the room.

I stepped out of the bed-and-breakfast and found that it was a marvelous day to walk.

I walked down Main Street from the East Village to the West, curioed in curio shops and browsed in art galleries and arts and crafts establishments. I bought a pewter ring and an inkwell with a hinged top for my writing desk, if I ever got one, or started writing again. By the time I returned to Monroe House, it was mid-afternoon. Eleanor sat on the porch swing, the blue suit in her lap. She had been crying sometime long ago, and now only the dry beds of her tears remained, like the waterless rivers of Mars. "Hi," she said.

"Sure, I'll go," I said. "Here. Have a pewter ring. I always wanted to see Fresno. They say you haven't lived until you've seen Fresno . . . and eaten a raisin. I was always kind of afraid of raisins, you know, because they look just like rabbit poop, and, well, I was always worried someone down at the raisin plant might make a mistake—"

"I'm sorry."

"It's really not that big a thing," I told her. "I can always choose to just not eat raisins."

"You were married in this suit, weren't you?" Eleanor asked.

"Ventura Courthouse. We changed in the bathrooms, before and after."

"God, I'm sorry, Parker."

"Damn it, me too."

"So you can't go, and I'm sorry for asking."

I sat down in the swing beside her. She held the suit by the shoulders, as if there were someone in it. I smiled at that. This Eleanor was quite a girl.

"What the hell, it's just cloth," I said.

And in truth, that's all it was.

So we drove to Fresno late that afternoon, leaving Monroe House locked up tight, not to keep burglars out, mind you, but to keep whatever was in, in. I found an old carpetbag, an honest-to-goodness facsimile of the real thing made sometime in the 1970s and left at the bed-and-breakfast out of good taste, no doubt, and loaded it with my clothes. Yes, my clothes that I owned and wore before Lily died. Shorts. Socks. All that stuff.

And the blue suit, too. My old luggage, a burgundy softbag, was just too memorable a thing to lug around, so I tossed it into the lost and found closet off the service porch.

Eleanor drove while I made witty conversation. I became aware that she wasn't listening when she turned on the radio and found a country music station. I knew she hated country music, so I switched the radio off and said, "I'll shut up."

After that it was just the broken lines ahead and behind, and shadows on asphalt.

The wedding rehearsal was to be held at a Baptist church in a Fresno suburb. When we pulled into the parking lot, it was already filled. Eleanor, ever the pragmatic woman, maneuvered the truck into a space between a tree and some concrete siding meant to keep the trash dumpster from rolling away. The sun had long since set, and we were long since late. But they found Eleanor a place between three of the most beautiful women I've ever seen, women of Lily's class and, if I had not been so dumbstruck in love with her memory, I might have admitted they were a tad prettier.

First there was Carla, at twenty-seven the oldest, with hair blond and in the family for generations, I'm sure. Carla had beauty that transcended youth. She would be a beauty in old age, with clear green eyes then and now, huge dimples and a chin that was firm and anchored all that was above it. Her figure was full where a figure should be full, and narrow where a figure almost never is.

"This is my friend Parker," Eleanor said to Carla.

"Parker," Carla responded with a voice that was cream and molasses with maybe a little honey poured in because, hey, we're God and we're not skimping on Carla, now are we?

"Carla," I said. "Nice to meet you."

Second was Della, who was an inch or so shorter than Carla, but otherwise just as beautiful. Della had a somewhat bigger bosom, or maybe it was just the bra she was wearing, who knew but Della and God? Her dimples were shallower than her sister's, her hair a shade darker, too, her eyes a shade lighter. She was drop-dead gorgeous and, I noticed with an eye every man develops over time, although perhaps not as clear as mine, Della would look wonderful in a bikini. Or if a man were really lucky, in less.

"Glad to meet you, Della," I said, shaking her hand, noting the sting of the finely groomed nails of each finger.

"I . . . I just can't get over, well, I . . . glad to meet you too, Parker," Della said.

Eleanor was third in line. Enough said there.

Then there was Cissy, who was the youngest at twenty-two. Cissy was the smallest of the four, with a build smaller than Della's and Carla's, but hugely more generous than Eleanor's. She too was blond, where Eleanor was brown-headed, her eyes greenish blue, where Eleanor's were brown, her complexion light and soft, like her two oldest siblings.

This answered a lot of questions, I realized.

The girls got back to practicing the wedding while I sat in a pew with Eleanor's mother, Ella, who was as beautiful as her daughters at twice the age. I could see a little of Ella in Eleanor (had Eleanor been named for this woman, I wondered?). Ella was pleasant and excelled at small talk.

"What do you do again, Mr. Parker?"

"Just Parker," I corrected her. "I used to write for a car magazine. Now I own a bed-and-breakfast where no one wants to stay."

"Why is that?" she asked.

"Because my late wife left it to me. . . ."

"No, I mean, why don't people want to stay—" And then she stopped as if her Depends had suddenly failed her. "Your ex-wife, you say?"

"Late. She died."

"I mean, you were married? To a woman?"

"Oh yeah."

This information had to be processed, so for a time Ella sat quietly with her hands folded in her lap while the minister, a youth of twenty-five, played director at the pulpit. Actually, this was to be a rather ornate wedding, with the taking of sacrament (Baptists?), plus several ceremonial procedures I didn't recognize, including special effects, a flower arrangement being lowered from the ceiling. What, no balloons? No released doves? Eleanor's mother interrupted my spectator sport.

"Excuse me, Mr. Parker, but was I mistaken? Aren't you a gay man?"

"I'm cheerful," I told her with the most inspiring smile I could concoct. "I'm often happy. I've had moments of bliss, fleeting, but moments nonetheless, but gay, no."

"We just assumed . . . because most of Eleanor's friends are gay that you—"

"That's very strange," I said, "as I think I know all of Eleanor's friends, and I don't think one of them is gay. Although the subject hasn't come up."

Hm. I could see Ella consider this new information. Something was up, no question about it, something about her daughter that she didn't know. Something . . .

"My daughter is a lesbian, Mr. Parker," she said with a voice that conveyed absolute assurance.

"Now that's really strange," I replied, "because she's never mentioned it, not once, not even when we're in bed together."

Ella stood up then and walked across the church to her husband, who was standing beside the groom's father exchanging jokes. Eleanor saw her mother's reaction and must have known I had said something to incite it. She looked to me. I smiled a simple *Who, me?* in return.

Eleanor's father, Billy is his name I found out later, who had not been interested in Eleanor's male friend enough to cross the room and be introduced to him, or me, rather, heard what Ella had to say and was already walking in my direction before she finished spilling the beans.

"Hello," he said forcefully, extending a hand, "but do I understand this right—you're my daughter's lover?"

"Billy!" Ella protested.

"No, no, it's all right," I said. "It's a legitimate question, coming from a father. I can see myself asking that question someday." Like hell.

I was crossing a Rubicon here, I could see that. What had begun as an innocent intrusion on my part was becoming somewhat more than that. I had no right to say these things, but it was clear, Eleanor was completely unknown to her family. I mean, it wasn't as if I were intruding into a cozy, tight little familial unit. These people thought their heterosexual daughter was a lesbian when I knew she wasn't. There was a reason Eleanor was the most isolated person I had ever known, with no friends that I knew of and a family that looked like refugees from a lederhosen festival while Eleanor was clearly a horse of a different color. I don't know, it just seemed like I was defending her.

"He has every right not to answer," Ella said in response to my silence.

"Well, look," I finally replied, "I'm not comfortable talking about our private life, what we do in the privacy of our bedroom—you know what I mean?"

Both parents were dumbstruck and merely looked at me like I had farted horrendously in church, and then taken credit for it. *Oh say, it was me!*

"I mean," I said, pushing forward, "I wouldn't want to know what you and Ella do in your bedroom, would I? But I know, I

think it's safe to assume—we can assume this about most couples, I think—you do share a bedroom, am I right?"

"Yes," Ella said.

"Right," Billy said, although the intonation of *right* was a little weak.

"We share a bedroom," I said, "Eleanor and I."

eleven

THE rehearsal went fast after that. I saw several groups of people argue silently across the room, the minister and Eleanor's father for one, Ella and her son Dougie for another. The three sisters huddled like a football special team needing a run-back to win, discussing something or other and looking at me as if I were an opposing linebacker. Eleanor was able to break away from the proceedings a few moments, long enough to drag me to the church foyer and ask, "What did you do?"

"Nothing," I said. "I told the truth."

"My mother gave me that 'I want to talk to you' look."

"Good. Probably a long time overdue."

But they again needed her to stand on the left, second in line among bridesmaids and sticking out like celery among pickles.

We drove in silence to the wedding rehearsal dinner, where someone, the bride's mother (probably at the advice of the groom's mother), had put our place cards at the second, smaller table where the children were going to eat. "There's been a mistake!" Carla shouted, as if she'd found another San Andreas fault line. "They've put Parker and Eleanor . . . ah, here." She moved our cards so that we sat between Carla and her date and Della and her date. Cissy switched her card with her date's card, so she sat beside Della, and Carla did the same, so she sat beside me. Eleanor's parents were across from us, so we were one big happy Glacy family, and me.

As it turned out, the minister and his wife wound up sitting at the table where the children sat, along with assorted teenagers and defrocked adults. The minister had to leave his table and come to ours to make his presentation, which was okay because the Glacy family wasn't listening.

"So," Ella said, leaning just a smidge across the table at us, "where did you two kids meet?"

"At my haunted bed-and-breakfast," I replied. I wound up with the Salisbury steak and potatoes, which were quite good. The string beans were a little overcooked, but nothing was chewy enough to keep me from answering with my mouth full.

"Your haunted bed-and-breakfast?" Billy asked. "Is that like . . . an amusement concession?"

"No, real place," I reported. "Real ghosts. Or ghost, we're not sure."

They all looked at Eleanor, who stared at her plate as if considering reproducing the mural from the Sistine Chapel in ground meat and mashed potatoes right there.

"And you just sort of fell in love?" Cissy asked.

Eleanor shot me a look. I knew that look. It was a Jack the Ripper look.

"Well, it's not quite that simple," I replied. "I'll have the apple crisp," I told the waiter as he went by, even though dessert was not being served yet and he hadn't asked.

"But I thought . . . we've thought, were led to believe, anyway, since high school, Eleanor, that you were a lesbian," Billy said.

That was it. Eleanor looked up from hell, retaining its intimate glow, and said, "Daddy, I never said I was a lesbian!"

"You never said you weren't!" Ella gasped.

Eleanor's expression directed at her mother said Ella was an idiot and a fool, probably an accurate assessment. I ate the last of the Salisbury steak and motioned for the waiter.

"Sir?" he asked.

"You know, this Salisbury steak was just . . . well, wonderful. I wonder if you might have an extra serving in the back?"

But Billy dropped his plate on mine with a klink! "Never mind," I told the waiter. Billy's plate was untouched. The food was still warm, too.

"All those years you led us to believe—!" Billy said, but then he stopped because something just dawned on him, struck him with the force of a chain-mail glove. He sat back in his tiny little fold-up chair and looked at me like one man admiring another. "You converted her, didn't you?" he asked me.

"I never said I was a lesbian," Eleanor announced to the table. "Della said I was a lesbian because I never could . . . wasn't popular enough in high school to . . . I didn't date!"

"You dirty dog!" Billy intoned. "You must be one hell of a . . . one hell of a man!"

I found no reason to deny that. I ate more of Billy's Salisbury steak and grinned.

"I don't understand, Billy," Ella said. "What do you mean by 'convert'? A lesbian is a lesbian, right?"

"Right," Cissy contributed.

"Hell no. Eleanor just never . . . never had anything to compare it with, that's all." And here his voice dropped so only the immediate twelve or so rehearsal dinner attendees could hear. "Only women were interested in her, so she became, what— accustomed, that's it, accustomed to, well, you know—!"

The mashed potatoes weren't mushy either, as they are so often at these events. They were fluffy, whipped rather than mashed, and had a buttery flavor.

"But then Parker here saw her, maybe as a challenge, I don't know, and he gave her what every real man gives a woman— and I'm not talking just about sex here, I'm talking about attitude, I'm talking about manliness, I'm talking about—!"

"I'm not a lesbian!" Eleanor shouted.

Everyone up and down the table, and at the other tables too, stopped chewing or gabbing or looking bored and turned their eyes on we few at the Glacy part of the table.

"Let me say this right now," Eleanor said, standing up. "I'm not a lesbian, I never was a lesbian, I am a heterosexual woman, okay?"

Well sure, okay, fine with me, no problem, all gestures or words from up and down the table.

"Eleanor, sit down!" Ella hissed. "You're making a spectacle of yourself!"

Eleanor sat down. "And not one person in this building didn't think I was gay because you and Daddy and Della and Carla and Cissy and even Dougie, for god's sakes, have told everyone we know that I'm a lesbian when I'm not."

"It's denial," Carla said. "She realizes she was misguided all those years, and now she denies what this man has done for her."

This man being me.

"Converting a bull dy—" Carla began, but wisely shut up as Eleanor began to reach for her.

"Leading a confirmed homosexual back to righteousness is an act worthy of God's blessing," the minister said, having sought refuge from the table where now children, perhaps some of them destined to be gay, were having a food fight. "We've all loved Eleanor all these years, and prayed for her—"

"You've p-p-prayed for me?" Eleanor stuttered.

"But God saw the wisdom of sending a man," the minister said, "to whom He gave masculine graces strong enough to lead—"

Cissy stood up. "You can't convert a lesbian into a straight person!" she asserted angrily.

"And how would you know that?" Ella asked, doubtful.

"Because I'm gay," Cissy reported, and then remembered her

male date sitting beside her and turned briefly to say, "Oh, sorry, Steve."

No kiss for you on the doorstep, Steve. No Motel 6, either.

AFTER the dinner was over, Carla and Della cornered me and we just had a wonderful time talking and, well, yes, I must admit it, flirting. It was almost like seeing in stereovision, although Della was just a little smaller and Carla was just a little more dimpled. They thought I was something special because no matter what you say, years of believing that someone is a lesbian can't be dispelled in an instant. I had taken their sister and made a woman of her. A heterosexual woman, which in their eyes was redundant, Cissy's admission aside. There's also the sister competition thing, what belonged to Eleanor being more attractive than if I had not been Eleanor's. As we talked small talk and laughed and I explained Eleanor's position as manager of my bed-and-breakfast, among other properties, and how we came to meet, and yes, there really was an evil, foul ghost occupying the place—another piece of cake?—I began to imagine what each of them looked like stark naked. I can't defend myself in this regard because—and fellas, you'll back me up on this—I'm a guy and this is what we guys do.

I just happened to look across the room where Eleanor, her mother, her father and Cissy were having a heated conversation and caught Eleanor's eyes, which said she would kill me later, and stop flirting with her sisters. I just grinned back because really, I had done nothing wrong, told the truth in every instance, and was enjoying the company of not one, but two truly beautiful women.

WHEN we were in Eleanor's pickup, she backed up over the parking bumper that held the trash dumpster in place, slammed the gearshift into drive, and squealed out of the parking lot. "I take it," she said, "you don't want to sleep with half a dozen men in my father's den?" she asked.

"How do you mean that?"

"I told them we would be more comfortable in a motel, which you're paying for," she replied. "I told them—"

But suddenly there was Ella, standing in front of the pickup and beside their family car. Eleanor stopped, and I rolled the passenger window down. "Don't forget your fitting," she told Eleanor. "It's at nine."

"I'll be there," Eleanor said. "Roll the window up, Theo."

"Theo?" Ella asked.

"Parker's his last name. His real first name is Theo."

"Actually, I prefer Parker," I said.

"Theo! That's a darling name!" Ella exclaimed (really, *exclaimed*).

"Roll the window up, Theo," Eleanor said. "We're going now."

I rolled the window up. Eleanor put the truck in gear.

"You didn't have to get nasty," I said.

Eleanor looked at me for an instant with an expression that said, *You are at this moment the most vile human being on the face of the earth.*

I paid for two motel rooms with an adjoining door. Eleanor's side was locked. I knocked but gave up after a while, turned on the TV and raided the honor bar for Toblerone chocolate and some pretzels. She came in around ten-thirty and sat on my bed. She was wearing her nightgown now, short, filmy, flippy-floppy, she didn't care—it was as if I had become one of her gay friends, had she actually made any male gay friends.

"Give me chocolate," she ordered, and I tossed what remained of the Toblerone at her.

"Look at it this way," I said. "Your parents don't think you're gay anymore. You're not gay, so that's a good thing, right? Cissy has come out, and she is a lesbian, so that's a good thing too, right? So what's the harm?"

"They think you're the reincarnation of Samson and Hercules," Eleanor said. "They think you're Superman!"

Well, they could think what they wanted.

"They think you're so damn manly my lesbian ways just collapsed before you and your horn—Gabriel's horn," she finished, just to make sure I didn't misinterpret what she was saying. "Walking around my walls and blowing your . . . Oh, crap, they think you're such hot stuff!"

"Eleanor, I was just—"

"And don't think I didn't see the way you were looking at my sisters!" Eleanor said, and did I note just a hint of jealousy creeping in there?

"They're beautiful women. If I hadn't looked at them, now that would have been unnatural."

Eleanor considered my argument. Yes, she had grown up hearing just how beautiful her sisters were, how lovely their hair was, and their skin, and their eyes, and their other attributes. "Yes, they are impressive human specimens," she suggested playfully. "That Carla, what a rack!"

"Eleanor!"

"And I've seen them out of the corral," Eleanor went on. "Perfect shape. More round than deep. Areolas that point to the stars."

"Eleanor, Carla's your sister," I reminded her, disgusted at the direction of this conversation, and interested at the same time.

"Now Della, she's got a rack, too. It's a little smaller than Carla's, so she compensates by wearing a Wonderbra. They're perfectly shaped, too," she continued, rising from my bed, strolling toward the door that linked our rooms. Her index fingers pointed toward the constellation Orion. "Again, to the stars."

"It's not appropriate for one sister to talk about another," I said.

"Why not? For nearly a decade they told everyone I was a lesbian."

"It's not the same thing."

"Now Carla has the perfect bottom, and her legs—she keeps her entire body tanned, I'm sure you noticed. Della's afraid of sun damage, and her bottom is what you would call, well, you—" and here she had to think a moment. "You would say she had extra-strong landing gear. But it's shaped nicely."

She was grinning from ear to ear, because by this time in our relationship Eleanor knew I was a guy, just a regular guy who responded to women in the way guys always have and always will. I wanted to see Carla and Della stark naked and in a friendly mood, and she knew it. Theoretically speaking, of course.

"And the thing is, Theo," she whispered at the door, "the thing is, you can have either one of them, because they'll think they're stealing you from me!"

She slammed the door shut and locked it.

She took my chocolate with her.

twelve

THE wedding was lovely. In all this time I haven't mentioned the bride, but she was lovely, too, if one overlooks the slight gap between her front teeth which gave her a Terry Thomas look. I'm speaking of the late English character actor Terry Thomas. Adelaid—she was called Addie, the bride— didn't have Terry's mustache, of course, nor his comic gait. She was attractive, really.

Her dress was white silk and lace, with a bodice that rose to her neck and a back that was mostly missing. Unfortunately, Addie was nervous and apparently developed some sort of rash across her back that generous applications of powder couldn't hide. It was under her arms, too, which the dress exposed as she held her wedding bouquet.

It's for reasons like this Lily and I were married before a judge.

By this time Eleanor had become more civil toward me. After all, I hadn't attempted to sabotage anything. My objective had been to drive her stock up in the family corporate environment, and I achieved that. She was still the least attractive Glacy, and that included the two males of the family, father Billy and the brother Dougie. But she was a real heterosexual woman, which, in Fresno, means a lot.

Cissy, alas, had reacted to coming out by accident by cutting her hair into a rather severe style and wearing jewelry in piercings that hadn't been obvious without the hardware. The holes,

I mean. She apparently hadn't slept well and had developed bags beneath her eyes. She wore pants under the bridesmaid's dress (Ella told me this), but the damn thing was so long, no one could see anyway.

Pastor Bob Ratchett (I learned his name only that morning) conducted a fine service, not nearly as ostentatious as I'd feared. The flowers descended from heaven, embracing the boy and girl in a horseshoe of various blossoms. Angels sang (six of the best voices from the church choir, I was told) for a photo moment (or, more accurately, twenty minutes), after which we all retired to the Elks Lodge three doors down the street, where God wouldn't mind too much if liquor were served.

All told, there were two hundred guests. Eleanor and I were lost in the mass of sweating humanity almost immediately. "No snide comments from you, Parker," she said, using my preferred name again. Everyone else had picked up the Theo monicker from Ella, of course, so now I was to be Theo until I got the hell out of there.

"I have no snide comments to make," I told Eleanor, who I might add looked quite good. Her sisters had given her some tips on makeup, or maybe even applied it for her, which brought out her eyes and lips and cheeks. The dress was cut to make it look like she had breasts and hips, and her skin, which was always her best feature, was even better beneath a light dusting of powder. She smelled good, too, although not of vanilla, my favorite.

Della lassoed me first. She pushed through the crowd like a destroyer powering through the waves, right to where I was standing in line for libation. "Eleanor, you don't mind if I borrow Theo, do you? Just for a moment? You'll have him back in two shakes of a puppy's tail, and in good condition, I promise."

Eleanor took my place in line because by this time she needed a drink too. Della, meanwhile, dragged me across the hall to a private room whose door she shut behind us. As good as Eleanor looked, and I had told her several times she was the bee's knees, there was no way she could compete with Della, who may have been the most attractive woman I ever stood beside. She took her time, looking me up and down like I was a prize bull brought in for stud services, before she said, "I just wanted to say—"

"Yes?"

"I just wanted to say, I'm flabbergasted!"

"You are?"

"I never thought Eleanor . . . I mean, we love Eleanor, don't get me wrong. She's too bookish, and she doesn't care a whit about clothes or makeup or anything that helps a woman be, well . . . a woman. And god has not seen fit to give her . . ."

"Feminine attributes?" I suggested.

"She's as flat as an ironing board," Della reported sadly. Curious that these two women should discuss their respective chests, and within hours of one another. "But you know that!" Della continued. Everyone knew that, I noted to myself.

"Never in my wildest dreams for her—we love her dearly, you know, even though sometimes it doesn't seem so—never did I expect her to bag a man as, well . . ."

"Manly?" I suggested.

"No, that's not it," Della said. "Uhm, ordinary—Yes, that's it! Ordinary . . . as you!"

"Ordinary?"

"I don't mean you're not good-looking, because you are."

"Thanks."

"I find you very attractive."

"Good to know."

"My point being, you are a reach for her in the couples department."

"I am?"

"Absolutely. And that's why I know it's love, and not some

kind of temporary lust like most men get when they look at your body. You have no idea how many men want to just do me because of my figure. I have to be very careful."

I was past being insulted at being called ordinary by this time and was honestly curious about Della's perspective.

"You have to be careful," I said, prodding her on.

"They see my body, but they don't see me," Della said. "But with you, you must see Eleanor as she is, because, frankly, she has no body to look at, really, although I've always thought her face is pretty. Isn't her face pretty?"

"Oh, very," I commented dryly.

"I mean she's not bogged down with these dimples and things. She's got a plain face like most models have."

Now I hadn't ever thought of that. Eleanor's face was honest, straightforward, and plain, in the terrain sort of way.

"People have always had a hard time seeing Eleanor for who she is, but it's clear to me you two are in love. I mean, no one could shoot grins or dirty looks back and forth at each other with such abandon and not love one another, right?"

I didn't answer, but she must have seen an answer in my expression, which from this side of my skin was just dumfounded.

"So I want to say thank you," Della told me, wrapping her arms around me and holding me tight like a close member of the family, her rather large chest pressed against my bonier one not worth mentioning because we're family now. I knew she was sincere, she wasn't trying to cut in on her sister—a part of me found that disappointing—and I was touched by the fact that she really did love her plain sibling and was happy for her.

When she pulled away, I noted that her makeup was ruined and she would have to go replenish it, or whatever one did to so much powder and oil. She left the room and I was alone for a moment before Carla entered. Damn, it was hard to tell the two sisters apart.

Well, there was one way.

"Any more at home like you?" she asked coquettishly.

"Broke the mold," I said, "during production."

"That's just too bad," she said. "I always found older men, particularly distinguished, gimpy men, a real turn on."

She meant my cane and limp, one leg shorter, or longer if you prefer, than the other. I shrugged sadly. Sorry, no can do.

"Well, just as well. Eleanor needs you more than I do, I suppose. But you must be one powerful lover."

Deny this? No.

"Look, I really didn't come in here to flirt with you," Carla said. "In fact, I shouldn't even be toying with it because you're my lesbian sister's . . . well, now my other lesbian sister's beau, and I want her to be happy."

"She's a great girl," I said.

"You think so?" Hm. Carla was not completely convinced. "I mean, she's always been a little . . . strange. But you know that."

This seemed like the perfect opportunity to find things out about Eleanor, my friend Eleanor. "Not completely," I replied. "I'm not sure I know what you mean."

"Well, she was the first Glacy girl to buy a vibrator, even though she's third in line."

"Really?"

"Said it was for her shoulder. She said she had a bad vertebra or something."

"In her shoulder?"

"And she would go into the bathroom with it and massage for hours on end."

"Really?"

"But Della and I knew what she was really doing. I guess maybe Cissy had a clue too, now that I think of it."

"Ah," said I, trying to look as normal as a person could who had been given intimate details of his friend's masturbatory predilections.

"She used to read these books, too." Well, everyone said Eleanor was bookish. "*Delta of Venus* was her favorite. By Anaïs Nin. We all thought it was just some literary thing or other, but then Della read one of the chapters, and then we all read it. It's a sex book!"

"Really?"

"And she never had a date. Not one. All through high school."

"Was she really that unattractive?"

Carla struggled with the issue. "I never thought she was bad-looking, just different. She's allergic to perfumes, you know, so sometimes she would wear vanilla, which smells nice. And she was allergic to most makeup in those days, although makeup's mostly hypoallergenic today. But . . . Eleanor's been down on herself her entire life. There's a reason, I guess you already suspect what it is."

Yes, I suspected what it was.

"Mom's summer of love?" I asked.

Carla laughed. "Yes! Summer of love! That's very good!"

She couldn't quite bring herself to say it. Having no scruples myself, no fear of invading people's private lives, I asked, "Who is Eleanor's real father?"

"He was the Pastor of the church back then," Carla said. "He's moved on now, to Nebraska, I hear, which is a kind of penance itself, I guess. My dad used to drink and raise hell and treat everyone bad, my mom worst of all. She needed something and the minister, he just gave it, that's all."

Timely gift well received, apparently. So Eleanor was named for her mother, a gesture of commitment, maybe, or a way to assert pride where none was obvious. Eleanor. Ella.

"Eleanor knew—we all knew, because they decided not to

hide it," Carla went on. "They made Cissy just to prove their marriage was strong. And it has been, ever since. But Eleanor, she's been down on herself all her life. Not as pretty as the other Glacy girls, not as popular. Hell, not as Glacy as us, either."

Poor Carla could not see the upside to any of this, but there was an upside because an outsider like me could tell, Eleanor was smarter and deeper than all the other Glacys put together.

"She has intimacy problems," Carla said finally. "With boys who would ask her out. With friends at school. With us, even. But now she's found you, Theo. She's found a man who will love her because of who she is and not because she's got big tits or looks good in a bathing suit."

I said nothing, because I was a thief in my host's house.

"Would you do me a favor?" I asked Carla.

"Sure."

"Would you send the minister in to see me? And don't get any ideas, okay? I'm just going to have a talk with him, and not about marriage."

THE minister arrived ten minutes later. I sat him down and told him about my bed-and-breakfast. I told him everything, about Lily, about Eleanor, about the sex issue that seemed to thread through the entire matter.

"And they're dreams, right? You're just talking about dreams?"

"So far, except for the noises, and I think they might have a natural explanation."

"Exorcism, that's a Catholic thing," Pastor Bob said.

"That's what I hear."

"I guess we could bless the place. Ask the Holy Spirit to cast demons out, although that's really a Foursquare Church kind of thing."

"All I'm asking now, just for the moment, is you come spend a night at the bed-and-breakfast, on me."

"Spend a night in a haunted house?" Clearly this didn't seem like the best idea in the world to Pastor Bob.

"Well, I would be there," I suggested.

"And Eleanor?"

"No. Not Eleanor. I think maybe Eleanor's the source of the problem."

thirteen

SOME people drink a little. Some people drink a lot. Some of the former people get drunk as a goose; some of the latter show not a sign of intoxication. Eleanor was a former who decided to give the latter a try. As the reception went on Eleanor became more and more intoxicated, on more and varied successive drinks, until finally she was as blotto as an animated duck.

I, on the other hand, drank a small quantity of bourbon, the only reaction to which was that I needed my cane less.

At one point Eleanor stood up before the gathered celebrants and announced that not only was she not a lesbian, she was a virgin. The people at the reception, particularly those on the other side of the aisle, the bride's side, were so astonished by this that a pall of silence settled over the place until I stood and began clapping. Soon Eleanor received a standing ovation.

Of course, I and a select few knew that she had had carnal knowledge of one, and possibly a series of plastic bananas with batteries in them, but no matter, none's the wiser.

When Eleanor began to amuse herself by voicing that she should lose her virginity to some lucky fellow at the reception, I decided it was time to go. Prior to this Billy and Ella approached me regarding the virgin thing and I just shook my head and grimaced, assuring them that their dear daughter was merely having fun with them.

So I drove the Ranger. We stopped once for gas and once for vomit, one a pickup, the other a delivery. By the time we neared

Cambria, Eleanor was sobering but sick, moaning, "Please tell me I didn't—"

"You've lived a life of rectitude, Eleanor. It had to pee out sometime," I told her.

"In front of all those people!"

"Yes, and your image has changed, that's for sure."

"Cissy told me I should have stayed a lesbian."

"I'm sure that's Cissy's perspective."

"I told them I was a virgin!" she realized.

"Not to worry. I told everyone I've filled each one of your orifices with every pointy or protruding part of my body, including elbows and earlobes."

"God, I was so drunk. . . ."

Now that didn't deserve an answer.

I drove past Cambria and San Simeon up the coast to a Vista Point, one of those cleared spaces along the highway and beside the sea where one may stop and view the scenery. It was past one in the morning by this time, a moonless night where stars fell across the sky like a blanket. I stopped the pickup and stepped out. Eleanor joined me a moment later, still unsteady on her feet and holding on to the passenger door with both hands.

"God, the sky is beautiful," I said, a whisper almost.

"Did Della make a play for you?" Eleanor asked.

"Your sisters love you more than you know," I replied.

"Carla?"

"She told me about the vibrator," I said, but didn't elaborate further. "She said you were isolated, even from a very young age. She said they all love you."

"We love each other!" Eleanor spat at me, as if I had suggested the opposite.

I said nothing, but pointed at the stars. Eleanor looked. "Yes, beautiful," she said. She was still wearing the bridesmaid getup, and it was stained from the unfortunate episode earlier when

Eleanor almost didn't get her head out the door in time. Our bags were in the truck. She almost toppled making it to the bed of the truck, found her bag, unzipped it.

"I'm going to change clothes, so don't look."

"I can't promise that," I replied with a smile.

"You don't even think I'm attractive!" she said, slurring half the words.

"You're a beautiful woman, Eleanor Glacy, and you can't trust yourself with me because I'm a man."

She tried to unzip the dress in back, fouled the zipper, then pulled the outfit off over her head. She was wearing almost nothing, nothing on top certainly. She bent down and removed her shoes, tossing them into the bed with the ruined, meant-to-be-used-once dress. She pulled on a pair of pants, zipped them up, cinched the belt, then dove into the bag looking for a shirt.

I saw this briefly in the passenger side-door mirror, but looked away, back at the stars. She found a flannel shirt, buttoned it wrong, leaving one side of the bottom lower than the other, then circled the car to be beside me. She carried two soft-soled shoes and handed them to me. "If you please," she said.

She sat on the truck seat while I, like her prince, pulled socks onto her feet, and then fitted each shoe, tying each lace. When she stood up I began to rebutton her shirt, from the top down. She watched me hopefully, as if I might stop at one button or the other, unbutton them all, and then take her.

The possibility occurred to me.

Had she the figure of Carla or Della my fingers would never have gotten this close to her chest without sexual intent. As it was, her tiny bosom was quickly swallowed by fabric as I buttoned the flannel shirt.

When I was done, I found that she had been looking at me the full time.

"So now you know, don't you?" she asked.

"About the vibrator? Yes. About the hours spent in the bathroom massaging your vertebra, yes."

"My sisters have blue eyes, I have brown. My sisters have big—"

"I know you're a bastard. Your family still loves you, Eleanor."

"My mother loves me," Eleanor spat. "I am my mother's daughter. But Daddy isn't Daddy, and my sisters are really just half-sisters. . . ."

"It doesn't matter."

"Yes, it does!"

"It doesn't matter now, because everyone's grown up and that's in the past. Your father loves you. Probably not as much as he loves the others, but that's the way of the human heart, Eleanor, and you can't fault him for that. It's a miracle he loves you at all. A miracle."

She stumbled to one of the large boulders the state has lined these scenic stops with so cars won't roll into the sea, or into the rocks and surf below. She sat down. The truck headlights were still on, the engine still running, so I shut them off. I sat on the hood of the truck because it was still warm. Eleanor would not feel cold for hours yet, alcohol in the bloodstream acting as heater.

"How old were you when they told you?" I asked. Honesty. I had a friend who was adopted and during that period in our history it was felt that honesty was far more important than comfort, so his parents were told to tell him he wasn't their biological son as early as they could. He had been six. He never recovered.

"Seven," she replied. Close.

"How did they put it?"

"They said Mommy and Daddy had made Dougie, Carla, and Della, but then they were apart for a while, so Mommy and this other man who remained nameless because of his profession made me. But then Mommy and Daddy got back together and they made Cissy. It didn't matter that Daddy didn't help to make me because he loved me anyway and he would always be my Daddy. Pretty neat, huh?"

"Did your parents separate for a time?"

"No. I found out who my father was when I was twelve. He had left our church by then and went on to another. He and my mother had an affair for two weeks before Pastor MacDonald's guilt got the better of him and he confessed to his wife. My parents became Baptists after that."

"Ever try to talk with him?"

"Once. Over the phone."

"How'd it go?"

"I was a 'child of sin,' he said. He asked me to go to church every day and pray that my body and my soul not be damned forever because of what he and my mother did."

"Concise. Not particularly compassionate, but concise."

"Not everything is a joke, Parker."

"On the contrary, Eleanor, dear Eleanor, almost everything is."

"I've been screwed up my whole life," Eleanor told me. "I was the ugly daughter. I was the bastard daughter, because somehow people found out. My parents were very honest and forthright about things. Forgiveness and all that. From God. From the community."

Stupidity is part of the human condition. I didn't have to say this. Some wisdom need not be spoken. We all know it.

"Occasionally boys in high school would ask me out, god knows why. I couldn't say yes. I thought maybe it was because I was a bastard. You know, the 'Say Yes' gene. My mother couldn't say no, maybe the same was true of me."

THE HAUNTING OF CAMBRIA 🕊 115

"Eleanor, girls stopped saying no a long time ago."

"We're talking about feelings here, okay? Even men know about feelings, don't they?"

"Remotely," I replied. "Go on."

"And I felt . . . dirty and sometimes worthless. I tried to kill myself three times. No one mentioned that, did they?"

I sat up, slid from the hood, found my footing. Her family talked about homosexuality and infidelity but somehow forgot to mention that their daughter/sister had tried to take her own life?

"No," I replied after a time. "No one said anything about that."

"I was in therapy for a while," she went on. "I thought if I just got away from them, created a new life of my own, then . . . things would be better. So I came here to Cambria."

"Have things been better?"

She grinned after a moment. "Yes, actually, they have. I know a lot of people in town. They've all been nice to me, everyone except that electrician, Mr. Coake, and apparently he's nasty to everyone."

Ah, I no longer had to take Coake's nastiness personally.

"I don't have a lot of friends yet, but I'm . . . learning. I've made you into a friend, haven't I, Parker?"

"Bosom buddies," I replied.

"So, you can grow out of your problems, or solve them, or whatever."

"I've always believed that," I told her earnestly. "I've always believed in hope."

She had talked herself out of a depression, and mostly intoxication. She stood up and breathed the ocean air. Behind her, waves rushed to the shore and crashed with magnificent explosions. We had only the parking lights to guide us, but above, the stars were truly magnificent.

"There's just one thing," I said to Eleanor as she stood beside me and stared up into the vault of heaven.

"What's that?"

"I'm evicting you."

"This isn't fair, Theo!"

I was back to being Theo again. I had better get used to it, I thought.

"Look, Eleanor, if it turns out something happens and you're not there, then, great, you can move right back in and continue to be terrorized."

"What if something doesn't happen?"

"Then it tends to suggest—I wouldn't say prove, but suggests—you are the cause of the events."

"Theo—"

"Listen to me. I'm having your minister out. Maybe a deacon or two. You can get a room at The Bluebird on Main Street. Their prices are reasonable and the place has local color. Maybe I'll even take you to The Sow's Ear for—"

"This isn't fair!"

"We'll have some other people sleep over. Maybe somebody else from out of town who has no preconceptions about the place. You can sleep elsewhere for the night. If everyone sleeps the night through with no problems, then . . . Eleanor, women who have not had active sexual lives have been known to cause, I don't know, events."

"Aren't you talking about telekinesis?" she argued. "And isn't that usually when the female is a girl, not a woman?"

"Yes, and yes, but let's look at this rationally," I said, regretting it the minute I said it, because it suggested she wasn't speaking rationally. "You do have an unusual sexual background—"

"I have no sexual background!"

"You're ignoring the vibrator," I said.

"Not everything's a joke, Theo."

"Okay, right," I said. "Oh, listen, Eleanor, I know you've made that grim place your home over these past months, but we need to test this thing, okay?"

She agreed around the time she began to shiver.

fourteen

We arrived back at Monroe House at three. We were both so tired Eleanor went right into the bathroom to change into her jammies while I stood in the hall and put on cast-off pajamas. Did anyone really wear pajamas anymore? I wondered. But it was too cold to wonder long, and when I tapped on the bedroom door, Eleanor said, "Your converted lesbian's already in bed." I entered and found her with eyes already closed, covered to her chin with bedding, and acting as if she were fast asleep.

I took the opposite bed and turned out the light. I had a brief debate with myself regarding the merits of equipping each room with a Clapper—you know, those devices that allow you to shut off the lights from bed just by clapping your hands—but darkness made the argument moot and I was asleep almost instantly.

The glowing face of my wristwatch on the nightstand between us said it was four when the baleful calling began. Eleanor was already sitting up. I looked over at her and she made a face and said, "Did I forget to mention I scheduled this?"

I rolled out of bed and sat on the edge, waiting for the noise to go away, but it merely got louder. Eleanor sat down beside me. She was wearing boxer shorts I recognized from the used clothes bin and a sweatshirt marked COAST UNION XL, which I thought was pretty cute until I realized she hadn't had a chance to shower since the roadside incident where she vomited and she wasn't taking any chances with her own clothes.

I got the flashlight from the bedside table. She already had hers. We stood.

The noise became terrible, as loud as a shout and as mournful as a dirge. The walls seemed to shake with it. I looked to Eleanor, but she shook her head no. This was new.

We ventured to the door and opened it. Outside, beyond the influence of our two meager flashlight beams, Monroe House was as dark as a pit, and the sound twice as loud. I stepped out. Eleanor followed.

I checked the lights. Nothing, switched up or down. I waved my beam downstairs, at the front door and the entries to the lobby and the kitchen respectively. Nothing was moving but my hand, which I admit shook a little.

"It's coming from in there," Eleanor said.

Her flashlight beam was on the door to the master suite. She snapped off the beam. A red glow flickered from beneath the door.

"Turn that back on," I ordered. Eleanor pushed the flashlight switch and its puny light made an imperfect circle of yellow on the door.

I stood there for a time, considering. "What are you waiting for?" Eleanor asked. Now there's a question. I could imagine Napoleon being asked that very question at Waterloo, or Nimitz at Midway. "Oh, for chrissakes," Eleanor said and stepped past me. She wrapped her fingers around the doorknob and stopped, surprised.

"What is it?" I asked. She removed her hand and mine took its place. Cold. The knob was freezing cold. Literally. I turned it and pushed the door open. The wailing was a bellow now, so loud we would have had a hard time hearing one another, had either of us anything to say.

The light was coming from the closet whose door was wide open. Someone was standing inside there.

I tried the wall switch, with the same result. Nothing.

Eleanor stepped past me to get a better angle for a look at the closet. I had considered that, of course, but strangely my mind was thinking of other things. I was thinking about Lily and how she had loved this building, this room, that closet. So big. Big enough for all her clothes, her shoes, her hats (yes, hats). And I thought about how dreams are given substance, not by work entirely, but by making them so real in your mind that they have to be real in the world itself. And as I was thinking this, I was remembering our first night together and how her body pressed against mine made me feel, and still made me feel when I thought about it. I remembered the scent of her, artificial and natural, the smell of her hair and skin, the wonderful taste of her lips and tongue. I remembered just how much I had loved Lily—how much I still did—when she walked out of the closet.

But it was postmortem Lily who walked out of the closet, coroner's-slab Lily. One leg had been torn off, I was told—I vaguely remembered a doctor telling me that much later, long after her body had been reduced to ashes and buried in Maryland. Both legs were there now, but I could see the terrible rift in her flesh where her right leg had been ripped away. Her clothes were a mess, the knit shirt, the shorts. There was blood everywhere. Her skin was white and mottled a marble gray, the result of blood settling, I remembered reading.

Lily's skull was dented on the left side, pushed in, and blood had cascaded down onto her face, covering most of it. Now only her cool green eyes were untouched, because the lids were open and she was staring at me. She did not limp, as I did now, as she walked slowly toward me. In death she had full mobility. And the terrible crying, that horrific, mournful sobbing at the noise level of an orchestra, was coming from her open mouth.

Her hands were open to me, like Christ's are often depicted, as if inviting all the world to come embrace him, except in Lily's case one hand was twisted almost all the way around, broken at the wrist. She turned at the far corner of the bed and continued approaching.

"Parker?" Eleanor asked with just a hint of excitement in her voice, like she had just been bitten by a werewolf. I could think of nothing to say. Introductions didn't seem appropriate. All I could think of was that I had done this to Lily, more than killed her and mutilated her body, but helped to keep her here in this goddamn bed-and-breakfast with my occupancy of it and half-assed plans to restore it.

"Parker?" Eleanor asked again.

"Lily," I said.

Lily passed Eleanor as if she wasn't there. The bellowing continued, but rose in volume, as if this corpse were singing. Her arms reached out toward me. I wanted her to touch me. I wanted her to make me pay for what I had done. I wanted to be made clean again, washed in the blood of retribution. I was also scared as hell and incapable of moving.

Lily's hands, the straight one, the bent one, reached out for me and I did nothing. Well, I began to cry. That was it. I began to cry, for what we lost that day on the highway near the Piedras Blancas lighthouse, on a curve, at a moment when Lily put her feet on the dash and I marveled at her lovely legs.

Lily's fingers were reaching for me. The sound was a shrill bellow, like a wind, a shriek. Lily's eyes were so open and bright they glowed. I stood waiting, waiting for the inevitable.

But then Eleanor stepped between us. I saw doubt cross Lily's expression.

"You can't have him!" Eleanor said. Her voice was so low in comparison to the wail that I almost didn't hear it. But she spoke louder the second time, a shout. "You can't have him!"

Lily swung her arm with the broken wrist and hit Eleanor

across the cheek, sending her reeling. Then she began to take another step when Eleanor stepped between us again, her lip bleeding—how this could be so, I don't know, a corporeal ghost—and shouted, "You can't have him! *You can't have him!*"

The ghost swung again. Her arm broke and flew across the room. Eleanor continued to stand her ground as doubt and rage commingled in the ghost's expression before its light blinked out of existence, and Eleanor fainted to the floor.

For a long moment I didn't know what to do. There was complete silence in the room, the only light coming from the two dropped flashlights, their beams shooting crazily across the floor of the master suite. Then I heard Eleanor moan, and I dropped to her side. She was unconscious.

I picked Eleanor up, took her to our shared bedroom, wrapped a quilt around her and rushed her down the stairs and outside, to the porch swing, where I sat and held her until the sun began to warm us. She was out cold, and her lip started swelling long before her eyes opened, but when they did she smiled and said, "Pretty good, huh?" Well, it sounded more like, "Preddy good, hunh?" because her lip was swollen badly. Eleanor had been struck by a ghost.

The ghost of my late wife.

"You're a brave person," I said.

"Yeah, I know. Thurprithing, hunh?"

I don't know what came over me, but I leaned down and kissed her on her swollen lips. I lingered there, as grotesque as her swollen lips were, pressed gently against them. When I pulled away, her eyes were closed, as if she'd been trying to experience what a real kiss from me would feel like.

Like the dolt that I was, and am, it didn't occur to me to put an icepack on her lips, but she suggested it, and I went to retrieve some ice and put it in a baggy, and that in a dishtowel. She was sitting up when I returned, the sweatshirt that said

COAST UNION XL across the chest half-exposed from the quilt. She put the ice to her lips immediately.

"Thill think I'm the thourthe of all thith?" she asked.

I wasn't ready to answer that one. Probably not, I thought, but really, when you put all the pieces together, Eleanor had been the only person to experience physical manifestations— the finger bruises on her legs, and the swollen lips. She could be some kind of psychic projector who created the sounds and images and made them seem real.

I also didn't want to think Lily was a ghost harboring anger and hatred for me, even if I deserved it.

"I don't think it was her," Eleanor said after a moment, seeming to read my mind. "I think it's this house."

"It's not the Lily I knew in life," I said. "She could no more hurt me than . . . you."

That made her smile. Admittedly, I could have done without the smile. Any cop strolling by at that moment would have arrested me for beating a woman.

"It'th the houthe," Eleanor said again. "But we'll do it your way. I'll move out."

fifteen

L ATER, after the sun was well up in the sky, Eleanor and I went back to the master suite. We found the door to the closet closed, as it had been days before, and no sign of the events of earlier that morning. There were no severed arms lying nearby or blood or any of that. We got excited a moment when we found a single drop of blood, but then we realized that it was probably Eleanor's, from when she was struck.

If she was struck.

Eleanor was still wearing striped boxer shorts and the COAST UNION XL sweatshirt, her hair tied back into a ponytail, her feet bare. She looked cute as hell and noticed my looking at her. It made her grin, and me stop.

"When's Pastor Bob coming?" she asked.

"This afternoon. With a van of volunteers."

"How do you plan to feed these people?" Eleanor asked, always the practical one. I shrugged. I was prepared to buy their meals from the various restaurants in town. If there's one thing Cambria has more than its share of, it's restaurants.

"I'll come over, cook them breakfast, lunch, and dinner," she said.

"It's a bed-and-breakfast," I reminded her.

"You're asking them to stay in a haunted house overnight. The least we can do is feed them." There was that use of "we" again.

"Okay. Thanks," I told her.

Later that day, in the early afternoon, I drove her to the Bluebird Motel on Main Street. I made a reciprocal deal with them, trading nights in unused rooms once we reopened. They were being very trusting. But hell, it was Cambria.

Pastor Bob arrived about five-thirty driving an Astro van containing two deacons, a youth minister who looked too young to be anything but a youth himself, and the choir leader, a woman named Mildred. Mildred was very pretty and under thirty and was the fifth person in her family, and fourth generation of a line of Mildreds, to have that name. She went by Millie. I was told this as I shook her hand.

Inside, at the kitchen table, I explained what had happened after the wedding when Eleanor and I arrived back at Monroe House, a manifestation involving actual physical contact. It was decided immediately by Pastor Bob that Millie should go bunk with Eleanor. I agreed.

I didn't go into detail about which room had experienced what, and I placed Pastor Bob in the master suite and spread the others out in various rooms. I remained in the room with two beds, lying and telling them it wasn't our normal sleeping arrangement. We played pinochle (single deck, four-handed) at the kitchen table until almost nine, then retired to our various bedrooms.

I was awakened at six by Eleanor sitting at the end of my bed, wearing a flannel shirt and jeans. She'd raided the old clothes bin again. I'd created a trend.

"Anything happen last night?" she asked.

"Not as far as I can tell."

"I'll start breakfast," she said, standing, then with a grin, "I'm making cinnamon rolls!"

By the time I strolled into the kitchen, Millie and Eleanor were laughing and talking about something that had happened at their church years before, and I wondered at how Eleanor had seemed to loosen up. No one would call her weird now, I thought.

Pastor Bob and the two deacons came in next, followed minutes later by the youth minister, whose hair shot up in back like he hadn't had time to comb it. He had one of those short haircuts where all you have to do is pat everything down in the morning.

"Well?" I asked everyone.

"Slept like a baby," Pastor Bob said.

"Hey, this is a nice place," Deacon Jones (not the ex-football player) commented. "I bet the Mrs. would like this."

Deacon Mueller turned one of the chairs around John-Wayne style and sat. "Had a strange dream," he reported. "But the Lord Jesus Christ smote that old devil and I just went back to sleep."

Even Pastor Bob had to roll his eyes at that one.

My eyes met Eleanor's across the room. There was sadness there, because now even she had to admit that whatever was happening in Monroe House was connected to her, somehow. I felt bad for her. I felt bad for me.

The church group toured the town, snapped pictures left and right, had lunch on me at Linn's (I took the morose Eleanor along with us, so she wouldn't have to cook), and then we rendezvoused at The Black Cat, one of Cambria's newest restaurants, where I bought everyone dinner. Total cost for the experiment . . . Oh, to hell with it.

Sometime between Linn's and The Black Cat, Eleanor and I found ourselves alone in the Astro van.

"Last night doesn't mean anything," she asserted.

"No, but it suggests something, doesn't it?"

"What do you plan to do about it?"

"I want you to move out. Permanently."

She said nothing for a moment, merely stared ahead at

Leffingwell Landing, the spot where sailing ships from San Francisco used to unload their wares long before the road through Big Sur was finished. The church folks were posing by the waterside for pictures. "I don't want to leave," she said softly.

"It's just a rooming house," I replied. "It's just wood and paint and mildew."

"You don't want me to leave."

"Of course I don't want you to leave."

"We've become a team."

"I'm happy you think so."

"Who'll cook for you?"

"I'll buy Pop-Tarts, Raisin Bran, Cheerios—"

"No, I mean for the guests, after you reopen."

This was the first I'd heard of this. She wanted to be the chef of Monroe House. Damn, I should have realized. She hadn't stayed in a haunted house—or maybe haunted it herself—for more than two months without an ulterior motive. She wanted a job.

"Fine. You've got the job," I said. "But you can't stay at Monroe House. Not at night."

But that wasn't good enough. "You think I'm bringing this . . . haunting to your doorstep, Parker, but believe me, I'm not."

Pastor Bob came back to the van then, followed by a gaggle of fellow church members, and we went to dinner at The Black Cat.

WE said good-bye to the church bunch on the front porch of Monroe House. Pastor Bob, whom I was developing a real fondness for—never did he take himself more seriously than anyone else—leaned forward and whispered into my ear, "You should marry that girl, Theo." (I was still being called Theo, thanks to Eleanor's telling her mother about my real first name.) "You should marry her, because she's made to love just one man and it's pretty obvious to me that man is you. I'll provide the church and the minister for free."

The wages of sin are a discount marriage, at least with Pastor Bob.

I demurred. We all laughed and waved. The van headed back to Fresno.

When I turned around to go back into the house, Eleanor was sitting on the porch swing. I sat beside her.

After a time she said, "I belong here, with you."

"Eleanor, we barely know one another."

"No. You're crazy for me. Everyone sees it."

"If you're talking about those church folks, it's because that's what we've told them—you and me together!"

"I can see you're crazy about me," Eleanor asserted. "I can sense these things, Parker. Men don't know much more than what their organ tells them, but women feel things much more deeply."

I grinned. It just so happened that I believed this, up to a point, but this was no time to admit it.

"I'm sorry, sweetheart," I said, and it was the diminutive "sweetheart" one uses with children, and not the sexual kind. "I'm really, really sorry, but you've spent your last night in Monroe House."

"Then I should get the rest of my things," she said in a monotone.

"Yes, you should."

She stood up and went inside. I continued to sit on the swing, hearing it creak, watching the occasional car drive into the Brambles parking lot, which you can barely see from our front porch. I was going to miss Eleanor, if she chose not to work as the house chef. I suspected that if she did, we'd develop our own reputation in town. Maybe I could expand, create a real dining room out that side door. Eleanor's cooking was superb.

But if she chose to move back to Fresno, or up or down the coast away from Cambria, then I really would miss her because she was right, we'd become a team. Pals. Bosom buddies.

After a time I realized that she should have come back downstairs by now. I was suddenly worried about her. Whatever connection she had with this house might not want her to leave. It might . . .

I bounded up the stairs calling her name and almost tripped over the two bags parked outside the door of our room. They were her bags—neatly packed, it seemed—soft luggage, not lumpy or . . .

"Eleanor?" I called. I tapped on the door.

"Yes?" she answered.

"Are you okay?"

"You can come in, Parker."

I turned the knob and entered. There was one lamp on, the one between the double beds. She sat on her bed. She held the bath towel lengthwise so that it covered her, although I could see she wore no panties or bra (I don't think she ever wore a bra) because the sides of her body were exposed. She was naked, with a towel.

"Eleanor," I said (in retrospect, with comic sincerity). "What is the meaning of this?"

"Come in, Parker."

I closed the door behind me.

"Everything I own is in those bags outside. You own this towel. Want it back?"

I said nothing. I could think of nothing to say. My "What is the meaning of this?" question kept ringing in my ears.

"You think I cause . . . whatever it is that's happening here," she said, standing up. The towel shimmied a little as she stood, left, then right. "You think because I haven't . . . been capable of allowing myself to be naked with another person, because I'm a virgin, some kind of energy is . . . well, you know!"

I knew.

"I'm not completely sane, Parker. I've been crazy all my life. But for the first time, I can see it. I can see things clearly now. I'm in love with you, Parker. I'm in love with you and—" When had those tears begun to flow? I didn't remember them starting. I guess my eyes were on that towel, even though I had told myself that she wasn't attractive, she was just this tall, boney kid with an everyday face and—

"—know you love me. I can tell it by the way you look at me sometimes, like there's something here I can't see, that only you can see. Isn't that what love is, Parker, seeing something in the other person only you can see?"

"I don't know," I said. "My secret is that I'm stupid. I pass for smart."

"If I'm making this house haunted, or providing the energy for it through my virginity, then . . . I don't want to be a virgin anymore." Eleanor began to allow the towel to drop. It wasn't all at once, but in a few moments it was wrinkled cloth on the floor and she stood before me stark naked. "I want the first time to be with you. If you want me to stay after that, then I'll stay. If you want me to leave, then that's what I'll do."

But I was barely listening to these words, because I wondered how I ever thought this woman was ordinary, or too thin, or too tall, or too plain. Her face was angelic in its simplicity, honest, open, her smile a thrill to see. Her body was lean, it's true, but there was a womanliness to it that made her sisters look like, well . . . cows. Everything about Eleanor was subtle, every shape a nuance, every curve and turn of her body graceful and delightful.

She was still crying. How had I made her cry? I couldn't

allow her to cry. I rushed to her and wrapped my arms around her and told her not to cry, please stop crying.

"This is wonderful," Eleanor said. "This is very nice, Parker," she continued. "But could you please make love with me, because I've been waiting for a long time for that to happen, and I'd kind of like to get started."

I leaned back and saw the grin on her face.

You don't need to know the rest.

sixteen

Not every man goes to bed with a virgin. She was very curious about male anatomy. "Does it hurt when I do this?" she asked.

"No."

"How about this?"

"Nope."

"How about . . . ?"

"Ow!"

"Then I guess I can't tie it in a knot, huh?"

"No."

There were other issues. "Why can't we do it again?"

"Because we've done it three times."

"So?"

"So I'm not a machine, Eleanor. I've only got so much get up and go, and thanks to you, it got up and went."

"For how long?" Now this was a serious question.

"We can have at it, I don't know, maybe tomorrow."

"Tomorrow!?"

"Eleanor, there will be tomorrows, right?"

She was sitting up in the bed, challenging god to make her put clothes on. She just looked at me as if I were a ride at Disneyland that had just been shut down for maintenance. She grinned, and then she laughed.

"Thank you!" she blurted. "Thank you, Parker. It hardly hurt at all. Just the first time, a little, and then—"

I kissed her, in part to shut her up, in part to hold god's complaint against my body, in part because I hadn't felt this way about a woman, any woman, in so long . . .

Since Lily, dead now eight months and seven days and . . . so many hours, I don't know, I forget.

"Parker," she said with a look of mild surprise on her face, "I'm not a virgin anymore!"

I got up and took a shower, but when I came out she was still naked, divinely, subtly naked and sitting on her legs on the bed, looking out the window at the Cambria night.

"Aren't you cold?" I asked.

"I'm never going to wear clothes again."

Huh?

"I'm going to live in the wild and wander around naked and beautiful—I'm beautiful, aren't I, Parker? You can see it?"

"Like a doe," I said. "I see your muscles flex as you leap."

"I used to think I had to be like my sisters—"

"Cows, every one of them," I told her.

"Parker, I love them!" she protested, before giggling and saying, "every last bovine one of them! But I used to think you had to be like them. That everything had to wiggle or bounce. That you had to have something to strap down or hold up—"

I sat down beside her. Even though we had made love for hours, she smelled wonderful, her skin surprisingly warm. After the embrace broke, I leaned back. "You can't be beautiful and afraid, Eleanor."

"Everyone's afraid," she replied evenly, my naked philosopher. "Not everyone's brave."

I just couldn't stop myself. I held her for a time and warmed her. I opened my bathrobe and we warmed one another. Then I told her to either take a shower, or sleep alone. She went happily to the shower.

I lay back on the bed I used to sleep in alone—it was unruffled by our play—and wondered if the release of a virgin's pent-up sexual power was enough to release Monroe House from whatever it was that haunted it. Or would my betrayal of my dead wife call her forth to seek vengeance upon me, vengeance for worse than a simple mistake while driving, for true betrayal inside another woman?

When Eleanor returned, she was naked yet, her hair turbaned with a towel. She laughed as I looked at her. There was not an inch of unnecessary fat anywhere on her body, only lean muscle and supple skin. She pranced around the room for a time, inspected things on the top of the chest of drawers, studied a wall calendar three months late being turned, then finally leaned against one of the end bedposts.

"So," she said, "do I go, or do I stay?"

"When?"

"Tonight. Forever."

What do you say to a naked woman?

"Tonight, stay. Forever, we'll see."

"And if our little problem has gone, can I be chef here when you reopen?"

"Yes."

"And live on premises?"

"Yes."

"And make demands on the owner, day and night?"

"Eleanor, you should put some clothes on."

"So," she said after a moment's inspection, "there is no 'hard and fast' rule about how many times a night—"

"Eleanor!"

Yes, again.

SHE didn't want to sleep in the room with the twin beds, so we moved downstairs to the bedroom on the east side, which had a king-size bed. We slept spooned, first east, then west. Dawn came early and strong, light blistering across the carpet and onto the bed. When I woke she was already awake, eyes wide, covered to her ears with bedding.

"Parker, do you know what happened last night?"

"Yeah," I replied, "Not a peep!" By that I meant no noise, no manifestations, no ghostly activity at all.

"Oh, that, yeah," Eleanor responded.

"What is it?" I asked.

"I'm in bed with a man," she replied softly.

"With me," I said.

"I'm naked beneath these covers."

I could think of nothing to say to that. She was of course naked as a jaybird beneath these covers. Also, stored somewhere in my brain but easily retrievable were memories of hours of naked Eleanor in the room upstairs. Hours.

"So," I said, thinking that changing the subject might free her of any concerns, "what do you think of this wallpaper?"

"It's hideous," she said—we agreed on that—and squirmed beneath the covers.

"Do you really think we need wallpaper?"

"Parker, it's a bed-and-breakfast. You need wallpaper. Now, back to this issue—I'm naked under here."

I sighed. "Yes. I remember tucking you in. We slept naked, together, the night through. I'm naked beneath these covers too."

That information just added to her dismay. "Parker, I was . . . distraught last night. I mean, you were going to make me go away and—"

"Eleanor, I watched you for hours while you were gloriously naked. I made love to you, and you made love to me. What is the problem?"

"It's awfully bright in here," she said.

"Yes?"

"I mean, you saw me in really flattering light last night. I had the three-way lamp switched to the lowest level, and—"

I whipped the covers back, exposing her. Okay, it was not sensitive and it was not gentle, but it was effective because the moment I gazed at her, naked beside me, she must have seen the look of absolute adoration on my face because she grinned. I watched her sit up, back to me, and stand. Our various pieces of clothing had been left upstairs. She walked to the door.

"Thanks to you," she said, "I have to take another shower." She stepped into the hall.

Whereupon Eleanor Glacy, late a virgin and as akin to a exhibitionist as a Catholic nun, met Lillith DeMay, Lily's dear granny, who with her executive assistant Linda Hull and attorney Abel Gorman had gained access to Monroe House through an unlocked front door and stood at the small front desk, about to tap the service bell.

seventeen

AFTER Eleanor screamed and ran back into our room, I equipped her with a bedsheet, toga style. She went upstairs to get dressed while I, identically clad, went out to meet the Iron Granny.

"Lillith," I said, "You couldn't have come at a more propitious time!"

She said nothing, but looked me up and down as if it were indeed Roman times and she might be able to buy me and send me off to the tin mines of ancient Britain.

"My executive assistant, Linda Hull," Lillith finally said. Linda was forty, dressed almost identically to the Iron Granny in a gray suit, skirt for pants, and gray shoes. She seemed honestly amused by poor Eleanor's response to their entrance, and of course by me.

"My attorney, Abel Gorman," Lillith continued. Uh-oh. I now knew why she was here, of course.

I took them all into the kitchen and fumbled with the coffeemaker while Lillith fumed and the other two dawdled behind their chairs, waiting for their master to sit. But Eleanor burst in moments later wearing a long skirt and print blouse (how had I missed just how pretty and feminine Eleanor was?) and taking charge.

"Everyone, please sit down. I'll have coffee in a moment and breakfast in twenty minutes."

"We ate at the hotel," Lillith said.

"Rolls, then," Eleanor asserted, not to be put off by anyone in her kitchen. "And Parker, why don't you get dressed?"

"Yes, Theo," the Iron Granny suggested sourly, "why don't you deprive us of having to look at your unusual physique, hm?"

So I went upstairs, took the luxury of a shower, and descended the stairs twenty minutes later wearing my blue suit, prepared for war.

The unholy three were sitting at the breakfast table with Eleanor opposite, staring them down. I joined them at the table after pouring myself a cup of coffee. Eleanor tried to stand to get it for me, but I pressed her shoulder and said, "I can get it."

"You're getting around on your cane nicely," Lillith said.

I sat opposite her. "Thanks," I replied.

"Maybe you don't need it anymore."

"Spinal anomaly," I replied. "Alignment issues. Balance, that sort of thing. What brings you to lovely Cambria, Lillith?"

"I came to see my property," she said.

Hm.

Lillith looked to Abel, who set right in. "Mr. Parker, there are some issues we would like to clear up."

"There are?"

"Regarding the morning of the accident."

"Yes, I remember it clearly," I said, recalling the line from Casablanca. You wore blue, the Germans wore gray. "Go on."

Abel rifled through some papers in his briefcase and brought out a document I thought I recognized. I had made a statement in the hospital some weeks after the accident. The court has a name for them. Sworn affidavit.

"Now, according to your statement," he said, rolling pages back, "you and the late Mrs. Parker left Los Angeles that morning at about eight, is that correct?"

"Yes."

"And you were married in Ventura about nine-thirty?"

"Uh-huh."

"And then you were back on the road immediately, arriving in Cambria by two that afternoon, yes?"

"Yes."

"One question we forgot to ask, did you stop for breakfast?"

"On the pier in Santa Barbara. There's a credit card receipt, I'm sure."

"Yours," Lillith asked, "or hers?"

Her meaning was lost on no one at the table. I treated it like a reasonable question. "I think Lily picked up the tab, but I could be mistaken."

"Then according to your testimony you and the new Mrs. Parker went to Cambria Shores Escrow and signed the final papers to buy this establishment, is that correct?"

"Correct."

"The purchase of this property was initiated in the maiden name of Mrs. Parker, so there was a delay while the papers were altered to reflect her new married name—and yours too, of course."

"There was a delay," I replied. "It could have been for that reason. I signed papers in our married name, my last name."

"Then according to your statement, you took Mrs. Parker to the Moonstone Gardens Restaurant for a drink."

"Yes," I said.

"Then you drove north on the Coast Highway, where the unfortunate accident occurred, killing your wife and badly injuring yourself, is that correct?"

Eleanor stepped on my foot before I could answer.

"No," Eleanor said, "Mrs. Parker had planned a surprise. They came back here and," Eleanor looked at me, "consummated the marriage."

"Then why did you have reservations at the Sea Otter Inn on Moonstone Beach?" Lillith asked.

Eleanor pressed harder on my foot. "Oh, well, Theo told me shortly after he moved here that one of his fondest memories of . . . was . . ."

"Who are you again?" Lillith asked.

"I was hired by the court-appointed conservator to manage this property. My name is Eleanor Glacy."

"Does that include 'managing' its purported owner, as well?" Lillith spat.

Eleanor thought about that a moment, *Yes, well*, before answering, "Mr. Parker and I have become friends."

Linda Hull, Lillith's assistant, smiled but looked away.

I was not comfortable lying about having had sex with my wife after we'd signed some papers. Legal, not legal, I didn't savor sullying her with duplicity. On the other hand, I knew what Lily wanted when she died—she wanted this lousy collection of lumber and paint to be ours, and in her absence, mine. I further knew there was more at stake than a little bed-and-breakfast. I knew the Iron Granny too well, by reputation at least, to step into this pile of manure.

"This obviously has to do with Lily's estate," I said as Eleanor's foot slowly withdrew from my shoe. "It seems likely to me that you didn't disinherit her when she married me, or possibly you didn't have time to, I'm not sure. Or maybe there were other trusts of which she wasn't aware that can't be withdrawn. There are other assets, yes?"

"We're not here to answer questions!" Lillith snapped. "Nor are we here to hide what is, after all, information you have a right to possess. Your attorney—"

"I don't have an attorney. At least, not anymore. I fired him after the insurance settlement."

"Then let me suggest that you get one, Mr. Parker," Abel said, ignoring Lillith's glare. "Your late wife's estate is sizable. I can't say how much because no one knows, and frankly, it changes day to day. Stocks. Bonds. Like that."

The silence was enviable. If we'd just had this kind of silence in Monroe House at night every night. Well, come to think of it, like last night, after Eleanor and I stopped playing house.

"Mr. Parker?" Abel asked after a time.

"I don't want it," I said.

Eleanor kicked me.

"All I want is this bed-and-breakfast, why I have no idea, but I do. Maybe because we bought it together. In any case, I'll gladly sign a waiver releasing Lily's estate to her closest blood relative—let me guess, that would be you, Lillith?"

"Yes, me," Lillith said. "No, you won't sign a waiver."

"Put in layman's terms, Mr. Parker," Abel said, "you can't bifurcate the estate prior to the completion of probate. Afterward you may make a gift of whatever you wish to Mrs. DeMay. However, there are tax ramifications for both of you, taxes that will eat up a sizable portion of the estate."

"You didn't consummate the marriage!" Lillith barked. "Therefore it is not a legally binding marriage, therefore her estate belongs to me! Including this, this . . . ugly, ugly building. That wallpaper is oppressive!"

"This may come as a shock to you, Lillith. I hope so, but Lily and I were screwing our brains out for months before the marriage and—"

"And it doesn't matter," Abel said. "Your status then was as lovers. No implied property commingling at all. But as husband and wife, in a community property state—"

"You can't prove the marriage wasn't consummated!" Eleanor said.

"There is the issue of the timeline," Abel said. You know, it's a sorry state when the one person you like most in a negotiation is the lawyer representing your opposition. "It's a matter of record when you left Moonstone Gardens."

"There was a license. There was a ceremony. There was a judge," I said. "I doubt consummation figures into it, even if we didn't consummate, which we did."

"One might think not, Mr. Parker," Abel replied matter-of-factly, "but in truth there are precedents which support otherwise. To return to the issue at hand, it's a matter of record when you left Moonstone Gardens."

Matter of record, matter of record . . . I remembered there was a waitress and the manager, both nice people. We told them each separately that we were newlyweds. We paid the bill—did they time-stamp the bill? No, wait, I paid the bill around the time Lily went to the bathroom, but she actually drove here to leave the bags, so . . .

"We came here for a quickie," I said.

"There wasn't time!" Lillith certainly knew what a quickie was.

"You don't know your granddaughter," I said. "She was . . . wonderful . . . but she was also unpredictable. Doesn't matter. Abel, take this into court and smoke it. If you win, god bless ya. If you lose, send the check here."

"Get yourself an attorney, Mr. Parker." He was already refilling his briefcase and preparing for war.

"I don't pay you to hand out free advice," Lillith said to him.

"I'd love to sit and visit with you folks awhile," I said, "but as you can plainly see, until we get this wallpaper changed, we're closed. Also, I have a brand new lover here and I don't think her engine has been idling, if you know what I mean."

Eleanor beamed at being proclaimed my lover to all present.

"You dishonor Lily's memory!" Lillith said. "It's too early. You should still be mourning!"

"You sad old woman," I replied. "I'll mourn Lily 'til the day I die. Don't bother locking the door on your way out."

AFTER we were alone in the kitchen, Eleanor said, "I'm sorry for stomping on your foot."

"Glad you did. Kept me awake."

"Thank you, for telling everyone we're . . . a couple."

"I said we were lovers."

"Yeah, that's what I mean," Eleanor said. She was twisting and turning ever so slightly in front of me, like a cat underfoot.

"Eleanor?"

"We haven't done it in here yet," she meowed. "Not here in my kitchen."

I was losing weight.

IT's a funny thing that happens to you when you first fall in love. Think back. You were a different person. You were a brand-new adult. All of a sudden this troublesome, hairy, and often disruptive organ that god or maybe nature equipped you with made perfect sense. You shared it. You made someone you liked a lot very happy in short intervals, and their troublesome, disruptive equipment made you happy, too. And in between, you saw a person as he or she really was for the first time. Open. Unhidden. Life made sense.

Releasing this energy and giving it to a lover changes you in other ways too. In Eleanor's case, she bloomed. No more long dresses. She stole jeans from the lost-and-found bin and cut off the legs, rolling up what remained of each pant leg until you could almost see her . . . well, rolled them up high. She tied shirts beneath her little chest calypso-style, exposing her flat, muscled tummy. She got her hair cut short. She started wearing lipstick and a light dusting of makeup.

And people began talking. I heard some of the things they said.

"What's gotten into that girl?"

"Who's gotten into that girl?"

"You know, I never noticed before, but she's kind of a looker, ain't she?"

"Wow, look at those legs!" This from a fourteen-year-old.

She walked different, too, with a kind of prance, or maybe animated gait would be a better way of putting it. She wasn't always staring at the ground anymore. And she smiled, and that made me smile, and as you well know, smiling makes other people smile, so we were a smiling bunch of folks in Cambria, where people already smile far more than anywhere else.

Now I had very little to do with this. Oh, I was the object of her passion, yes. But really, the change was there, waiting to happen all the time. I was just the lucky son of a bitch who was standing nearby when it happened.

And damn it, even I had to admit it, I was falling in love. All over again.

eighteen

WE forgot about the Iron Granny and her legal retainers and set about enjoying the summer. Walking the sand was difficult for me—my cane drove into the grains like an oil-well bit, throwing my balance off—so I stayed closer to the hard land, where the sea rarely visited. Eleanor, however, loved running in the surf, dancing and prancing in it, her new shorter hair bouncing as no other part of her lovely body could. I bought her a new bathing suit, a bright yellow one-piece that clung to her lean anatomy like paint. She looked glorious in it, and several times reported in wonder that someone had come on to her.

"Choose," I would say each time, "this gimpy old man, or that handsome, sound one." She always chose me, foolish girl.

Choosing the new swimsuit was an adventure itself because Eleanor, in her newly discovered sexuality, wanted to buy the skimpiest, tiniest bikini available. Now I've not mentioned this before, and I do so now only with the greatest reluctance, but Cambria is not a bikini kind of town. There are towns to the south, Seal Beach and Huntington Beach as examples, where year-round rutting (*rutting*, a word I learned from Lily) is practiced. No, Cambria is more a one-piece kind of place, or maybe cut-offs and shirttails. So when she held up the bikini from across the shop, one tiny piece of cloth held between two fingers, the other, even smaller piece of cloth in the fingers of the opposite hand, I shook my head no.

"Why not?"

"I don't think there's enough cloth there to cover your palm, not to mention your—"

"But you said—!" She had to lower her voice here. "But you said I was sexy!"

"Oh yes."

"That I have a perfect body."

"Perfect in every way."

She grinned. "Why shouldn't I show a little of it?"

"Eleanor, you're a property manager in a town so small everyone knows at least rumors about everybody else."

She thought about that a moment.

"You might get a little more business—from the men—and lose a whole lot of business from the women."

She continued to think. I looked through the rack of one-piece suits. "Do you have one of these that'll fit her?" I asked a saleswoman.

She looked Eleanor over. "Oh, honey, there are women who would die for a figure like yours. You can never be too thin, or too rich!" And she winked before disappearing into the back.

She took the smallest size, a minor problem lengthwise that she appreciated for what it showed, but otherwise the suit fit perfectly.

Several weeks into our love affair I realized that Eleanor had held pent up a whole set of desires and yearnings for years and years. Such as the night she said, "Let's go skinny-dipping."

We were driving back from Big Sur, not far from the accident scene where Lily had died but going in the opposite direction. The shore is coarse here, rocky and inaccessible except in a few spots, one of them from a vista point. "There! There!" she said, pointing to an empty vista point parking area. I pulled into the area because Eleanor was already naked and I intended to talk her back into her clothes, but before I could say a word she was out the door and running for this one path that led down to a small beach.

I took my cane and a flashlight from the glove compartment and followed her down, almost tripping and falling twice. I found her playing chicken with the surf, running up to it, and then retreating away as it surged toward her. Laughing too, of course.

"Eleanor," I said with just a tinge of anger in my voice because I was tired and feeling really gimpy and going naked in public was something I had given up, oh, a decade ago at least.

"Come on, come on, come on!" she said, suppressing shivering because she didn't want me to talk her out of this adventure. She unbuttoned my clothes as I buttoned but eventually I could see that I was going to lose, because the cane kept slowing me down. By the time she pulled my shorts down and directed me to step out of them I was resigned—okay, and a little turned on by my sea siren girlfriend—when a rustic male voice interrupted us with, "It's sure a good night for it."

Eleanor screamed and ran back up the trail to the vista point, where she found that at least four cars had pulled in during the interim and tourists were standing about looking at the nearly full moon. She dashed inside the pickup and quickly began getting dressed.

"She was a virgin until recently," I said by way of explanation to the rustic voice in the shadows. The sea breeze wasn't all that cold, and I felt a little too foolish to go scrambling to put on my clothes.

"Yeah, had one like that too, once. Married her. Just put her in the ground two years ago next May, damn it," he said. I saw his outline, the fishing pole, something burning, maybe a cigarette, maybe a cigar, from which he didn't inhale.

I pulled on my shorts after snapping them in the breeze to rid them of sand, then the pants after the same routine.

"Buried my first wife too," I said.

"Disease?"

"Car wreck."

"Oh, the cane. I see."

I didn't bother with the shoes or the socks, just stuffed the latter into the former. I pulled on my flannel shirt.

"Got to hold on to these moments," the voice said. I guessed he was maybe sixty-five or seventy, and not in the best of health, either. "She won't be a vixen always," he said, "or you burdened with one."

"She's not a burden," I replied.

He laughed. "No, not that one."

"You come down here often?" I asked. "At night, I mean?"

"I keep hoping to die here, but so far, no luck."

I understood. Or at least, I thought I did. I'd almost died myself, and for a time, death was preferable to life, coward though that I am.

"Sorry I waited to say something," he said as I turned to go, "but she was so damn lovely, it made me proud just to be a human being and in her presence. You tell her that."

"Good luck," I told him.

"Got to happen sometime," he said.

Every now and then I go back, but he's not there. Don't know how lucky he was, whether death took him, or left him.

When I arrived at the vista point, fully clothed of course except for my shoes and socks, I found Eleanor in the pickup. She was dressed to the last button, sitting very properly like she used to do all the time with her hands folded in her lap and her shoulders straight as if taking an oral exam. I got behind the wheel but didn't turn the engine over.

"What took you so long?" she asked.

"Had a nice conversation with that guy."

"He was about to watch us have sex!" she said with an edge to her voice.

"No, or he would have kept his trap shut," I said. I told her what the man had told me, about being in the presence of such beauty as she danced in the surf that it made him feel proud to be a human being. Her eyes softened then.

"What's he doing down there?" she asked.

"Fishing. Dying. Cancer, maybe. Maybe loneliness. Something."

"Oh, that poor man."

I got us back out on the road before she began crying. "I'm not like this," she said after a while. "I mean, I wasn't ever before."

"Want to go back?"

"No," she said softly, then, "No! You love me, don't you, Theo?" Yes, here I was, Theo again, and having to like it.

"Yes, I love you," I replied softly, "and sometimes it makes me proud to be in the presence of such beauty."

"I won't always be beautiful," she said.

"Oh yes you will."

WE made a pact. "We'll restore Monroe House together. I'll work for free, but afterward you guarantee me one year as chef. Agreed?"

"Eleanor, there may not be a Monroe House. The Iron Granny might take it from us."

"Then that's the way it is." She held out her hand and I took it.

The nights had been haunt-free for a month. Free of disturbances of almost any kind. We moved into the master suite, slept like minxes when we weren't doing that other thing minxes are famous for, and enjoyed living country style. I bought a couple of hand steamers and we started on the first floor removing the old wallpaper, which we learned was layered. Each layer got progressively better until we reached the innermost paper, which was light and airy and lovely, flowers in a field. Unfortunately, that layer had to come off too.

Eleanor, as it turned out, had wonderful taste when it came to interior design. Beyond choosing new wallpaper, she rearranged the furniture, bought and installed new curtains, and organized things to give the rooms more space and better views from the beds. We moved all the heavy faux antiques to a side room and had a garage sale. We started antiquing, but the truth was, we didn't have the capital to replenish all Monroe House's furniture with real antiques. We went catalogue shopping online using Eleanor's tiny little iBook computer. Our faux antiques arrived in boxes and we stored them all in the buggy shed.

Oh, the buggy shed. I've forgotten to mention it. It was the real McCoy, built at the same time as the house, with room for six buggies inside. There was a time when people could rent a buggy-and-one or a buggy-and-two, depending on the horse-power desired, and take rides out into the countryside, which even today is minutes from Main Street. It must have been a side business because Monroe House was not built to accommodate guests. There were still two buggies inside, one still on its wheels, all of which ignited ideas in my mind.

But the biggest idea, the one I hadn't shared with Eleanor yet because I didn't want to scare her, was turning Monroe House into a dinner venue. It would remain a bed-and-breakfast, but in the evening it would convert into a restaurant. There was room to expand a dining room off the east door. The kitchen was large enough. But I didn't mention it because scaring Eleanor scared me.

ONE night I awoke and Eleanor was gone. Her side of the bed was a valley of cloth, the covers shoved aside, her slippers missing. I glanced in the direction of the bathroom but there was no light beneath the door. I got up, slipped into my own house-shoes, found my robe draped over the wing chair near the bed, and called out, "Eleanor?"

I opened the door and stepped out. I saw a form at the base of the stairs. "Eleanor?" I asked.

"Down here."

I flipped the light switch. Nothing happened.

"Be careful coming down the stairs," she said.

I came carefully, one leg, then the other and the cane, until I was behind her and she scooted her tiny bottom over to make room for me.

"Wiring's gone," I said.

"No, it's back." By *it* she didn't mean the wiring.

I said nothing for a long time, because I had been so sure, so damn sure that whatever it was that had haunted this place was gone.

"Maybe it is just the wiring," I suggested.

"I could hear the wail," Eleanor reported. "It woke me up."

"I didn't hear anything."

"No, it was . . . soft. Diminished. Not powerful anymore. It was almost subtle."

"Damn it, then," I said.

"And I saw her again." A chill exploded along my spine. Oh Lily, please don't come haunt me! "She stood at the foot of the bed," Eleanor continued, "and just stared at me—at us—with an icy rage. That's the word for it, rage."

"Was it Lily?"

Eleanor shook her head. "I don't know. Same hair color, and skin. But the clothing was all wrong. Old-fashioned. And it was dark."

"You saw this?"

Eleanor shook her head. "It was a dream. Then she opened her mouth and I heard the wail," she continued. "I woke up still hearing it, but not nearby, from downstairs. So I came down for a look."

Eleanor's bravery scared me. "You don't go anywhere alone," I told her. "Not when these things happen."

"It can't feed on me anymore, Theo," she said, looking at me. "But what are we going to do, tell people they can't bring their young girls along with them? No virgins. No emotionally distraught children, or—"

"No. Obviously not."

"People will come. When they do, they'll wake up what almost sleeps here and bad things will happen."

I put my arm around her. She was shivering. The endothermic among us have a hell of a time holding onto heat. She laid her head on my shoulder and I felt a tear drip onto my sleeve.

"We've got to beat it, Theo," she said. "This is going to be our home and our livelihood, and we've got to beat it."

"Somebody knows something," I said. "All ghost stories are mysteries, you said. Somebody knows something."

nineteen

THE lights came back on around five. We had coffee and fresh rolls Eleanor whipped up at the kitchen table. I brought a tablet from upstairs and some pens.

"Where's the icing?" I asked, as the rolls were naked on top.

"You're getting fat," she said. "We don't need the icing."

"Eleanor!" I protested. For a time there I was losing weight, but at some point Eleanor's cooking overtook Eleanor's demands of me and, well, I was developing a spare tire.

"And a man who can't do his duty is a useless man," she said with mock sincerity.

"It's your fault," I said. "Your cooking."

"Eat less of it," she responded, tousling my hair. She smelled of vanilla. I hadn't realized for a time, but the vanilla came from her baking, not as a perfume. "So, what do we have here?"

"We're making lists. Phenomena. Suggestions?"

"Well, the power always goes out. Maybe it draws power from the lines."

I wrote, POWER GOES OUT. DRAWS POWER FROM LINES?

"It prefers to visit in your dreams," I said, musing.

"Corporeality requires power," Eleanor responded.

"Which it had, from you and your pent-up emotions."

"I had some things pent up, it's true, but I'm not sure they were my emotions," she joked.

I wrote, VISITS IN DREAMS.

"Yet, sometimes the dreams become reality when you awaken,"

she said. "The marks on my legs, and the time it tried to tear my nightgown off."

"Don't forget the Lily doppelganger that hit you."

I wrote, LEAVES REAL EVIDENCE. CORPOREAL. CAN HURT PHYSICALLY.

"And there are two of them, a man and a woman," I said.

"How do you know that?"

"That thing in the master suite wasn't Lily—God, I hope it wasn't Lily. . . ."

"It wasn't," Eleanor said.

"But it was female. And the thing that attacked you was definitely male."

Eleanor was standing behind me, watching me print words on the tablet. I wrote, TWO GHOSTS, ONE MALE, ONE FEMALE.

"I'm not sure it's either sex," she said after a time. "I'm not sure of anything like that, Theo."

"You're not sure it's a ghost?"

"I'm not sure I know what a ghost is," Eleanor replied after a time. "All I know is, whatever is in this house, it hates and it uses the most powerful of human emotions against us. It used my isolation and self-loathing and pent-up sexual desire to power, well, what happened. And now that it's deprived of that, thanks to you"—she hugged me from behind—"now it's drawing energy from wherever it can."

"Maybe we can kill it," I suggested.

"How?"

"Turn the power off for a few days. Take a run up to Monterey. Let it . . . pass away."

"I have things in the freezer."

"We'll move it to one of the neighbors'."

"Theo, you own this place and you don't know you have a walk-in freezer?"

Hm, actually, no.

"I'll hire one of the restaurants to store the stuff. How much is it?"

"Not much," Eleanor replied, plopping down on my lap with a grin. "More than'll fit in a home freezer, but if one of the restaurants has the room . . ."

The Brambles had the room. They didn't even charge me, a professional courtesy for when we reopened.

I HAD the power turned off at two-thirty-seven p.m. Thursday, but instead of running up to Monterey for a weekend getaway, Eleanor had another idea. We went looking for historians.

We started with the Cambria Historical Society and its proprietor, Ms. Clagg, a woman of demure stature. Cambria is not lacking in historians, professional, casual, and long-lived. But most of the histories were of the Leviticus variety. You know, so and so begat so and so, and opened a hardware store, and they begat so and so, who moved to San Luis Obispo, got married and bought a Starbucks franchise, and they begat . . . When we told Ms. Clagg what we were looking for, she said, "Oh, you want scandal. We don't document scandal here, you know. We're a civic organization."

But she gave us referrals. We heard stories.

"There was a multiple murder there during Prohibition," Delilah Sykes told us. Referred by the society, Delilah lived in a house just off Bridge Street, which as you may recall leads to the town's biggest cemetery. It was a lovely little house with one bedroom and a parlor the size of a pamphlet. She served tea from a tea set with a cozy covering the little teapot. I then noticed that she collected them—teapots adorned every shelf and free plane in the small parlor, even the top of a new plasma TV set.

"Seven people, as I recall," Delilah Sykes told us about Monroe House. "In the kitchen. Gunned down."

"Oh, my," Eleanor said.

"Yes, the worst murder in Cambria history," Delilah continued, blowing air across the surface of her tea. I couldn't help noting that her dentures whistled.

When we mentioned the murder to Chester Colt, who lived up in the pines in a relatively new cabin, he said, "Phew! Crap, every word of it." Chester's cabin was plastered with photos of hunting trips, children and grandchildren, old cars he'd once owned, his late wife in Africa, Europe, Asia, even a few with an earlier Chester beside her instead of behind the camera. He was alone now. There were piles of clothes and other things we didn't investigate here and there around the place. There was also an odor—not a stench, really, but something that women know how to get rid of and men of Chester's generation do not.

"Nobody ever got shot dead during Prohibition in Monroe House," Chester continued. He was tall and lean, with skin that didn't fit anymore. "A man fell down the back staircase and broke his neck. That was in the late thirties, I think, or maybe forties. I forget. Anyway, at the autopsy they found he'd been shot six times during his lifetime, each at a different period in his life—how they figure that I don't know—and survived each round, so maybe that's where the story started. . . . But there was a rape."

Eleanor and I exchanged looks.

"It's actually a pretty good story, if you want to hear it."

Did Chester think we were there for some other reason?

"There was a beautiful woman, most beautiful woman in town," Chester said, lighting his pipe. "I remember her, even though I was just a kid then. One of the Leicester girls." He pronounced it *Lie-ster*. "You probably haven't heard of the Leicester family. Prominent at one time. Moved out of town right after. In those days rape was the woman's crime. Anyway, she was much sought after, 'cause she was a real pretty thing. Don't recall her name. Let's call her Marie. She finally chose this one feller over another, some said because he had more money. Forget the name, now. Paulson, maybe, or Rawlins, something like that. Anyway, they came up from Morro Bay where he was a fishing boat captain and rented a room in Monroe House to seal the deal."

Chester stopped, like he'd just said something awful, but Eleanor smiled and waved and told him to go on.

"Well," Chester said, "this other feller, the loser, don't know his name either. Let's call him Mike. He followed their car with the wedding trappings on it, staying just far enough behind not to be noticed. He saw them go into Monroe House. He walked around and he steamed.

"Meanwhile, upstairs, Paulson and Marie retired to their room. It wasn't like it is today—you've got bathrooms and closets right there in the rooms nowadays, right?"

"Right."

"Well, not in those days," Chester told us with a grin to note how much things have changed. "Bathrooms were a social thing back then. Located at the end of the hall, probably. I was in Monroe House once years ago but I don't remember. Anyway, Marie asked Paulson to go out on the veranda and have a smoke while she prepared herself for the marriage bed. Paulson went downstairs, lit a smoke, and decided to take a little walk. Somewhere along that walk Mike snuck up behind him and hit him with something hard. There's a joke there, but with a lady present, never mind. Knocked him clean out.

"All we have is Marie's story now. She was modest, she said, so she turned out the light and got under the covers to wait for her husband. Mike went into her bedroom and when Marie said nothin', he said nothin' either. He just took his clothes off and had her. She claimed it was dark and she didn't know it wasn't her husband, so she put up no fight at all. There wasn't a torn garment or any of that.

"Later, come early in the morning but well before dawn, Paulson or Rawlins or whatever his name was, he came to and called the constabulary. They went into his room at Monroe House and found his wife and Mike fast asleep, having exerted themselves mightily over the preceding several hours."

This story was so absurd both Eleanor and I laughed.

"No, no, there's a sad end to it," Chester said, "funny as it may seem at face value. Mike was arrested for rape, but he continued to insist he was invited in by Marie, whose husband had gone missing. He claimed Marie thought Paulson was a coward not to make a woman of her, so she invited Mike to do the deed, which he did. He was never prosecuted.

"Paulson, now, was the laughing stock of the county. He couldn't take the fall. Either he was a fool, or his wife was a slut, so of course she was a slut. He divorced her forthwith.

"Her family disowned her, too. They owned the biggest store in town back then and people voted with their money. Hell, way people thought back then, she could have been a slut. So here she was, penniless and homeless and famous—or infamous, if you like—so you can imagine what became of her. There was this brothel down in San Luis Obispo and even though she was a good Christian girl—at least, before that night people said she was—a couple of months later she sold herself so as not to starve to death. And because she was famous, almost every man in the county, many of them her former suitors, went down there and paid five dollars and took what might have cost them a lifetime otherwise."

Silence consumed everything in the room except the sounds from the fireplace. Chester tapped his pipe against the brick hearth, emptied the ashes.

"That's awful," Eleanor whispered.

Chester barked a laugh. "Of course it is."

"What became of her?" I asked.

"Her looks went. Looks go first, don't they?" Chester said. "She died of some drug or other, or maybe it was whiskey, who knows, less than ten years later. Now that," he finished, pointing to each of us with the stem of his pipe, "that's a real ghost story."

WE compared notes in our room at the White Water Inn on Moonstone Beach. "That's some story, about Marie," I said with a laugh.

"It's not funny. Women didn't have many choices back then, and her choices were stolen from her."

"You think she haunts Monroe House?" I asked.

"No."

"Then there's the gangsters being shot in the kitchen."

"That would be famous. Like the Saint Valentine's Day Massacre in Chicago," she said.

"Well," I commented when my arms filled with a hundred pounds of warm woman, "there are more names on the list."

Yes, more "historians" to question.

twenty

THE phone call came just before ten p.m., a time when most Cambrians are asleep in their beds with the lights out and the sidewalk rolled up. It was Ms. Clagg, the director of the Cambria Historical Society. Eleanor answered it, but I heard Clagg's voice clearly over the receiver. "I'm sorry to call so late," she said.

"It's okay. We're still up," Eleanor said.

"I hope the names I gave you were some help."

"Yes," Eleanor told her. "Chester in particular."

"He's quite a storyteller, isn't he?" Ms. Clagg said. "Well, I don't want to keep you up any more than I have already. I just wanted to say your visit got me to thinking. I remembered that we have several boxes of items left over from one of the owners of Monroe House. I didn't know which one. The boxes were here when I joined the society. Anyway, I found them, the boxes I mean, and inside one of them is a journal. It belonged to the original owner, the man who built the house, James Monroe."

As soon as she hung up, Eleanor turned and used her long, thin legs to push me toward the edge of the bed. I had suggested that we could stop by tomorrow and pick up the boxes and journal, but Eleanor was so excited she wanted them now.

Eleanor wore pajamas and a robe, but as I was the one who would have to get out and retrieve the boxes, I insisted on clothes. Layered clothes. It was forty degrees outside with a blustery wind off the ocean. Ms. Clagg lived in a two-story house with a view of the sea over a descending knoll of pines in

Liemert Estates, on the landward side of the highway. As soon as our pickup (*our* pickup, like Monroe House was *our* house) pulled into the driveway, her porch light switched on and her door opened. She wore a thick robe over flannel p.j.'s and mukluks. The boxes were already on the porch.

"Go inside! It's cold, damn it!" I barked at her as I picked up the small boxes with the journal sitting on top. "And thanks!"

"Goodnight, Mr. Parker," she said sweetly and retreated inside. The porch lights stayed on until I slipped behind the wheel, having left the boxes in the bed of the truck. I handed the journal to Eleanor.

As I drove, Eleanor's eyes pored over the journal as if she'd found a true artifact of the Christ. The overhead light revealed a period journal, printed gold filigree over a green canvas cover, the sort of ledger book that could have been purchased in any stationery store at the turn of the twentieth century. Eleanor flipped through the pages, which were in fine condition, as if made yesterday. The light was too dim to allow reading, but she excitedly pointed out drawings of plants which were surrounded by text. I had to push the book away once from blocking my view or I would have run into a tree.

Back at the White Water Inn, Eleanor was out of the truck before I had it properly parked. She rushed to the door of our room only to realize I had the key. I took my time placing the truck in park, turning off the engine, getting out, locking the doors, as Eleanor danced in front of our room.

"Theo!"

"Coming, coming," I said, walking slowly. She poked me when I unlocked the door, and she rushed inside.

I changed back into pajamas while Eleanor scoured the journal.

"Well?" I asked.

She read from the flyleaf. "Personal Journal of Dr. James T. Monroe, Botanist. The next line reads: National Geographic

Expedition to Amazon Basin, 1898." Eleanor grinned up at me. "Pretty neat, huh?"

"Yeah, pretty neat."

Eleanor thumbed through the used pages, which extended to the halfway point of the journal before ending. She flipped through the pages again as I joined her on the bed, kicking off my house shoes. "Look," she said. "He drew a bunch of plants all through the book, or at least as far as it goes."

"Photography was still cumbersome back then," I suggested. "A good botanist was expected to be able to draw his subjects."

"He's not bad," Eleanor said.

"Was. Past tense, Eleanor."

"Right," she said in a dismissive tone as she continued to rifle the pages past her nose. "He has lousy penmanship, though."

I took the journal from her and flipped back to the title page. Monroe's hand was sure and meticulous, what you would expect from a Victorian, or Edwardian, whichever it was in 1898. I turned to the first entry and found the opposite, tiny writing with ligatures compressed and text made even more difficult to read by a tropical humidity that had caused the ink to spread. I recognized the scribbling as something other than writing even so.

"It's not writing," I told Eleanor. "I think it's shorthand."

"Shorthand? Does anyone still use shorthand?"

"In executive suites, maybe. In court, too. But back in the nineteen hundreds it was all the rage. The newest software for writing, if you will. A lot of Victorians, particularly the science enthusiasts, used shorthand. There were competing shorthand languages."

"How do you know all this?" she asked.

"I could never sleep in class," I said.

"We'll have to find the right shorthand language and translate it."

I took the book from her, placed it on the as yet unopened boxes that we would get to tomorrow, put another log on the fire, and climbed back into bed with Eleanor. We were both tired. I fell asleep with her fingers stroking my shoulder and didn't dream once of Dr. James Monroe or his house.

WE pieced this together later. It must have happened this way. While we slept at the White Water Inn on Moonstone Beach, a hitchhiker by the name of Phil Becker had thumbed a ride up from LA to wherever. His ride lived in Cambria, so he found himself stranded on a small two-lane highway in a small town at two in the morning. He walked around a little and saw a dark house, no lights on at all, not on the porch or in any of the rooms downstairs or upstairs. He might have knocked on the door, just to see if anyone was home, and when he heard no response, he broke the glass insert in the front door and unlocked the door.

We later found some of the rooms ransacked, the fridge door open, as was the walk-in freezer. Phil was looking for a meal. He found some bread in one of the breadboxes—Eleanor is fond of archaic things, so she has four—and wolfed down at least one loaf of wheat bread, slice by slice. He also found our liquor cabinet, broke the lock, and chose one of the cheaper bottles of Napoleon brandy to drink from.

We found the master suite, our bedroom, rifled. He used one of the storm lamps we keep on premises for obvious reasons to light his way as he went through Eleanor's things, then mine, finding nothing worth stealing. It must have angered him, because he tore one of Eleanor's skirts, one of her old ones that was ankle-length, and strew the floor with our clothes.

Two days would go by before we returned from Moonstone Beach, a mere few hundreds yards away, and found his body on the staircase. He was spread out like a dropped mannequin, mouth agape, skin white as rice, with mottled bruises near the lower portion of his body—blood settling—and his eyes wide open forever in surprise and fear.

The autopsy they performed later down in San Luis Obispo revealed that he'd died of a heart attack.

Phil had been twenty-four.

twenty-one

THE next morning as we were getting ready for the day, Eleanor and I each took a turn looking through the Monroe boxes. At least once during the ensuing decades someone had moved these items, because the boxes had ads for Breezy Soda and Uncle Albert's Palmade printed on their sides, products out of manufacture since the mid-thirties, I guessed.

The larger box contained a framed photo of a man, woman, and child. Judging by the clothes they wore, the photo was taken sometime in the late nineteenth or early twentieth century. There were snapshots probably taken with a Kodak box camera, again mostly of the woman and child holding hands or standing on a sidewalk and waving in a frenzied sort of way that made the woman's hand fan across the photo. She was lovely, the woman, and with a quick change of clothing might fit right in in Cambria today. There was one photograph of the man—Monroe, probably, although nothing was written on the back of the print to indicate identity. He stood in roughly the same place holding the child in his arms, her pudgy legs and spring-fresh dress making a statement about gender and class for a time gone and nearly forgotten. It was obvious he loved the little girl dearly, but he tried not to share that fact with everyone who would see this picture. His face was stern, officious, and respectable.

There was a smaller receptacle containing photonegatives of various plants.

The smaller box contained letters from unknown people about unknown events and circumstances. There was a diploma from Boston University. James Monroe had received a doctorate in botany there in 1893. Another certificate (a rarity in that day and age) indicated that Lila Bonny Monroe had been born to James and Celia Monroe on February 22, 1895. Lila, I thought, a name so similar to Lily's.

There were several books on botany, a volume of poetry by Shelley (Ozymandius predicting the coming of the Great and Terrible Oz himself), a book on parenting ("Discipline" an early chapter title), two tin windup toys, Coldstream Guard and Union Soldier, both of which still worked (I suspected they had been Monroe's toys as a child, not his daughter's), and strangely not surprising, several samples of wallpaper. Even then, Monroe House defied good wallpapering, it seemed.

At the bottom of the smaller box was a blueprint, what's called an *as-built*. It was Monroe House. I refolded the blueprint very carefully and returned it to its place in the order of things, at the bottom of the box.

"This is probably all that's left of them," I said to Eleanor over the sound of the shower spray.

"What?" she shouted.

"When you get out," I said, but I never repeated it to her because when she stepped out of the shower she had ideas of her own to share.

"I want to stop by the bookshop," she said. She meant Tiller's Books, where she formerly worked. "Maybe the shorthand is a common one."

"Better hope he didn't create it himself," I said. "Victorians used to do things like that."

She gave me a look like she'd just bitten into an apple with guests.

In all, we interviewed twelve people in three days, most of them in their nineties, although there was one who claimed to be 103. There were all kinds of stories, none of them really convincing or possessing what you might call connective tissue with what we were confronting. Eleanor really enjoyed herself—she liked old people in the same way she liked old things and old customs. She was bookish, and intense, and thoughtful and considerate of the feelings of the old people.

I fell asleep twice.

There was a story of prohibition gold hidden somewhere on the Monroe House premises, in retrospect complete rubbish of course, but at the time it kept me awake. The problem with oral history is that it changes, word to word, person to person, in ways too slight for a third person to recognize, someone who actually knows the whole thing. And then that story gets passed on, and it gets passed on, and before you know it a coven of witches was caught dancing naked around Monroe House and were stoned to death, or maybe burned, if there was enough lumber available. At any rate, the value of real history is that it's written at the time of the events it records. If there are discrepancies, they're challenged and corrected in short order.

The only thing all these people agreed on, and they were women, mostly, as it is a curse (and maybe a blessing) that men die and leave them alone—they all agreed that there was something evil about Monroe House. One old woman said, "I have guests up from Southern California all the time. As you can see, I can't board them here, in this tiny place. But I have never, ever recommended Monroe House to any of my guests for an overnight stay."

"Because . . . ?" Eleanor prompted.

"Because everyone knows there's something evil about that place."

"So, great," I said, as we left the last of them, "not only do we have a bad reputation as a bed-and-breakfast, but we're also known as *the* repository of evil in Cambria. We should see if that's noted in our ad in the Yellow Pages."

Eleanor had checked with Tiller's Books. The shorthand how-tos that Tiller had in stock didn't correspond with the dialect used in Monroe's diary. Eleanor put her little iBook to use and went online looking for additional information about shorthand. She found a site devoted entirely to various shorthand languages, some going back hundreds of years, and left a query. The site operator e-mailed back that she would take a look at Monroe's scribblings for a fee. I drove Eleanor into the village, where she scanned several of the journal pages and e-mailed them to the shorthand expert.

WE had packed our bags earlier, so I drove us home, where Eleanor went inside ahead of me and found Phil Becker's body sprawled out on the staircase. She didn't even scream. She simply walked back out to where I was trying to grasp all four bags at once and said, "There's a dead man inside."

Somehow this didn't surprise me either. I called the Cambria Volunteer Constabulary (actually, that's a traditional name—it's the County Sheriff who man the cars now) and a female deputy arrived in less than two minutes to inspect the premises.

Eleanor and I sat on the porch swing, glum.

"Yep, dead, two, three days," Deputy Cathy Nielson said. "Power's off in there, you people know that?"

"We turned it off," I reported.

"Just come back from an extended vacation?" she asked.

"We were gone three days," Eleanor said.

"Now I've heard of cheap," Cathy replied and walked to her unit to call the various agencies that handle dead bodies.

"That poor man," Eleanor said. It was one of her catch phrases. A stray dog might elicit, "That poor dog." A limping woman would cause her to say, "That poor woman." A dead man sprawled on our staircase drew the comment, "That poor man."

"He broke in," I observed.

"Doesn't mean he had to die for it," Eleanor said.

"I didn't say anything about retribution," I replied, still glum and starting to get a little irritated myself. "There's a half-empty bottle of our brandy in his hand, and some bread from the—"

"And he's welcome to it," Eleanor said.

"Well, yeah—now."

"It's so unfortunate," Eleanor sighed. "He just happened along while we were gone and—"

We looked at each other. Happened along while we were gone. . . .

"We turned off the power, Eleanor."

"No!" she clamored.

"What if it was hungry?" I asked. "What if it was starving! There was no electrical power to draw on, so what if it . . . enticed this hobo to just wander in and make himself at home." I thought about it a moment. It made perfect sense. Without electrical energy, it was dissipating, beginning to dwindle to nothingness. Earlier we'd witnessed the same event on a smaller scale as it was deprived of Eleanor's energy.

"It scared him to death!" I said an instant after Eleanor.

"Theo, it's really alive!" Eleanor exclaimed.

"Yeah, and it's hungry."

SOME hours later the coroner from San Luis Obispo, the county seat, removed the remains of Phil Becker from our bed-and-breakfast. Well, not all the remains. Eleanor opened every window—I didn't think there was that much of a stench, as it had been cool and only three days, but she insisted. Then we scrubbed a stain that Phil had left on the carpet—not in the days after his death, as he decomposed, but as he died. The stain was formidable. We finally rolled the carpet up and took it to the buggy barn for later disposition.

It began to get dark. I lit one of the storm lamps, then several more, as Eleanor, ever the practical one, drove down to The Cookie Crock market to buy something for us to eat. We had sandwiches and diet soda over lamplight.

"Here's to Phil," I said, raising my glass.

"Phil, sorry," Eleanor said, clinking her glass against mine.

"So," I said, "now the place has killed someone."

"How do we know it hasn't killed before?"

"Good question," I replied.

"But you know, we're jumping to a big conclusion here. I mean, yes, Phil may have been scared to death by some kind of manifestation, but . . . we can't be sure there's a connection between Phil breaking in and the, uhm, what would you call it, the entity, enticing him in."

Eleanor had a point.

We slept like children in the arms of their mother that night, each comforted by the presence of the other, and hoping that whatever it was that lived in our bed-and-breakfast wouldn't harm us.

The next morning, after some thought, I devised a test to see if Monroe House was enticing victims to enter it. I retrieved canvas chairs from the buggy shed while Eleanor bought us an ice chest at The Cookie Crock and stocked it with sodas and other edibles. I placed a couple of beach umbrellas on the lawn, and the chairs beneath them. We sat, Eleanor and I, and waited.

Morning went.

Eleanor read a Stephen King novel. Eleanor likes her Stephen

King. I read Tom Clancy. Finishing one of his books makes you feel like you've done something.

Early afternoon came, and went.

Then in mid-afternoon we saw a hawk hovering over Monroe House.

"Look at that creature," Eleanor enthused. "It's magnificent."

It hovered and it hovered for an hour and twenty minutes. Every now and again we'd look up, shade our eyes and marvel at how the hawk could float like a kite, but without the string to keep it in place.

"We should warn it," Eleanor suggested after it became evident it wasn't going to just fly away.

"Earth to hawk, Earth to hawk," I said, "You've been painted by enemy radar."

"The house will kill it," she said.

"Will it?"

The hawk hovered for another half an hour, and then dove as if hunting a mouse for the roof of Monroe House. It landed with a squawk, flopped-hopped to an eave, and dropped beneath it.

"The hawk is down," I said.

Eleanor, feeling guilty, said nothing.

An hour later a squirrel made a dash for the basement. Ten minutes later, another squirrel followed the first.

It was late afternoon now, four sodas past noon, and Eleanor couldn't sit anymore and watch the animals leap to their deaths. "Theo, we've got to turn the power back on."

"And let it live?" I asked.

"Yes! Yes, let it live. Just give it enough power to stay alive, until we can think of something."

"No," I said, sensing that the fear these lower life-forms would generate could never be enough to keep it alive.

"Theo, we're killing these animals!" Eleanor said, her voice rising.

"There aren't enough animals in Cambria to keep this thing alive, Eleanor," I told her. "There aren't enough—"

George, the neighbor's dog, a big Labrador retriever, loped across the street. Eleanor had taken a shine to the dog, and it liked her, too. I've always been rather indifferent to animals unless they're cooked and on a plate, but I do appreciate people who appreciate them, sensing in them something I lack. Eleanor saw George and immediately kneeled to pet him, but he sashayed past her, heading for Monroe House.

"George!" Eleanor screamed and ran after the dog. I got up and gave chase, too, but George was too fast for us. He darted beneath the porch. It was too close to the ground on this side for me, but Eleanor slid beneath the wood and the ground and scrambled after George.

I ran up into the house, then down into the basement from the lobby door.

The basement was filling up with dead animals, birds, rabbits, mice, other dogs, and Eleanor had landed in the middle of their rotting corpses as she screamed and tried to pull George back.

I grabbed the animal by the collar and pulled it toward the stairs. George resisted, even tried to bite me, snapping at my legs. I ignored him as much as possible. "Follow me!" I shouted. If given a choice, Eleanor would have far preferred my giving help to the dog than her. Tough woman that she is, she stood from the carnage and followed me.

We retreated to the buggy barn, where I locked the door while looking for a chain for George's collar. Eleanor, who wore her short jeans and a top tied calypso-style, was stained head to foot with decaying flesh from the pit in the basement. She was sobbing and trying to find air to breathe that wasn't tainted by death.

"Here," I said, pulling her to a spigot. It took a minute to get the hose screwed on, but I sprayed her off on high pressure. All this time she kept saying, "Turn it on! Turn it on! Goddamn it, Theo, turn the power back on!" and rubbing her body clean of dead flesh.

I paid extra for emergency service and had the power back on in two hours.

twenty-two

I T was after dark when the power came back on. We wandered inside and sat listlessly at the kitchen table. Eleanor made a pot of coffee, then went upstairs after the water heater had a chance to prime itself and took a long, long shower. I read an old issue of The Cambrian and learned that we'd missed a performance of *Death of a Salesman* at the Pewter Plow Playhouse, the local theater. Eleanor came back downstairs wearing her bathrobe. We said nothing to one another for more than an hour.

And then it hit me. "We'll tent the place," I told Eleanor. "That way, nothing goes in, nothing comes out. Then we'll shut off the power."

"Tent it? What do you mean?"

"Like we're having it fumigated."

Eleanor said nothing for a few minutes before, "Are you willing to take that chance? I mean, we don't know what this place is . . . we don't know how it's calling—things, people—inside, do we?"

"It doesn't matter if they can't get inside."

"What do we do, stand guard for a week or two to make sure?"

"Nothing will be able to get inside, Eleanor," I asserted. "They'll stake the tent down. I mean, those things are designed to hold dangerous poison."

Eleanor wasn't convinced. "We need an expert," she said. This was tantamount to the old male-female argument about asking directions. Women are far more likely to put their faith in others, to seek "expert" advice, while men are more self-reliant—they're pathfinders, and yes, they do sometimes get lost or shoot off their big toes.

"We tried getting an expert," I said. By which I meant our furtive phone calls to popular television shows.

"I can look on the Internet," she said.

"We can both look on the Internet!" I replied. "I'll look for a cheap extermination company!"

THAT night, a large land mass lay between us in the king-size bed, and for the first time since our relationship began, Eleanor slipped between the sheets wearing a nightgown, and not play-fully naked. We lay in the dark for a long time before I said, "Eleanor, I'm not responsible for those animals, or Phil Becker."

Silence.

"Eleanor . . ."

"Yes, you are," she replied softly. "So am I."

"We had no way of knowing. . . ."

"We sat out on the lawn under an umbrella, Theo!" she growled at me. "We, we were spectators at a killing! As for Becker, we saluted him over food, clinking our glasses together like his death was meaningless. It wasn't meaningless, Theo. It wasn't."

For the first time I was deprived of her heart, her breath, the warmth of her body, and I missed her.

I FOUND a company that would tent the entire place for two weeks for a very reasonable price. Eleanor found a psychic from the Bay area and a professor of paranormal studies from Occidental College down in LA, both of whom were interested in investigating our "incident" further, the psychic only after being assured she could write a book on the subject. I agreed to hold off tenting while the two "experts" conferred.

Too proud to take the cold treatment, I moved my digs over to the room with the double bed.

Once, late at night, four days after George almost succumbed to the house, I heard the wailing again and came out to the landing to find Eleanor sitting there in the dark at the foot of the stairs.

"Careful coming down," she said.

The noise was from everywhere, and nowhere. I sat down beside her, saw that she was wearing one of her new satin nightgowns and nothing else, and gave her my terrycloth robe. "No, you need it," she said. I didn't say anything. I had hardly said anything to her for days, resenting that she was hiding herself from me, resenting the loss of the woman I loved.

"The power's out again," Eleanor said, referring to the phenomenon as if it were a natural event.

"You mean, it's consuming it," I said.

"Whatever."

"Why do you think it's only during the middle of the night? The power thing, I mean?"

"I don't know," Eleanor said. "You don't suppose . . . it has another source of power during the day?"

"Yes! *Yes!* Solar power. It soaks up the sun! It's a sun bather! The tent will kill it. You just wait and see."

"Theo, you promised to wait. . . ."

"I'll hold off until the 'experts' have had their chance," I told her.

Silence. Except for the wailing, of course, distant, growing more faint. Finally it was gone.

The hall lights came on.

We looked at each other. She looked sleepless and haggard. Maybe I did too. We turned together and ascended the steps, even though she had to wait for me and my cane. At the top of the steps she took my elbow and pulled me into the master suite, where she removed my robe and then lifted her night-gown over her head.

"I need your body heat, Theo," she said, sliding beneath the covers. I followed her after dropping my clothes to the floor. "I need to be held," she whispered.

The synergy of our bodies soon made us both warm. She cried for a time, I didn't ask why. We had nothing to do with the death of Phil Becker, and as for those animals, the pit of decaying flesh in the basement, since limed and hauled away, proved that the house had been supplementing its diet for months, maybe years. And yet Eleanor took her role in the affair personally. Here is another observation about women, most of them anyway: they're life-givers, not life-takers. If it was necessary I could kill someone and not think about it twice—if it was necessary. But most women operate from the opposite dynamic. "That poor man," Eleanor had said about Phil Becker, "that poor dog," or "that poor woman" about others less fortunate than herself whom she'd seen as her life progressed. Women who don't possess the life-giving dynamic, or who suppress it or kill it in order to be more like men, and hence more competitive with them, lose far more than they gain.

Before we got out of bed that morning she wanted me. Needless to say, the same was true for me. We made love, and I cracked a couple of my weird jokes so she would laugh. I wouldn't let her out of bed, wouldn't relinquish contact with her skin, with her lips, with her eyes. And when she finally did steal from the bed, I wouldn't stop looking at her lovely body and naked grin, so she threw a pillow at me and ran into the bathroom.

That afternoon the first of our "experts" arrived, Madame Ouspenskaya. Okay, her name wasn't Ouspenskaya, it was Henderson, and she didn't refer to herself as madame, but I was already disposed to reject anything she might offer. She was merely an impediment to my grand scheme, the tent, the glorious maneuver that would rid us of whatever it was that lived in this bed-and-breakfast.

We put Janice, Madame Henderson's first name, which she insisted we call her, in one of the first-floor rooms where we'd finished installing the new wallpaper and furniture. It's a nice room with a view of the lawn and part of the front porch. "Oh, this is lovely," she said, already failing to sense the evil that lurked in Monroe House. "It looks new."

"We just redecorated," Eleanor told her.

"Have you two been together long?" Janice asked, a seemingly casual question, but perhaps useful later when she concocted her gobbledegook.

"Just a few months," Eleanor answered. "I used to be property manager here while he was vacationing in a coma, but he woke up and now I'm just his concubine." Eleanor's sense of humor was beginning to parallel my own.

"How sweet," Janice said, as if Eleanor had told her we were newlyweds.

"Actually, we're pretty happy, except for the house, of course."

"It's just a house," Janice said. "It's sticks and stones. What two people have together when they love one another, now that's important." And almost in the same breath, "Is this sink new, too? It's quaint." It had red filigree around the basin and matching knobs. Of course it was new.

"It's retro," I said. "Victorian, but with a drain."

ELEANOR accompanied Janice Henderson as she walked the property while I played solitaire on Eleanor's little Macintosh computer. I kept losing as I tried to listen in on the conversation. Janice said, "Oh, this is a hot spot," and darn it, it was in the master suite that she said this, too. "Hm, I feel something here," she commented in the hallway between the two bed-rooms upstairs.

But she got only four steps down toward the basement before she stopped, said something negative, and they retreated up the steps and closed the door. It still smelled a little down there, lime or no lime. It was the smell, I assured myself.

Janice also perceived something in the kitchen, which was not the best of choices, because Eleanor loved the kitchen, worked in the kitchen, and made food in the kitchen that certainly had a quality-of-life effect on me. They talked like two schemers, as if the house could hear them, and in mock disgust I stood and went out to the porch to swing myself like a boy in kneepants.

That night over dinner Eleanor told Janice Henderson everything about the house, including the months she occupied the place before I got there and what happened to her. I advised against this—let's allow the psychic and the professor of paranormal studies to discover their own ghosts, I said—but Eleanor wanted to make sure they had the full story and knew what they were dealing with.

"You were a virgin?" Janice asked in true surprise.

Eleanor squirmed in her seat a little, played with the Yankee pot roast on her plate for a second, moving things around with her three-pronged fork, and nodded. "Yes, well, I . . . I wasn't ready to—"

"And you were how old?"

"Twenty-three."

"And afterwards, the house seemed to rest?"

Eleanor gestured yes between throwing me a *don't you dare enter this conversation* look.

"Well, I don't wonder," Janice said.

Eleanor continued with the story, about how the haunting returned but at a much lower level, how finally we realized that it was stealing electrical power in order to live, and how we turned the power off and poor Phil Becker died and we discovered that the house was drawing prey inside, to be killed to feed its needs.

"Have you ever heard of anything, you know, a haunting like that?" Eleanor asked.

Janice considered the question for a moment, then held her plate up to ask for a second helping of Eleanor's Yankee pot roast, which Eleanor was happy to provide. Janice pushed some of the roast around with her fork for a moment, then said, "It sounds like it's alive."

"Yes," I replied. "It does."

"Ghosts aren't alive. They're energy, and we're not sure how that energy gets replenished, but . . . as a rule, they don't kill and consume."

I was beginning to appreciate Janice. She was a touchy-feely psychic, it's true, but she had a head on her shoulders.

"I mean, we kill living things, ingest them, digest them, and transform that matter into energy. This—what are you calling it, anyway?—this entity seems to be doing the same thing."

"I've called it Ralph for some time now," I said with a broad smile. "Eleanor has other names for him/it, which we won't mention at this table."

"And it's intelligent, too," Janice said.

Of course, we'd known for some time that it was intelligent. It mimicked people we knew, and quite well, too. But having Janice say the words made an impact on both of us. We shared a look that didn't go unnoticed by Janice.

"What do you know about the history of this house?" she asked.

Eleanor told Janice about Monroe and the journal we couldn't read because it was written in shorthand.

"May I see it?"

Janice spent half an hour poring over the journal, as unable to decipher it as we were. She marveled at Monroe's artwork, the finely drawn plants, leaves and flowers of the Amazon basin.

"There are photographs, too," I said. "Negatives, actually." Janice wasn't interested in those, however, and suddenly shut the journal.

"It may have happened later," she said. "Whatever it was that happened to this place may have occurred after Monroe and his family left." She shoved the journal across the table to Eleanor, who put it back into the larger of the two boxes.

"Now, for the big question—is it safe to sleep in this house?" she asked. After a moment Eleanor and I pulled our gazes from one another.

"It needs real energy to, what, make itself solid," I said. "Right now it's pretty weak. It might try to scare the pants off you, though. You should be aware of that."

Janice was a little upset with this news, we could see, but didn't turn down the peach cobbler served minutes later, which, unfortunately, Eleanor wouldn't let me eat.

Late the next morning, well before dawn, I heard a scream explode from downstairs, followed by an "It's okay! Never mind! I'm all right!" Eleanor slept through it, and I just turned over and went back to sleep. Later Janice told us that she'd seen headlights from a car on the street outside swing across her wall and thought . . . well, you'd have to crawl inside Janice's head to know what she thought she saw, but it couldn't be nice.

twenty-three

R EALLY?" Tom McCorkindale asked when I met him at his
car in front of Monroe House and, with some prodding,
told him the entire story. "I mean, it eats birds and dogs and
things?"

"Eats probably isn't the right term. It kills them, we think to
absorb some kind of electro-biometric energy."

I was looking for the hardware. In Steven Spielberg movies,
professors of paranormal studies usually showed up with a van
filled with electrical monitoring equipment. McCorkindale arrived in a modern VW bug with two leather bags stuffed behind the front seat. He wore a golf shirt and slacks, and
sunglasses on his brow. He looked to be thirty, was what Eleanor
would call later (to my annoyance) "throbby," by which she meant
heartthrobby, a heartthrob sort of man.

"What's electro-biometric energy?" he asked.

"You know, juice, power. Electricity," I said finally.

Tom grinned. Yes, he was dealing with amateurs.

"And why do you think . . . ? Oh yes, the power that goes out
in the middle of the night, during the wailing." Tom nodded to
himself, mulling that over. "But that raises the question, why in
the middle of the night—oh, sunlight," he said, turning his gaze
toward the roof of Monroe House. "Of course."

"Of course."

"But how does it absorb it? Through the walls? Are you suggesting that your house is a living thing?"

"All theories," I told him. "I'm starting to get a tan standing out here," I said. "I'm developing a bald spot, right back here, that's really susceptible to—"

So we lugged his two very large, very expensive, very German bags toward the house. "You've got your equipment in here?" I asked.

"What equipment?"

"Don't you have meters to read, you know, electrical charges, temperature density, that stuff?"

"Oh, that. I used to use that stuff, but the damnedest thing was, we discovered it was all reading itself. You know, one device would pick up the electrical field of the other and so on. And then we realized houses are surrounded by electrical charges. The wiring in the walls, household appliances. It made hand-held stuff worthless. Now, we've got some remote monitors developed by the CIA and sold on the open market that we could lug down here, or is it up here? But that would take the dean to sign off on the whole thing—you know, capital expenditures and so forth—so I guess the answer is no."

"We brought in a psychic," I said as if mentioning that we'd replaced all of the mattresses in the place with horse manure.

"Oh, who?"

"Janice Henderson."

"Oh, Jannie! She's a sweetheart, isn't she?"

"You're friends?" I asked.

"Acquaintances. She's one of the more sane psychics out there," McCorkindale said, and then in a barely audible voice, "You know, most of those people have a few screws loose in the head."

Well, his attitude wasn't disdain for all psychic-kind, but it was something.

We put Tom in the room opposite Janice. It was identical, freshly renovated by Eleanor and myself right down to the plumbing fixtures, a blue motif rather than red. "Hey," Tom said, "pretty nice. Look at that sink."

Eleanor had said the sinks would make the rooms.

THAT morning a young man driving an old VW beetle drove up to the curb. He left the engine running, trotted up to the front door, knocked, and when I said, "Yes?" asked, "Theodore Parker?"

Uh-oh, I thought, *here's the Iron Granny's work.*

"Theodore Parker, Theodore Parker . . . Oh, I think that's the name of the guy who died here last week. You read about it in the *The Cambrian*?"

"Yeah, right," he replied and dropped a thick business envelope at my feet. "You are served."

While Eleanor, Janice, and Tom told stories that went bump in the night, I thumbed through nearly sixty pages of legal gobbledygook, not one of which I understood except the first, which stated that Iron Granny was suing for possession of Lily's unmeasured estate.

"I'm going to have to get a lawyer," I told the three sitting at the table. "Too bad our ghost isn't an attorney. Now, him, I'd hire!"

I tossed the paper into the corner catchall and joined the conversation.

LATER in the afternoon there came a rapping at our door. I answered it again, after thinking about sending Eleanor, but hell, I was already served, so what worse could go wrong? At the door stood Abel Gorman, the Iron Granny's legal muscle, and a woman I presumed was his assistant, thirty years younger, beautiful, and also carrying one of those expensive briefcases.

"Abel," I said, "what a coincidence. I was just served with—"

"This morning? Ah, we're right on time, then."

I didn't invite them in. I stood and waited. Time passed. The woman smiled. I've met my share of female attorneys. The ones whose mouth muscles haven't atrophied and so are capable of forming a smile are rare. Her smile revealed perfect teeth, perfect lips, and made me turn my head just a little to the left and look into her eyes, which were pale, pale blue and clear as rainwater. Her hair was blond, her suit gray—skirt below, not pants, revealing very shapely legs.

"Mr. Parker," Abel said, "my firm is no longer associated with Mrs. DeMay."

"No?"

"We broke off our relationship with Mrs. DeMay several days—shortly after our last meeting, the meeting with you, you may remember?"

Oh, I remembered. The woman was becoming self-conscious that I was inspecting her so closely, so I pulled my eyes back into my head and turned to Abel. "Did the Iron Granny fire you because you acted so, ah, decently toward me and my associate?"

"No, actually, our ties were broken over another matter, and initiated by my firm. May we come in?"

I suddenly realized that I was being rude. I pushed the screen door open. They entered.

"This is Laura Karczek, one of our associates." Karczek is pronounced *Car-check*.

I shook Laura's hand. It was warm, soft to the touch but gripping my hand with a firmness that said, *I am a competent woman.*

"Ms. Karczek," I said.

"Laura is fine," she said, releasing me from formality.

Abel accepted his role as host in my mental absence with grace. "Laura, this is Theo Parker. Mr. Parker was briefly Mrs. DeMay's son-in-law."

"I'm so sorry about what happened," Laura said, and I knew by the tone of her voice, her body language, and the sincerity that beamed from her clear, powder-blue eyes that she was indeed sad about my loss.

"Is there somewhere we can go to talk?" Abel asked.

The kitchen was out. "I've got a psychic and a professor of paranormal research in there conferring with Eleanor," I announced. They waited for an explanation, and I wondered if perhaps I'd already explained too much. "We found a dead man in here last week."

"A dead man?"

"There," I pointed at the stairs even as I looked at Laura. "He'd been dead several days."

"What? You didn't notice?" Abel asked.

"Oh, no, no," I said, "We vacated Monroe House for a short period and turned the power off so we could . . . kill the ghost."

"Kill the ghost?" Abel's voice was beginning to reveal perturbance. He was a legal guy, a brief-and-tort kind of man, and ghosts didn't inhabit his world except as ploys in court cases.

"The house is haunted, Abel," I said, guiding them to the lobby where I sat them down, Laura on the circular settee (Eleanor's idea, the round settee, and a good one) and Abel on a love seat. "Can I get either of you something to drink?"

"Something with bubbles," Abel said.

"Do you have brandy?" Laura asked. "It was a long drive and my eyes are locked on the center line. I've got a headache."

I offered her Tylenol or aspirin, but she said brandy would do the trick.

Once in the kitchen I let Eleanor know we had attorneys in the lobby and to be prepared to come to my aid with something loaded.

When I brought the glass of 7 UP and a brandy snifter to them, Laura had opened her jacket, revealing a lovely business blouse with ruffles up the bodice. Abel had opened his jacket too, but who cared? I gave them their libations and took a seat in the wing chair, a remnant from before renovations began.

"You've done a nice job with this place," Abel said. "It's not so damn creepy anymore, haunting aside."

"Thanks. That's mostly because of Eleanor."

Laura questioned this with a look. "Eleanor is his property manager and what, Theo—close personal friend?"

"Our bedroom is at the top of the stairs on the left," I said. I don't know what possessed me to say this, to bracket it in such bold terms, but Laura acted as if I'd mentioned having bought milk at the store.

"Look, Theo, let me come to the point. I am constrained by law and ethically as well from representing you in your defense of Mrs. DeMay's suit, and your inevitable countersuit."

"My inevitable countersuit?"

"Yes, of course. For the mental anguish caused by her accusations and attempt to steal from you what is clearly your property, by law and moral rectitude."

"Accusations?"

"I am also constrained to share what was then attorney-client privileged information," Abel continued. "Laura here will testify that I have in no way briefed her regarding the finer details of this case. She has obtained some information regarding the case in the course of her duties at Kriegel, Gorman, and Stein, overheard conversations at the water cooler and so on, although none of that information could be classified as 'privileged.'"

"No," Laura confirmed, "it could not."

"However, being a good attorney in her own right, Laura has learned that several of your associates at *Li'l Deuce Coupe* magazine will testify of your intention to marry Lily DeMay for her money. One may testify that you and he talked about Ms. De-May's death and what it might mean for you, were you to inherit."

The ramifications of this statement thundered in my head. I had had no conversations with anyone about Lily's money, or for that matter, Lily herself, except to say what a lucky guy I was because she was . . . Well, I didn't exactly go into detail about why I was lucky. All of a sudden I could see how conversations could have been misconstrued. It was common knowledge that Lily DeMay was a DeMay of the DeMays, and I'm sure more than a few men had made a run at her because of that. The fact that she was drop-dead gorgeous had something to do with it, too—which for an instant brought tears to my eyes because she had been beautiful and young and laughing mere moments before she died. But what was it Lily had said to me? "You're the only person here I like?" Had some of the losers, the guys who'd made a run at her for reasons close to what they were now accusing me of, offered to testify against me?

Then the worst-case scenario hit me. "They're prosecuting me for murder!?" I asked, at the decibel level in excess of a shout.

My shout silenced all talking in the kitchen, and a moment later Eleanor came out and sat down on the end table beside my wing chair.

"No, no, please let me explain," Abel continued.

"I'm Eleanor Glacy," Eleanor said, introducing herself to Laura.

"Laura Karczek. I'm Abel's associate." They shook hands.

"No one of any importance, or for that matter sanity, is going to say you attempted to kill your late wife," Abel said. "But there will be accusations that you bragged about the marriage and speculated that if Lily DeMay were to die, which she subsequently did, you would inherit a great deal of money."

"I didn't know anything about any great deal of money," I told them. "Lily mentioned the inheritance she was going to receive from her grandfather's estate. It was barely enough to cover the purchase of this bed-and-breakfast, and we were planning to borrow against the real estate so we could get the money to renovate."

"Well, as I said during our initial meeting," Abel said, "no one knows how much money Lily was going to inherit. But for legal and tax reasons—none of this involving me, as I am not a tax lawyer and it's a matter of record—Lillith established an irreversible, iron-clad trust for her only granddaughter, a trust containing several million shares of DeMay stock, plus bonds and cash. She attempted to get it changed when Lily announced she was going to marry you and buy this building. Lillith's long-term plans for Lily were that she take over the company, and obviously Lily didn't want to do that."

"How much money?" I asked.

"As I recall, you offered to give it back," Abel said with a little smile.

"The offer stands," I replied. "How much money?"

"A guess—"

"It's only a guess," Laura said.

"Half a billion dollars."

"Or maybe a billion," Laura suggested.

"Or possibly two billion dollars," Abel finished. "We just don't know."

It then became clear what Abel Gorman and his firm, Kriegel, Gorman, and Stein, wanted with me. He wanted to represent me because if I won, I became the Iron Granny's official heir. It was also clear that, all legal mumbo-jumbo aside, while Laura Karczek would be the attorney of record, Abel Gorman would be running the show.

"Can she win this case?" I asked.

"As I mentioned during our initial meeting, there are precedents that support her position—nonconsummation of the marriage—"

"They consummated," Eleanor piped in.

"Yes, well, open to debate, that issue. Then there's your intent. Did you marry her for her money with the intent of . . . killing her later? We don't know—can't know what Lillith De-May is willing to purport, and possibly pay others to testify to. My guess is that it's going to get nasty, and it's going to get public."

"What about our position?" I asked.

"Well, as you said yourself, you had a license, you had a ceremony, and you had a judge. That seems pretty strong to me. If I were her attorney—and I used to be—I would attack your character, the minutiae of the legalities, what are referred to as loopholes. Were all the necessary documents signed, *i*'s dotted, *t*'s crossed . . ."

"I can get all that for you—"

"Not necessary," Laura said. "They're all a matter of public record. I had them pulled Tuesday."

"At this point we don't represent—" Abel began.

"You're hired," I said.

"Then there's the matter of contingency, or retainer."

"What percentage would your firm take for contingency?"

"Half."

"Retainer," I said more promptly than was necessary. "I'll write you a check."

Laura would stay with us for several days to interview me and Eleanor and get a feel for the sort of people we were, for legal reasons. She'd put together a file on both of us. They didn't have to say my relationship with Eleanor coming so close on the heels of Lily's death didn't help our case.

I gave Laura the last renovated room, one toward the back adjacent to the kitchen with a view of the pines on the hills separating us from Pacific Coast Highway, whose flitting broken lines had given her a headache on the drive up from LA.

I dropped her bag on the bed while she removed her jacket. I noticed the sweat stains beneath her arms, and she saw me noticing. "I need to clean up a little," she said. "I get nervous in new situations. And it's been a long day. And Abel insisted I drive because he had to drive back."

"Long drive."

"Theo?"

"I prefer Parker," I told her. If she called me Parker, she'd be the only one to do so anymore.

"Is this place really haunted?"

"Very," I said. "Do you believe in ghosts, Laura?"

"I don't disbelieve in them."

"Leave your business card wedged in the door frame," I suggested to her. "Ghosts are scared to death of lawyers."

twenty-four

I CAME into the kitchen to find Eleanor sitting alone at the
table. Monroe's boxes were stacked on the table again. Obviously, Eleanor had briefed Tom our scientist regarding the journal no one could read. Eleanor was sipping from a glass of red
wine and staring out the kitchen window at a pine tree that
blocked part of the view of an empty lot where we thought
about constructing a flower garden with a gazebo.

"You okay?" I asked.

"Yeah," she replied softly.

"Where's our team?"

"I sent them out to walk around the East Village. See the
sights."

"It's a nice day," I said.

"Uh-huh."

"Thinking about the billion dollars, right?" I asked.

"Yeah."

"It's a lot of money."

"Yeah."

"You think it would change everything," I said.

"Yeah."

"It would, I guess," I said. "With money like that, I guess it
owns you."

I poured a glass of iced tea and sat down beside her. She was
wearing shorts—it seemed that she always wore shorts now,
sometimes even when it was a little cold, because I and others

had told her she had pretty legs. She was wearing shorts and one of my button-down shirts, a blue one, whose tails hung down in front and back.

"We could travel," she said, and then after a long moment, "if there still was a 'we.'"

"Of course there'd be a 'we,' Eleanor," I said, not completely sure of it myself.

"Laura's very pretty," she said, and, as if to balance things, "Tom's a little throbby himself."

"Throbby?"

"Heartthrobby. It's a term from junior high school. I don't know why I dragged it out."

"Oh," I said.

"With a billion dollars," Eleanor continued, still staring out a window without a view, never once having looked at me, "you could do just about anything you want."

"Yeah. Sure."

"Have . . . just about anyone you want."

I put my hand on her arm. It was strangely cold and didn't react to me at all. "You can buy some people," I told her, "but some people you can't."

"Yes, but those people you can charm," Eleanor replied and turned and smiled at me as if she was trying to charm my pants off, and damned if she didn't.

"Change everything," I agreed.

"Hard to trust other people. Hard to trust yourself," she said. "Yes, Theo, it would change everything."

"You doubt me?" I asked.

"I'm not insane," Eleanor replied. "And I have feelings too."

I COULDN'T stand the conversation in the kitchen. I went to the pantry, found a fresh bottle of our best cognac, the kind that says V.S.O.P. on it, god knows why, and a fresh brandy snifter. I took them to Laura's room. I thought her headache may have lingered and she could use relief. Her door was open. She left it open, or maybe it drifted open—yes, I recall, this door has a tendency to drift open if not closed properly—and Laura was unpacking her suitcase. She was wearing a teddy, not a fresh one but something she'd worn on the trip up from Los Angeles I could tell, because of the wrinkles. Voyeur that I am, I stood with the bottle of cognac and the snifter in my hands for some moments and looked at her. She had released her mane of blond hair, which hung to the middle of her back, and as she bent over removing this or that piece of clothing, her thighs tensed and released, her bottom flexed and relaxed. The teddy was one of those that sort of hung down in the crotch area and left ample room in the back. She was very sexy, and I began to think about what Eleanor had said, that billions of dollars would change everything.

I could have Laura, I thought, and then dispose of her. Yes, I thought the word, *dispose.*

I could have every manner of human female, black women, Asian women, blonds and brunettes, redheads—

"Parker?" Laura had turned and seen me standing in the doorway with the bottle of cognac and the snifter in my hands. She wasn't miffed that I had seen her in her underwear because, maybe, she also saw I was no longer looking at her, but at all the women who would come after. The planes I could buy, the boats to cruise the Med, everything I could do with a billion dollars—

"Parker?"

"What? Oh. I just thought . . . I just thought you might want to keep a little headache medicine in your room."

She was concerned for me, I could see, maybe because she was used to men ogling her and clearly I was not, or at least was no longer ogling her. She took the bottle and snifter from my hands before I could drop them.

"Thank you. That's very sweet. But as you can see I'm . . . involved."

"Yes, I can see that."

"So, I'm going to take a shower now."

"Good idea."

She took the door in both hands and slowly began to close it.

"I'm sorry," I said. "For . . . I mean, the door was open and I—"

"I can tell, Parker, you're not that kind of man."

"No."

"But that doesn't make me any more . . . *dressed.*"

"No."

"So I'll see you at dinner."

"Okay."

The door clicked shut, firmly this time. I stood before it for some minutes thinking not about Laura's lovely body, or the intimacy of her that I had glimpsed, or even what Eleanor had said to me, but what a billion dollars could do and how it would change everything.

AT dinner, Eleanor and I put on a good face of being tellers of ghost stories.

"You mean, we might hear or see something tonight?" Laura asked. Clearly, the thought no longer scared her so much as excited her. Of course, there were five of us at the table, and Eleanor had lived here for several months, and then me, so . . . it was safe, right?

"Probably," Eleanor replied. "When it happens, it usually happens between two and three."

"Keep the flashlight beside your bed," I suggested, "or under the other pillow, so you can find it in the dark."

"Theo is being dramatic," Eleanor said. "If you're concerned, light one of the storm lamps and turn it low. There's one in every room."

"From what Theo and Eleanor have described, I'm not sure it is a ghost," Janice said.

"I agree," Tom concurred. "It acts more like a corporeal being, a creature that needs sustenance." Thus far, I could see little difference between these two, one a scientist and the other a psychic.

"Then again," Tom said, "there's always the possibility that what we're witnessing here—if we are witnessing anything," he added, to keep his professional distance. "What we're witnessing is the missing link between psychic phenomena and hard science. What if we learn that after people die, they continue to 'live' by other means, by absorbing energy through some kind of osmosis instead of digestion?"

"Why here?" Janice asked. "There've been thousands, tens of thousands of documented cases of hauntings, many inexplicable. Why should the answer present itself here?"

Eleanor had cooked a wonderful dinner, even though I could tell she wasn't in the mood for it. Her eyes avoided mine the entire evening. She wore a dress whose design was taken from a Renoir painting, cinched at the waist with a thick brown belt, and shoes with large square heels. Laura wore jeans and a heavy sweater and walking boots. They were a contrast in womanhood.

Tom took another bite of beef Wellington and chewed, thinking it over. "The intermittent power outages, not unusual in themselves in other cases, but proven to be connected here with . . . whatever this thing is. The dead man. The animals attracted to the pit below."

"The basement," I corrected.

"Call it what you will," Tom continued, "but for the first time, we've got a connection between the manifestation itself and its life needs. Why do ghosts haunt? If they haunt," he finished, again protecting his professional standing by not admitting their existence. "Emotional turmoil has always been associated with hauntings. Killings. Beatings. Mourning. Suppressed sexuality. And now electricity."

This was becoming too ordinary for Laura. She leaned forward and looked at Eleanor at the head of the table. "I just can't believe you stayed a virgin until you were twenty-three! I mean, how'd you manage that?"

It was meant in fun, of course. Laura was saying she couldn't possibly have suppressed her sexuality for all that time, but Eleanor, the part of Eleanor that had kept her a virgin and isolated and self-hated, remained within her just enough to cause her to freeze.

And instead of withdrawing and at least doing no more harm, Laura tried to make it better. "I mean, I couldn't have . . . I went completely out of control when I was sixteen and I—boy crazy, you know. Couldn't get enough . . . of them."

Eleanor stood up. The look on her face said it all.

"I'm sorry," Laura said.

Eleanor went into the kitchen and turned the light off.

I excused myself and followed her. I found her standing at the sink, palms against the stainless steel, leaning in on her arms and crying into the drain. "What's the matter with me?" she asked.

"Nothing. Nothing's the matter with you."

"I'm so screwed up, Parker," she said, using that name for the first time in months. "I'm just . . . screwed up."

I wrapped my arms around her. She tried to shrug me off, but I held on to her anyway, and after a moment she accepted me like a coat and began to bawl unreservedly. I let her weep until there were no more tears and she sucked air as if I'd squeezed all of it out of her.

"I love you, Eleanor," I said. "I love Lily, too, and I'll always love Lily. But now I love you, too, and I can't think of what a day would be like without you in it . . . just as each day without Lily hurts. You make it hurt a lot less, but it still hurts."

She turned. It was dark and her face was a shadow. "I'm not as good as Lily, Parker," she said. "I'm not as pretty. I'm not as smart. I'm not as funny or witty."

"You're a liar," I said, and meant it.

Her wet face buried into my shoulder. I held her for the better part of an hour. When we finally reentered the dining room, we found it vacated by our guests. I heard laughter from the front porch. I told Eleanor to go upstairs and prepare for bed while I dealt with our guests. She walked past me, out the screen door to the porch. I followed.

"I apologize," she said to them. Laura was leaning against the railing, while Tom and Janice shared the swing, each at opposite ends with the knee of one leg meeting in the middle. "I'm an emotional ninny sometimes," Eleanor said. "There's another one! Ninny! I haven't used that word since junior high school either!" She laughed.

Laura left the rail and hugged her.

"I was an ass, Eleanor," she said. "A woman knows when the time is right. For me, unfortunately, there was a slut phase I went through when I was sixteen, and I've regretted it ever since, so I guess I was making myself feel a little better by making you seem to be the odd one. The truth is, I'm the weird woman here, not you."

It was a nice gesture. Eleanor hugged her back. They would become friends, I could see.

Damn it.

Just kidding.

Eleanor and I escorted Laura to her room, and I lit her storm lamp, turning it so low the room was bathed in a mellow yellow glow. Tom had already closed his door by the time we got there. I tapped, asked if he needed anything. He replied, "Go away. I'm conjuring!"

Janice's door was open. We leaned in. "Everything okay?" Eleanor asked.

Janice was wearing the oddest pajamas I'd ever seen, full of wide pleats top and bottom and flared at the ankles. She'd bought them in India, she said. "No, I'm fine. I promise not to wake you when a car's headlights cross the wall there."

I'd forgotten to mention this to Eleanor, gestured that I would, and we left.

Upstairs, in our bedroom, the one chosen for us by Lily and fate, I made slow, soft, sweet love to Eleanor and asked her to marry me.

"We'll just see," she said, showing no surprise or reaction to my offer.

"We'll just see what?" I asked.

"How well you satisfy me."

But afterward, as she lay beside me, my breath flowing across her shoulder, hers over my chest, she whispered, "Yes, Theo Parker, I'll marry you," and we fell asleep.

twenty-five

THAT night after Eleanor and Theo left Laura, she prepared for bed. An efficient woman, she had packed an extra large T-shirt to use as a nightgown, among other compromises limiting the size and weight of her baggage, but decided to save it instead for possible wear the following day. Laura had a problem soiling clothes, particularly under the arms.

She left the storm lamp lit, but turned it down almost to the point of extinguishment. The room was dark but with shadows that allowed her to see her way into the bathroom if she needed. She slipped beneath the covers, pulled them up to her chin, and lay quietly, listening to the house.

Laura had never slept in a house purported to be haunted before, and in truth, it scared her a little. A man had died here, of a heart attack, it's true, but he was no less dead. She was a rational person who worked her way through law school with the aid of a small scholarship and by waiting on tables. People often misjudged her because she didn't look like a lower-class kid from Milwaukee, but she was.

An hour passed and she didn't fall asleep. She heard Eleanor and Theo making love upstairs, something almost impossible not to hear with the ambient noise level in the house dropped to almost zero. She also heard Janice Henderson snoring in the room next door, a mild, steady rhythm. Tom McCorkindale's room was beyond Janice's room, across a hall. No sound from there. The refrigerator in the adjacent kitchen hummed. The sound was comforting.

Lacking sleep, she ran Theo Parker's case over in her mind, and then considered the people she had met that day. Tom was cute and he was available, although she thought he might be gay. She thought Theo was a little spooky, but then, men who are about to inherit billions of dollars just might be allowed a little leeway in the spooky department. She also thought Theo's relationship with Eleanor was somewhat unformed, like concrete that hadn't dried yet. Theo was attracted to her, she knew, although not as a person yet, just as a blue-eyed blond woman with a good figure. Of the two men in the house, he was the better-looking and probably the smarter, but he was just a little wrenched. She liked Eleanor and recognized in what she did to the younger woman a trait she hated in herself, which was to make others look small so she could look better. She had experienced it before and tried to control it. Eleanor hadn't deserved to be treated the way Laura . . . Well, she'd chastised herself once for that. Live and learn.

Around one she heard footsteps in the hallway. She thought maybe Tom couldn't sleep and was going out onto the front porch for a smoke, or whatever men did these days with smoking declining in public acceptance and practice. Maybe he was going out for the brisk fresh air.

Laura knew she was a pretty girl and that her looks sometimes invited unwanted attention. She also knew that you didn't have to be pretty to invite unwanted attention. She was wary. Her sister had been raped, pulled into a car off the streets of Milwaukee when Laura was nine, raped repeatedly by two men, and then dumped like trash, alive but naked, beaten and traumatized hours later in a public park. Afterward her sister was incapable of forming a lasting relationship with any man and was unmarried to this day.

For Laura, her dad saved men. Her dad was the font of all wisdom. When she asked him about her sister and the rape years later, when she understood what rape was, at least the physical part of it, her father had said, "Laurie"—he called her Laurie all her life, until he died four years ago—"Laurie, sex makes men crazy. Sex usually doesn't make women crazy. Women have other things to do that. With men, they don't see the little person in here," and he poked her brow twice, so she'd know what he meant. "What they see is what's on the outside. You're starting to grow up now and it's time you knew this. They see your figure, they see the color of your hair or maybe that you've got a pretty smile. They see all kinds of things, little, big." He laughed. "Elbows, I love your mother's elbows, Laurie. They drive me crazy to this day! Anyway, they see your legs or your bottom. They see all these things long before they see you. So the thing is, you've got to be patient. You've got to wait. Because eventually most crazy men will see all those physical things and they'll eventually look up and they'll see you. If they don't like you, all that other stuff is meaningless, at least in the long term. If they like you, if they love you, all that stuff is meaningless too, in the long term. A woman's looks is kinda like the streamers down at the used car lot. You know, they hang from a wire overhead and flap in the breeze and they're all different colors. They say, 'Look at me!' But they've got nothing to do with the cars on the lot."

"What's that got to do with Kathy?"

"There are different degrees of madness," he told her.

"But Daddy, they almost killed her!"

The question hardened her father's face. He had wanted to lead her away from the brink, but here they were, staring right back down into the insanity that had almost taken the life of someone they loved. Laura was hardly old enough to understand what drove people, women as well as men, to extreme acts. Her body was just now developing a figure.

"Sex, mixed with other things, hate, humiliation, anger, can drive some people over the top. These men were not your every-day, 'Think I'll make a fool of myself' guy kind of crazy. These men were really crazy and so help me god, if I ever get my hands on them, I'll kill them. Now go play, and remember what I told you."

She forgot what he told her for a while when she was in high school, when the crazy boys all wanted to touch her breasts or squeeze her bottom, and later, when she had sex with them, like dissatisfied used-car buyers they'd move on down the street to another lot. But eventually Laura Karczek remembered that her beauty was just a streamer, not really important in itself, and righted her life. She became a lawyer, at first to prosecute crim-inals, she thought—rapists, maybe—but eventually just to prac-tice as a profession. Laura Karczek was a practical woman.

The footsteps stopped. Laura's hands, which had been down by her sides, pulled up to the top of the bedding. Her heart jumped a beat, anxiety only, not fear, but then the steps began again, slow so as not to awaken anyone. Laura took this as a sign of consideration. You could hear a pin drop on the far side of the house at this time of night.

Laura tried to turn her thoughts to other things. Abel's giving her this case was a major break. True, he and the other partners would make most of the major decisions, but for legal and ap-pearance reasons, Laura would represent the firm in court, with maybe another associate in the second chair. She had been with the firm two years, working second chair in a myriad of cases, and had had the misfortune of meeting Mrs. DeMay only twice. She took some satisfaction in the fact that she was going to beat this woman in court. DeMay's case was flimsy, to say the least.

The footsteps were closer outside in the hallway, heading not toward the front door and the porch outside, but back along the corridor, past Janice's room, toward hers. Recognition that she might be the destination of the man whose shoes were causing the floor to creak sent an immediate chill through her. She was new to this space, she was naked beneath these covers, and she suddenly doubted that she could call out for help. This latter was just a fear, like in a dream where you think you can't move until you discover that you can, but the fear was real.

Laura Karczek considered the possibilities. One, it was Tom or Theo acting like crazy men. In that case she was worried about her nudity, because nudity makes talking sense to a man a little less effective. But the door was locked, she remembered locking it herself and pulling hard on the doorknob, twisting it hard several times. She couldn't imagine either man trying to rape her. Tom had pretty much ignored her all night, although she did catch him looking at her breasts several times. Streamers. But then there was Theo, standing at the open door with the brandy that afternoon as she was changing, looking through her, not at her. Could that be the madness her father talked about? Would she have to fight Theo Parker, her client? Because Laura was not going down without a fight.

The footsteps approached. They had to be no farther than four or five feet from her door now, coming closer. She thought about leaping from the bed, running into the bathroom and shouting for help. But she didn't know if the bathroom door had a lock on it, and she knew the bedroom door did, she'd checked it, and if she had to face someone, she'd rather do it in a larger room with more maneuvering possibilities.

Her father had given her more than advice, she couldn't forget that, and it gave her courage to stand her ground, or lay her ground, as the true situation was.

The footsteps ended at her door. She saw a strange light glow dimly from beneath the door. Was he lighting a cigarette? There's no smoking in public places in California, she thought crazily. But this didn't look like a match light. It was an almost orange glow.

Then the door just swung open. The latch didn't turn, the knob wasn't twisted, it just swung open, revealing a huge man standing in the doorway. It wasn't Tom and it wasn't Theo, but a much bigger man, a man with a body used to work, a man who would be hard to fight off.

He started walking toward her bed. She could see his eyes now, and they were crazy. Even in the darkness she could see just how red they were, bloodshot and glowing with an evil intent. He would rape her, tear her streamers to shreds, and kill the little person inside.

Laura watched him approach. Her heart was pounding so hard her body shook with it in the bed. And yet she didn't move. Could she move? It was a question she couldn't answer. A thousand times she had wondered what she would do if someone tried to do to her what they did to Kathy, her older sister, and in each of those scenarios she had acted. But now the man approached her bed where her naked body lay waiting, and she questioned whether or not she could move.

Or make a sound.

When his arms reached out for her, Laura Karczek pushed back her covers just enough to reveal her father's eighteenth-birthday present to her, the Lady Smith & Wesson .357 Magnum, and she began firing. She didn't warn him, she didn't plead with him, she didn't negotiate in any way. Instead she emptied the gun into the brute, with each succeeding round pushing his reeling body back to the door. She heard it go *thud* outside.

twenty-six

IWAS halfway down the stairs when I realized I was naked—Eleanor and I had made love and then fallen asleep. The gunshots woke us up. I turned to go back up, but Eleanor tossed a robe at me and shot past, descending the stairs. She was busy tying a robe around herself too.

We reached Laura's room and found Janice standing in the doorway. Tom rushed up behind us. The lights were out, of course. Flashlight beams danced in the dark hallway. I flipped the wall switch several times to make sure there was no power. I stepped into the room and found Laura sitting on the bed, sheets swaddled around her waist and naked above, methodically reloading some kind of pistol.

"What happened?" I asked.

"Someone tried to rape me," she said with a calm voice that suggested to me she was anything but calm. "I killed him."

"Laura, put the gun down, honey," Janice said. Eleanor stepped around her, pushed the door closed enough so that no one could see in, and then realized I was already in the room.

"Get out," Eleanor said. I said nothing and stepped out of the room. Several minutes passed while I inspected the bullet holes in the hallway wall, six of them in a neat row, going left to right as if following a progression of some sort. "Okay, you can come in now," Eleanor said.

Janice, Tom and I went into the room to find Laura sitting where she'd been before. The gun was in her hand again. She spun the cylinder, snapped it into place, and slid it beneath the covers. She was wearing a T-shirt and jeans.

"Who was he?" she asked, like some character from *NYPD Blue* after taking out a perp. Tom and I exchanged looks. "Well," she asked again, and then shouted, "*Who was he?*"

We didn't quite know what to say.

"He's got some ID on him, doesn't he?" Laura leapt off the bed and marched into the hall. There was no body. "Where is he?" she asked. "Did he crawl away?" She flipped the hall light switch, but of course the power was off. She grabbed the flashlight out of my hands and trotted down the hall. It was at this point that I realized she'd brought the pistol with her.

"Where is the goddamn electricity in this house?!" she bellowed, like an angry animal.

"Laura," I said softly, just in case I startled her and she turned abruptly and emptied the pistol into me, "Laura, we told you about the—"

We heard the wail. It wasn't nearly as weak as it had been even several nights before. It was loud. It was right here, next to me, and everywhere.

The lights came on. The wail ended abruptly.

"Theo," Tom said from the bedroom. I gladly left the hallway to the Laura Light Armored Division and retreated to the bedroom. Tom was kneeling in front of the bullet holes in the walls, the same ones I'd inspected from the opposite side. "Look here," he said.

There was blood on the wall. Splatter.

"Guys," I said, "have a look."

Eleanor switched on the room light, which brought the splatter pattern into bright contrast with the field of flowers portrayed on the wallpaper Eleanor and I had put up just last week.

"See?" Laura said forcefully, pointing with the pistol's barrel. "There was a man. I shot him."

There was no question about her missing. The only question was, who could take such wounds and survive? The answer, of course, was no one.

I've often wondered why people retreat to the kitchen in times of crisis, and that morning I found the answer. A kitchen table is a wonderful device to lean on. It holds coffee, it holds milk, it holds people, propped up on their elbows with their brows buried in their palms.

"Well," Tom said, "You got me. This place is haunted."

"There was a man," Laura said. "He was going to rape me. I shot him."

"No, dear," Janice said, really the most awake and brightest one there. "He may have tried to rape you, although I doubt that. He may have tried to harm you, of that I'm almost certain. But was it a man? No, I don't think so."

"Explain the blood splatter on the walls," Laura ordered. "Let me rephrase that," she continued, the lawyer in her reaching out. "Can you explain the blood splatter as being anything other than human?"

"Looked human to me," Eleanor said. "I would have shot his dick off, too."

Now this was a side to my intended bride I had not seen before.

"She didn't 'shoot his dick off,' honey," I replied. "Judging by the bullet hole pattern on the wall, she shot him in the region of the chest repeatedly as he was propelled out of the room. You're a good shot," I said to Laura.

"Deadly," she replied into her black coffee.

"We're missing something," Janice said. She was eating ice cream. I don't know why, but eating ice cream at nearly two o'clock in the morning seems perverse. "He's trying to communicate."

Now that was an interesting observation.

"He?" Laura asked. "Now you're admitting it's a 'him'?"

"Well, maybe 'it' is more accurate," Janice said. "But whatever is here, ghost or . . . whatever . . . it can take corporeal form from time to time and do some real damage."

"We already told you that," Eleanor said.

"Yes, but I never believe dilettantes," Janice replied. "Sorry. And afterward, that howl, that awful gloating howl, like it had said 'Boo!' and wanted to take credit for it."

"An egotistical ghost?" Tom wondered aloud.

"It was a man," Laura reiterated.

"There was no blood trail," Janice said.

"There was blood splattered *all over the goddamn wall*!" Laura replied with just a hint of irritation.

"If it's trying to communicate, what's it trying to say?" Tom asked. He yawned halfway through the question, and I suspected Tom was one of those people who need their eight hours and no less. A strange personality trait for a ghost hunter.

"He's trying to say, 'Don't mess with me!'" I replied to Tom's question. "I tried to kill it. I'm going to kill it."

Everyone but Laura knew the details, but no one felt like enlightening Laura just yet. She had the gun stuck in her jeans. I tried to keep myself from looking at her chest, which clearly was braless beneath the T-shirt. Eleanor smirked at me once as my eyes darted away.

"I was going to bring this up earlier," Janice said, "but what right do you have to 'kill' it?"

"It's on my property," I replied. There you have it. The right of the property owner. Let them eat cake, or in this case, let them eat nothing.

"Oh, well then, please allow me time to pack," she said.

"It kills people." This from Eleanor.

"Maybe. Maybe it just goes 'Boo!' and things die of their own accord."

Tom raised his coffee cup, as if to present a toast. "Then let's hope it doesn't say 'Boo!' to you."

"I agree with Theo," Janice said, ignoring Tom's remark. "It's saying, 'Don't mess with me.' It used massive amounts of energy to become corporeal so that it could go into Laura's room. I don't know what would have happened if she hadn't had a gun—it might have murdered her—but the bullets flying through its carefully, painfully maintained physical reality were enough to cause it to dissipate. It had enough energy left afterward to laugh at us."

"I'm going to kill it," I said. "For Phil Becker's sake, if for no other reason."

"Who's Phil Becker?" Laura asked.

"The guy who died of a heard attack."

Laura pulled the gun from her waistband and laid it on the table. "Phil should have carried a gun, and asked questions later."

KNOWING its pattern, that it had used up all of the energy it had to do any harm this night, Tom and Eleanor went back to bed. Janice, Laura, and I continued to sit in the kitchen and consume carbohydrates in copious amounts. "So," I said to Laura, "Nice gun."

"My dad gave it to me on my eighteenth birthday. He would have given it to me sooner, had it been legal." When I questioned this with a look, she explained, "My sister was brutally raped—'brutally,' why do I modify the word *rape*?—and he gave all of his daughters guns, and taught them how to shoot."

"Anyone innocent ever get hurt with one of those guns?"

We looked at each other over the crevasse of the gun issue. "Not yet," she said.

"People die in car wrecks all the time," Janice said, "and no one outlaws cars." Then she realized what she'd said, recalled Lily and how she died. "Look, I'm sorry. I'm just tired."

"No offense taken."

"It was a man," Laura said again, reasserting her belief that it wasn't a spirit who had invaded her bedroom.

"Then where did he go?" I asked.

"I don't know," Laura replied. "Does this place have trap doors, sliding panels, anything like that?"

I wished Eleanor hadn't gone to bed because I would have liked to ask her. As it was, my experience with Monroe House was too limited to be sure. "I don't know. Let's go look."

I turned on the hallway light, then all the lights from the adjacent rooms with the doors wide open. I dropped to my knees and began looking, tapping here, tapping there, waiting for a sound that suggested some kind of material difference on the opposite side. Laura dropped to her knees and began to inspect the hardwood floor. Janice spooned another glump of ice cream into her mouth and said, "Oh my lord," disdainfully.

I worked my way down one wall, then the other, looking for a hiding place of some kind. It didn't have to be very wide or impede on the room opposite in any significant way. I was really looking for nothing, of course, because nothing was there.

"Have either of you fearless detectives considered that there's no blood trail down this hall?" Janice asked. "You put six .357 Magnum rounds in a man's body—well, presuming he hasn't split in half, there's likely to be a blood trail."

I could tell that Janice was really annoying Laura and that the lawyer desperately needed to believe that there was a rapist and that she'd gotten him dead between the eyes, or mid-chest, where they really teach you to aim.

I gave Janice a look and she shrugged, turned, and wandered into Laura's room. We continued to search in vain for another moment or two before Janice called, "You guys better come see this."

I stood, helped Laura to her feet (and noticed her breasts jiggle—I'm a guy, what can I say?), and we went into her room.

Janice was inspecting the six bullet holes. The blood splatter was gone, the holes dry and round, fiberboard dry and flaky, wallpaper torn and crisp, the glue that bound the wallpaper to the fiberboard wall granulated.

"That's the thing with ectoplasm," Janice said, finishing the last of the ice cream, "here today, gone today."

WE lingered in the kitchen until almost four, when Janice declared that she was going to bed, stood, and left the room. I stood up too, but Laura remained where she was sitting.

"Aren't you tired?" I asked. Now there's a smart question. Of course she was tired.

"I'll just sit up, I think."

You can't shoot a gun when you're asleep. She was scared to death. "Look, you can sleep with us," I said. "With Eleanor and me," I explained.

"I beg your pardon?"

"We have a roll-away bed in the upstairs closet. I'll put it in our room. It's already made up."

"Oh, that's . . . very nice of you."

"If I get randy in the middle of the night, don't worry, Eleanor keeps me on a short leash."

She laughed, but she didn't want to.

I pulled the roll-away bed from the closet, opened the door to our suite, flipped on the overhead light, and pushed it in, Laura right behind me.

Eleanor stirred sleepily in our bed. "What?"

"Laura's going to sleep with us, honey," I informed her.

I don't think her eyes opened. She snuggled back into her pillow. "Okay," she mumbled. "You two go first."

"Right-O," I said, releasing the latch that allowed the bed to unfold. "I've ruined her sense of humor," I explained to Laura.

"Couple of months back . . . she would have insisted on going first."

"Very funny," Laura said.

"Just one thing," I told her seriously. "No more bang-bang. You call for help. We're just, what, two feet away. Agreed?"

"Agreed."

"In fact, I would feel more comfortable if you gave me the—"

"No."

"Okay." I was naked beneath my robe, so I grabbed a pair of pajamas from the chest of drawers and went into the bathroom to change. When I came back in, Laura was already in bed, her jeans and T-shirt arrayed across a chair moved to be nearby. I suspected the .357 Magnum was hidden beneath the jeans. I happened to glance at them as I too climbed into bed, the one with my fiancée in it, and we turned off the lights.

"Goodnight, John-Boy," I said.

"Did I mention, Theo . . . I knew you were warped from the first moment I met you?" Laura said.

"Did I mention that when we met I didn't look up at your face for at least five min—ow!"

Eleanor. Short leash.

twenty-seven

I LAUGHED.

"No, really," Janice said, "it—whatever it is—is trying to communicate. I think we should listen to what it has to say."

We were taking coffee and rolls in the dining room. Eleanor was smiling as she brought the various items out from the kitchen. It was almost as if Monroe House were a real bed-and-breakfast, and she was running it. It was a mystery to me why that notion should give someone such pleasure, because I was beginning to think living in LA wasn't so bad. Sure, there was overpopulation, the gangs, a twenty-hour rush hour, but hey, no ghosts that I'd ever met.

That morning in the bathroom Eleanor had cornered me as I came out of the shower, grinned as she grabbed hold of me, I won't say where, and said, "You can look and you can flirt all you want, but you touch and I'll whack this thing off and mount it." She was responding to my playful banter with Laura the night before.

"Eleanor, such violence! And you know I was just having fun," I replied. She kissed me for a long time, such a long time in fact that we had to take another shower, this one together. Now as I observed her bringing her specialty rolls to the table and asking Tom or Janice or Laura if they wanted this or that, I couldn't help but remember that morning and the warning she'd delivered with mock seriousness. Well, come to think of it, maybe not so mock.

"Theo?" Janice said.

"He prefers 'Parker,'" Eleanor said sweetly, "why, I don't know. I've never met a more egotistical man."

"You'd better keep an eye on him," Laura said playfully, "he's a hound dog if I ever saw one." She had recovered from the previous night's encounter with ectoplasm, or at least appeared okay. She drank Earl Grey with one packet of sugar, not two, and ate a slice of Eleanor's date bread slowly, in pinches, as if the date bread were a feast and she had all the time in the world to eat it. It's how women keep their figures.

Eleanor gave me dry toast and black coffee. Period. During her moments in the kitchen, I snatched slices of date bread and gobbled them down.

"Theo?" Janice again.

"I'm sorry. I was thinking about food and women and that usually uses up all of my available consciousness."

"You can handle both at once, huh," Tom commented dryly. "I can usually handle only one."

"Communicate," Janice prompted. "It's trying to communicate."

"Yes. And I know what it's saying. 'Don't screw with me.'"

"Janice channels," Tom said. "That's what she's getting at."

No one said anything for a moment. I hadn't even heard the word *channel* used in this context in nearly a decade. It had been all the rage fifteen or twenty years ago, and of course in the nineteenth century as well, when all manner of ghosts were conjured and some of them photographed. Many photographers used blatantly phony double-exposure tricks to superimpose family members or vaguely human, foggy images standing behind the séance participants.

"You want to have a séance?" I asked.

"Yes. If you don't mind."

Mind. Mind. Did I mind? Well, did I want to be in contact

with whatever it was that haunted Monroe House? The immediate answer to that was no. The brute that attacked Laura last night also manhandled Eleanor numerous times "in her dreams," but with enough force to bruise her legs. The creature had sent a decidedly real, postmortem Lily out of the closet in the master suite to . . . do what? Kill me? Would it have killed Laura? Did it ever try and kill Eleanor?

"Janice, sure, have a séance," I said. "I'd be interested in learning just what it wants."

"I thought you said you know what it wants?" Eleanor asked in a rare stationary moment.

"Yes. It wants to feed. Eleanor, before I came to Monroe House, did you ever think it would kill you, or harm you in a physical way?"

"It did harm me."

"No, I mean . . . worse. Kill you, maybe?"

Eleanor considered the question a long moment. "I don't know."

"You were terrorized, certainly. As the dreams progressed—"

"Dreams?" Laura asked.

"We'll bring you up to speed in a moment," I told her. "As the dreams progressed, your legs were bruised. You had the sensation your clothes were being torn. Terror increased, yes?"

"Yeah, I guess."

"The first time we saw it"—I searched for a word—"become *tangible*, when Lily, the dead Lily came out of the closet, I . . . didn't know that it would hurt me, exactly. I was terrified, I mean, but I—"

"But it did hurt me, Theo," Eleanor said softly. Her lips had been swollen for hours after the encounter.

"Yes, but you protected me. You stood between us, between me and the terror. You stood between it and its objective."

"What are you saying?" Tom asked. He'd been particularly quiet this morning.

"We drink milk, don't we?" I asked. "Do we kill the cow?"

"We also eat steak," Tom replied.

"Exactly. We get sustenance different ways."

"That man was going to rape me last night," Laura said. "Rape me, then kill me. I know it."

"How do you know it?" Tom asked.

"Never mind how I know it."

"Laura," I said, "please."

"My sister Kathy was raped and almost killed when I was a kid . . . What else could he have wanted?"

I blatantly took a piece of date-nut bread. Eleanor saw me do it and frowned. But it was so good.

"Let's consider—Eleanor was hung up on sex and self-worth issues," I said as her sharp eyes sliced through me. "Sorry, honey, but we need to talk about this. I thought it was because she was a virgin—" Sharp eyes again. "But now, maybe . . . something else was at work. When I came here, I was feeling so guilty about Lily, about killing Lily in the accident, that I—" I couldn't finish the sentence because the truth was, I was still hung up on what I'd done, turned my eyes from the road to look at Lily's lovely body. If I had acted quickly enough when the SUV crossed the line . . .

"Theo?"

"Right. I was so emotionally distraught over the death of my wife that I provided fodder—I was milked, emotionally, like a cow. First, the dream where Lily forgave me, which of course had the opposite effect and distracted me from protecting Eleanor, and later, in the suite, when the dead Lily walked out of the closet and Eleanor protected me."

When I said that Eleanor had protected me, Laura gave her

a little smile. Of respect, I think, that she had stepped up to defend me. They were going to be friends, damn it.

"Then Laura. Still traumatized over the rape and near murder of her older sister. Laura, if I may speak plainly about what I think of you?"

She laughed. She wasn't afraid of me or my opinions of her at all. Which of course was the point. She waved a hand. No, go on.

"Laura is a very competent woman, self-motivated—a tough, no-nonsense attorney who isn't afraid of standing up to anyone."

"I can be scared just like anyone else."

"Yesterday, as I delivered some brandy to her room—she drinks brandy for headaches—I accidentally walked in while she was changing. She was in her underwear—"

"It was a teddy," she explained to Eleanor, whose response was an "Ah" expression, as if teddies don't count because they're a lot of cloth.

"My point here is, you weren't startled, you didn't reach for something to cover yourself with, you didn't demand that I leave the room, you just . . . gently, kindly sent me away."

"I don't understand," Laura said, "what should I have done?"

"Well, you didn't pull a .357 Magnum and shoot me."

"Theo, I don't understand your point—"

"Last night, after the incident, you were livid with anger and at the same time numb with terror."

"Yes."

"Look, this is my point—we all are who we are because of what's happened to us in life. Eleanor's experiences with her father and her family led her to not think highly of herself, or trust her sexual feelings or—"

"Detail," Eleanor said. "Too much detail."

"Sorry. I . . . felt that I had killed my wife in a moment of carelessness. I still feel that, but to a lesser degree. Laura lived with the brutal fact that her older sister had been attacked and raped. Laura became someone that couldn't happen to, not in daylight, not in the blackest night. And yet here, each of us . . ."

"It milked us," Tom said. "It converts it into electricity!"

"What?" Janice asked. *Electricity?*

"Or maybe not," Tom continued, still enthused. "Maybe electricity is a medium of exchange. It takes emotions, strong emotions generated by strong past experiences, and uses it, eats it. And when it doesn't have humans, it attracts smaller animals—"

"Except they can't provide it with what it needs," I said, "so it switches from milk to steak."

"I remind you both, I put six .357 Magnum rounds into what looked like a man to me. If that man wasn't a man, why did he need to be physical?"

Well now, that was a question, wasn't it?

"Because . . ." Eleanor said slowly, "because he really was going to rape you, Laura. You've built up such armor around yourself the only way he can pierce it is by becoming real and doing to you what you fear most. He was going to have milk, and steak."

"We don't know what this entity really wants," Janice said, odd man out. "Everything you've talked about is just conjecture."

"Fine," I told her. "We'll have your séance. But I doubt if there'll be a meeting of the minds. After all, the dairy farmer and the cow rarely sit down to dinner."

Tom asked me to take him to see the pit where we found the bodies of all the small animals. Calling it a pit was a misnomer, as the basement floor was flat. Somewhere near the center of the house a slight sinkage occurred, probably no more than a foot. I didn't have it excavated, and after the lime had been poured over the remains, digging further made no sense.

As we descended the wood steps, Tom said, "Don't kid your-self. Janice is the real thing, if real things exist," he added with a laugh.

"Professional distance," I said.

"Nah, it's mostly just a habit now. But that's how you keep your credentials in the scientific community, skepticism. You've got to act like you're skeptical of the broccoli served at lunch. The truth is, scientists are the most fearful people I've ever met. They're scared shitless their professional credibility will be called into question because of some theory they possibly, perhaps, maybe, conceptually think may be true."

"If you can't attack the theory, attack the theorist."

"Exactly. But it does keep the frauds at bay," Tom said as he ducked under a floor beam. "The touchy-feely stuff is impossible to prove, because it's not reproducible on demand. That doesn't mean it doesn't exist. I've seen Janice do some pretty weird stuff."

"Such as?"

"Speak in Albanian, a rare dialect, too. I recorded it, then took it back to the university and had it analyzed."

"She channeled a dead Albanian?"

"Apparently."

"And that's not proof?"

"It's proof that maybe her aunt spoke Albanian, or she picked it up from a friend in college, or she got some tapes from the library and learned just enough to fool naïve college professors."

"Some things can't be proven."

"Some things won't be proven," Tom continued, squatting now above the white circle where I'd had lime poured. "Take a picture of a UFO, it's a photo trick. Bring back a piece of a flying saucer, it's just unidentifiable metal which they store away somewhere."

"They've done that?"

"Oh, sure, every major university has a closet full of the stuff. I saw a piece of metal once that couldn't be burned. We took it to a heat-treating plant—you know, where they apply case harden-ing to inferior metals by packing them in carbon and heating them—and this thing took everything they had, over three thou-sand degrees. Not a scratch. But that's another story. The thing is, Theo, there are some things science just refuses to look at. Is scared to look at, in fact. Unfortunately, those are the things that interest me. Look at your pit here—"

"It's not a pit. It wasn't more than a foot deep."

"You didn't dig, did you?" he asked.

"Well, no."

"My guess is it's a pit going down . . . I don't know, ten, twelve feet."

"Why a pit?"

"Accelerated decay causing soil degradation and collapse."

"I'm not following you."

"Digestion," Tom said.

twenty-eight

"THE thing about ghosts," Tom said as we strolled the lawn out in front of Monroe House—if you can call what we had in this water-deprived place a lawn—"the thing that interests me, anyway, is why do they haunt? Now, part of that we've already discussed—trauma in life, failure to 'go to the light' and all that. But really, that's not what interests me."

A hawk circled Monroe House, an ominous sight. Was it being drawn in or merely curious about a roof it hadn't marked yet? Do birds mark territory? Are birds territorial in any way? But the hawk flew off toward Moonstone Beach, wings thrusting to carry it over the hills and copse of trees in between.

"What interests me," Tom said as I looked back down at him, "is not the ghosts themselves—if there are ghosts," he said with a wry grin, "but the mechanism of the life-form itself. How are they sustained? Do they eat? Do they defecate? Is what we call defecation the phenomenon of ectoplasm?"

"Janice mentioned ectoplasm the other night," I said.

"Well, she was suggesting that the blood splatter we saw on the wall was a kind of ectoplasm, the material that ghosts create or find somewhere or, for all we know, manufacture, that gives them temporary corporeality."

"Why would a ghost need . . . flesh that could be blown onto a wall?"

Tom thought about that a moment. "My guess is . . . he

intended to have full and complete forced sexual intercourse with Laura, including ejaculation."

I stopped. Tom continued walking for a moment, noticed that he'd left me behind, and turned. "Surprised?" he asked.

"Yeah. I guess."

"These hauntings that include corporeality are pretty rare," he continued. "I mean, rare with a capital *R*. But when they do occur, they can get pretty nasty."

"Define nasty."

"Death and disfigurement, rape and mayhem, sometimes on a grand scale. There's a record of a haunting in Atlanta in the late nineteenth century—it's the south, right, so who in their right mind would take it seriously, but reportedly nearly fifty people died over six nights."

"How . . . Why did it end?"

"No one knows, but there was a fire in Atlanta that burned down most of the neighborhood, including the house. Maybe that had something to do with it."

I started walking again and Tom fell in beside me.

"Janice can't help us here, can she?"

"Candle in the wind," Tom replied.

"But what if it's the spirit of a dead miner, say, or one of the ranchers—"

"I don't think it's a spirit at all. I think it's a form of life. I think most hauntings are a variation on this form of life."

"Explain."

We left the property and found ourselves headed for Burton Drive, where there were shops that sold crystals and books about potions and other silly things that people bought. I wondered if there was some connection, if spiritualism, this little seaside town, and the thing in my house were all related in some distant kind of way, as if one sensed the other.

"I wasn't sure at first," Tom said. "I'm still not sure, but the guy who built the place being a botanist, that fits right in, you know? You've heard of the Venus flytrap," Tom continued, "the plant that eats insects? There's a whole class of such plants, big ones, little ones. Digestion is slow because the plants aren't equipped with bowels—at least, not as we know them. They often emit a sweet smell that draws their prey to them, where jaws snatch the insects up."

"I don't see the connection."

"I believe—" He smiled his "I am a scientist" smile and corrected himself with, "I *theorize* that there is a plant beneath your house. Its species, I *theorize,* may have begun like a Venus flytrap millions of years ago, attracting prey to its jaws by emitting an odor, or possibly a sound—that wailing noise we've heard, which would probably be a vestige today, and no longer useful. It's possible this species began to adapt in ways that distinguish it from other protein-consuming plants. I also *theorize* that as a defense mechanism, it developed intelligence probably quite different from our own."

"Underneath the house?"

"A defense mechanism. It could just as easily be hidden by a boulder or permafrost. But it had to have a way of attracting prey. It also needed to be omnivorous, like us, capable of eating anything. In fact, I think this species is far more omnivorous than we are. I think it can live—maybe for a short duration—by converting sunlight (like its other plant brethren), by eating almost any living protein-based creature—and by translating emotional energy into food."

"You've seen one of these plants?"

We stopped in front of a little shop called Moonstones, where wonderful glass art was sold. Light sparkled from within, sunlight reflected from a dozen different sources outside the shop and dispatched inside, where glass caught it and danced with it.

THE HAUNTING OF CAMBRIA

"No, I haven't seen one of the plants."

"So this really is just a theory!" I said.

"I think I can prove it." Tom said. "Here. With your place."

"How?"

"You remember our conversation when I first got here? We talked about how the house absorbs power during the day, after it draws power out of the electrical lines at night. You remember that conversation?"

"Yes."

"And I said, 'Oh, right, from the roof.'"

"Okay."

"Then there's got to be some, I don't know, vines growing from the plant to the roof."

"Where?" We'd seen no vines. There wasn't even any ivy growing in Monroe House.

"In the walls," Tom said with a smile, "in the walls. And probably the easiest place to find them would be in that little gable near the front."

WE didn't say anything to anyone when we returned to the house. I found a claw hammer in the toolbox, and Tom and I went to the drop ladder in the hall that led to the attic. Dust dripped from it in little balls, and seconds later, clouds. We unfolded the steps and ascended quickly, refolding the ladder and pulling it up behind us.

Light filtered in through slat windows. There were screens and glass. Not entirely uncivilized. Tom headed for the front of the building, walking gently across the flooring. I followed more warily. Every repair would come out of my pocket.

The little gable was an add-on, merely a vertical box, but the walls were lathe and plaster, old construction.

"Let me see your hammer," Tom ordered after he propped himself between two walls, legs braced.

"What are you going to do?"

"It's a double wall, Theo," Tom said. "I'm going to see what's between it."

"How much damage are you—oh, for chrissakes, here!" I gave him the claw hammer and stood to one side, recalling that builders of this period often used asbestos as a binding agent and fire retardant.

Tom leaned back and let loose with the claw end of the hammer. It took several swings before he got behind the plaster to the lathe, and then a dozen more to get a clawhold and pull a section loose and drop it to the floor.

He said nothing for a long moment. Then he motioned for me to come forward.

I didn't have to climb up to see it. It was a vine. A big, thick vine the width of a man's wrist, with leaves that were green and healthy even though there was no way they ever saw the light of day.

"Here's my plant," Tom said.

It had to be huge, vines running up all the walls, through the bedrooms and the bathrooms and the kitchen to the attic to the roof. Huge.

Tom opened a pocket knife.

"What are you doing?" I asked.

"I'm taking a cutting, of course."

"No! Don't! You don't know what—"

But the leaf sliced off without a fight. "I wish I'd brought a baggy," he said. "Here, hold this while I get more."

The leaf drifted down to the floor. I watched it fall in fascinated horror, because I knew this tip of finger we were slicing away had not gone unnoticed by its owner.

Tom took more cuttings—leaves, mostly, but also a cross section of the vine itself, which oozed a white sap that stank of sweetness. It didn't move as I'd expected, or whip out and strike

Tom or me. It merely remained stationary and allowed a human to prune it, as humans had been doing to plants since there were humans. It occurred to me that this thing might not be so terrible, that it was a plant, after all, something growing in the earth, like corn or wheat or a thorny bush. We had conquered all the world, why couldn't we conquer this pitiful, motionless thing?

Tom dropped down from the little tower. "This is the end of its vine, tip of the stalk," Tom said. "I doubt it grows more than another two or three feet up toward the roof. It's daytime now, and it's feeding, so it's busy."

"Can it move?"

"You've got me," Tom replied with a grin. "But one thing's for sure, the guys back at the horticulture lab are going to be analyzing these babies tomorrow morning. FedEx overnight, here we come."

Tom wrote a detailed e-mail, which he sent with his IBM ThinkPad over one of our phone lines. He borrowed several baggies from Eleanor's kitchen—we mentioned not a word of this to anyone—and I walked him to the local post office on Bridge Street, which also handled FedEx packages.

"There's something that bothers me," I said. "I'm thinking about the attack on Laura now—why would it want to ejaculate into her?"

"Not for reproductive purposes, certainly. It hasn't adapted that much. No," Tom continued, switching the manila envelope containing the baggies from one hand to the other, "I think it's a smart plant, maybe smarter than us in some ways. In its development it learned how its prey thinks—Hey, you know, I'm probably gonna win the Nobel Prize for this! Really! No shit!"

"Tom?"

"Oh, yeah, the rape—well, it was reproducing an actual rape, right down to the finer details."

"To reproduce it," I asked, "for Laura's reaction, or because it likes the idea of raping her?"

"I don't follow."

"Is it creating fear to feed on, or is it after sport?"

We were in line at the post office by this time, several people ahead of us, one behind. Tom considered the question. "I don't see that it matters," he said.

"Tom, terror is one thing, sadism another."

"I don't see that it matters," he said. "It was creating her most fearful event, right down to the finer details, and then it was going to kill her. Its intent is irrelevant."

WHEN we got back Tom went into the lobby to make some calls. I called everyone else out to the front porch and told them what had happened. Laura learned that we thought the creature intended to rape and kill her, actually take her life as she feared it might be taken since she was a little girl.

"I can drive you down to San Luis Obispo where you can catch the train into LA," I told her. She was wearing a bomber jacket artfully cut to fit her feminine figure. She pulled the butt of the .357 out of one of the pockets and allowed everyone to see it.

"I'm not going anywhere," she said.

"Laura, I'm closing the house. I'm going to have it tented and fumigated. I'm going to turn off all power to this place and kill it."

"No!" Janice snapped. "No. At least, allow me to—allow the séance to go forward."

"You can have a séance with the cuttings down at the college."

"You've got vines in the walls of your house, Theo," Janice said. "I don't know what kind of plants they are, but they're not ghosts or related to ghosts or even providing produce for ghosts.

Ghosts are the remnant of living human beings, not the projection of some giant rutabaga."

"Sorry, Janice," Tom said, allowing the screen door to slam behind him. "but you're out of the ghost business. At least here."

"I think the séance should go forward," Laura said.

"Me too." This was Eleanor, which meant she had my vote by proxy. The séance would go forward.

"I vote for the séance, too," Janice said with a triumphant laugh. "That makes three. Vote carried."

"You don't count, Jannie," Tom said. "You're what the vote's about. This place belongs to Theo here. What do you say, Theo?"

"Eleanor, darlin'," I said in my best fake Irish brogue, "if I said no, would I be welcome in that bonny bed of yours tonight?"

"No," she replied, "and maybe no other night, either."

"Séance it is, then."

twenty-nine

JANICE suggested we have something light to eat for dinner that night, which implied to me people might puke their brains out during our dance with the dead, but she pooh-poohed the idea. "You think better on less food," she said—curious, counter to my experience. In any case Eleanor, with Laura as her assistant chef, prepared salads with various dressings, with diced ham and turkey on the side for the guys. We didn't go hungry, I'll tell you.

Afterward, Tom and I retired to the porch with bottles of light beer. It was the only beer we had—I was in a German beer mood, but Eleanor had long since decided that we should eat less and exercise more. Eleanor had taken control of my body in more ways than were delightful, a possessive act that brings to mind another comment on the females among us. Once we mate, which is to say, once we become connected several times in that particular way, they begin to believe we never come apart, that we remain joined. And then if children are made, or if you prefer, "come along," because they're attached to her too while they're being created, then they belong to her, as well. Anything that stays too long near that vagina becomes her property, which she frets over and makes decisions about that ignore the fact that there is another human being there with territorial rights. There should be a sign posted that says, "Anything entering or exiting here becomes the exclusive property of . . ."

But we drank light beer anyway and listened to the silence, the glorious silence that is Cambria's greatest gift.

"You know many people here yet?" Tom asked.

"You, Janice, Laura, a female plumber, a drunken electrician, the woman who runs a grocery shopping service, um—the mailman."

"You're a real friendly guy," Tom observed.

"People keep introducing themselves to me," I noted. "Cambria is filled with friendly people. The thing is, I'm still in LA mode, so I can never remember their names or what they do or how I met them. You know, because in LA you don't remember things like that. In LA your friends live in Torrance, or Santa Monica, or Burbank—they're all professional friends, or friends based on shared interests, and not the people next door."

"Like I said," Tom commented again, "you're a real friendly guy."

"Yeah, it's probably me."

"Eleanor knows everyone, I bet."

"Everyone knows her. She used to be a little different. Shy."

"With legs like that?"

I gave Tom a look. "Just a friendly observation," he said.

"You think she's a looker?"

"Oh, yeah."

"Yeah," I said, "I think she's . . . pretty hot, actually. But when I first met her, I didn't."

"It's how women present themselves."

"Laura?"

"Nice presentation. Good legs. Good tits. But Laura would be like busting a bronco," Tom said with a laugh. "And you'd have to do it over and over, again and again, every night, because that bronco just ain't gonna stay saddle-broken."

"That what?" Laura said. She'd been standing at the screen door, flats of her hands poised on it ready to shove it open, which she now did. We turned and looked at her like a couple of boys with our pants down. Up came the zippers.

"I'm sorry?" Tom said, as if he didn't understand.

"I heard what you said," Laura told him. "And you're right, except neither one of you cowboys could stay in the saddle long enough."

"I'm dry," Tom said, shaking his empty beer bottle, and left the porch.

Laura joined me at the rail and stared out into the night.

"Talking about women is just about the most fun thing there is," I said, "second only to—"

"Yeah, we do it too. Do you think this one has . . . ? Do you think that one could . . . ? We do it too."

"Yeah, I know. I've snooped a time or two myself."

"I don't know how you could have thought Eleanor was plain," Laura said. So, she had been standing at the door longer than we thought. She'd been snooping. "She's got a model's fig-ure and a lovely face."

"I like the girl inside, too," I noted.

"Sure, she's got almost no tits at all, but some men like that—"

"This man likes that!"

For some reason we both laughed, like a couple of knowing rounders. "And she's funny, which you are too, but you're a guy, which ruins some of it."

"Sexual politics are strange. Things get in the way."

"Yeah, the fact that you men want to have every woman you meet, now that gets in the way."

"We do not," I protested. "I've had nary a carnal thought about the Iron Granny." In fact, it was hard to imagine Lillith DeMay having sex with anyone, or creating children, for that matter, or even being young enough to. But I was a guy who used a cane, whose hair had started turning gray recently (stress, probably), and who could see that he was no longer the person he'd been.

"So what do you think of Tom?" I asked.

"I don't think Tom's the kind of guy who could stay in the saddle, cowboy," Laura replied with a laugh. "Well, the truth is, I'm not sure Tom is the kind of guy who would even try to climb up onto the saddle."

Tom? Gay? Come to think of it—well, what in the hell did I know?

"You have a boyfriend?" I asked.

"I'm a woman attorney," Laura replied. "Have you ever met a female attorney with any boyfriends? Now, maybe if I make judge someday." The joke was lost on me, so I didn't laugh. "We spend our days in court and our nights preparing for court. We meet men who have wives who pick up their dry-cleaning and make dinners for them, and what they want from us is what they want to do to the opposition in court—get the picture? I do know some women attorneys who have husbands, come to think of it. One is married to a highway patrolman, but I think it's her marriage, not his. I know one who's married to a gardener. Really! He picks up the dry-cleaning and they microwave frozen food for dinner. Relationships like that are hard to come by. How 'bout you?"

How about me? Hm. Well, until recently I'd been a confirmed bachelor whose refrigerator was filled with beer and sodas and whose bed was more often than not filled with nothing. Then Lily, six weeks of coma, months and months of physical therapy, and—

"I fell in love twice this year. I must be ripe, or in bloom or something," I said softly.

"I can see Eleanor. You've made a difference in her life. She told me. What about Lily?"

"Same feeling, different colors."

"She still there in bed with you?" Now that was a strange question to ask. But the truth was, for a while, she had been there in bed with me, or more accurately, there'd been a hole in the bed where she used to be. Eleanor filled that hole and made it her own.

"Not anymore," I replied. "I mean, at first, yes, and for a long time, but . . . Eleanor."

"She's nuts for you," Laura said.

"She's just nuts, then."

"Afraid of this séance thing?"

"No. Why should I be?"

"Because Eleanor's gonna be there," Laura said, "and who knows, maybe Lily will show up, too."

I WAS on the porch alone for a long time when I heard Janice call my name. When I came in, I realized that Tom and Laura had talked, because they sat beside one another and she was smiling, not in her "tough girl, watch it!" mode but honestly laughing at something he'd said. Eleanor had left an open chair beside her, of course. I sat there. Janice was to my left.

"Lights," she said.

Eleanor brought a candelabra to the table and lit the three tall candles, then shut off the overhead lights. There were other lights on, one in the kitchen and one in the upstairs hall, distant and dim.

"I think I should say something about this process and what your expectations should be," Janice said. "I'm a white channeler. That means I change a little once I go into a trance—yes, Laura, it's a trance. I saw you roll your eyes."

"Sorry."

"No offense taken," Janice continued. "I will attempt to make contact with whatever spiritual beings are present. Some of you may see more than just me channeling the beings. Some of you may actually see them. Don't be afraid. They're just people who've passed on."

Tom said nothing at this, even though clearly he didn't believe it.

"I need someone to act as guide. Tom, you've done it before."

Tom had acted as Janice's guide before? Tom the scientist? "For the record, I don't believe in all this mumbo jumbo," he warned.

"All the better."

Tom nodded.

"Join hands," Janice instructed. Yeah, like I didn't see that one coming. To my right was Eleanor, then Tom, then Laura, and back to Janice, who had my left hand. For a long time nothing happened and I seriously considered removing my hand from the circle to scratch my nose. Then Janice's head fell back. Moments passed.

"Speak your name," Tom prompted.

Janice's head began to move back and forth, slowly at first and then with greater speed and severity. "No way out! No way out! There's no goddamn way out of here!"

"Speak your name," Tom said again, softly.

"Becker," she said, her voice deeper now, not masculine but as deep as her natural range could get. "Phil Becker. Where are you? *Where are you?* There's no way out of here!"

"Where are you, Phil?"

"I'm in the house, man! I'm in the goddamn house!"

"Why are you afraid?"

"Why am I afraid? *Why am I afraid,* you asshole! Look! Just look!"

"We can't see you, Phil. You'll have to tell us."

"On the stairs! Can't you see it on the stairs? *It's on the goddamn stairs!*"

"What?"

"My body. Oh god no, no, please no, I'm not, no, *I'm not*—"
Janice became still.

Eleanor looked to me for support. I shrugged. Laura grinned from across the circle of hands. It all seemed kind of silly, but at the same time, not. Of course, the death of Phil Becker was well known to everyone at the table.

Janice's head snapped back. She spoke in Spanish. Luckily, Laura spoke Spanish. "I'm an attorney and I work in LA," she explained to Tom, who must have questioned her with a look. She took over the interview as Janice spoke in Spanish, and Laura replied, then translated.

"She says she's a maid. She cleans the rooms. She sleeps in the maid's quarters—it's the room I have now. Had last night. A man comes to the door. It's late at night. She doesn't know any man, hasn't been friendly with any of the guests, has no boyfriend—*Slow down!*—yes, the door is not locked. None of the doors are locked. He comes in. Stop! *stop!* He's raping her. He's . . . oh my god, I think it's—Oh my god I think it's—What does he look like? Yes, yes, tall with, yes—"

Laura broke the circle, shoving herself to her feet, her chair scraping back across the hardwood floor.

Janice's eyes opened immediately.

Silence lingered in the room as Laura looked deep inside herself.

"He's killed before," she said softly, as if feeling the facts for the first time. "They've covered it up. The maid went back to Mexico, they said. There were others. A guest from San Francisco, buried under the house. A man from Chicago, another from Connecticut, two brothers from Germany, killed on successive nights, a little girl, six or seven, strangled by the man, choking, choking, *choking!*"

I grabbed her. I was going to shake her at first, like in the movies, but something in Eleanor's eyes made me see that what

Laura needed was parenting, so I took her in my arms and I hugged her close and told her it was all right, everything was all right, it would pass. As I did this, she continued. "There was a man from Paso Robles—where's that? nearby?—killed, and another woman and her husband, on their wedding night, and then a man in a tractor accident, and another man hit by the train, and—"

"Tractor accident?" Tom asked. "What tractor accident? What train?"

"And a car accident on Highway 1. Two little girls, their parents, the mother beheaded by the windshield, and an old woman dying of cancer, and another with emphysema, and men with heart attacks, and—"

Eleanor threw water over my shoulder and into Laura's face. She stopped immediately.

"Theo," Lily said.

I turned around slowly, Laura waking in my arms, and looked at Janice. There was no question it was Lily inside her. Her face had taken on Lily's features, and her voice was Lily's voice.

"Theo, do you hear me?" she asked.

For the eternity of a second I listened to what seemed like the echo of Lily's voice as it dissipated, like a ghost, from the dark room.

"Yes, Lily," I replied.

"Theo, the beast has us," she said through Janice's mouth. "It has us all. You've got to kill it, Theo. Please kill it."

"But Lily, how—?"

"Kill it, Theo, if you love me!" And this last a plaintive, piercing cry. "*Release us!*"

thirty

"GET out!" I screamed at Tom. "Get out now! Go pack your bags! No one is spending another night in this place!"

"But think! Think, Theo, how can some beast do this—tractor accidents and cancer deaths, and people dying of heart disease nowhere near here."

"No one is spending another night here!" I said again, Lily's voice still in my head. I was going to kill this thing. I was going to wring its neck, no matter what it was, animal, vegetable, or mineral.

Eleanor comforted Laura. They sat on the settee, Eleanor's arms around her new friend. Laura said, "It was like . . . like I saw it all. Murders, killings, over decades, different proprietors each making the same decision, protecting their investments."

"What about the tractor accident?" Tom asked.

"That, too, on a farm on the bluff above what is now the East Village."

"Cancer, you said, and heart attacks?"

"Yes."

"Not related to this house."

"No. Yes! . . . but no," Laura muttered. 'I can't explain it. They're all here! All of them!"

"It's capturing souls, Theo," Eleanor said. "Somehow, I don't know how, it captures souls, too."

"Prove souls exist!" Tom bellowed. "Prove it!"

"*It's an evil thing!*" Janice screamed. She remained seated at the round table, where each of us had sat not more than five minutes before. "It's an evil thing and it should be killed."

"Look, Theo, let me, just let me take this thing, let me study this thing, and I'll, I'll get the university to buy it from you. Name your price!"

"Go pack, Tom. You're not staying here tonight."

"*Listen to me!*" he shouted. "Listen to me, okay, just listen. This is the first time, the first time *ever,* that we've got proof, substantial, "here it is in my hands" kind of proof of the origin of the ghost legends. Substantiation, my man! Proof!"

"Kill it," Laura said. "Kill it, because if you drop dead now, for whatever reason, it will have you, Theo, forever. . . ."

"Well then, little miss attorney," Tom sniggered, "you can just go get a room at some hotel, because I'm not—"

"Get a room at a hotel!" Laura bellowed in reply. "*Get a room at a hotel!* I'm leaving the fucking county, you fool!" Laura stomped from the room to pack her things.

"She's right," Janice said. "This thing has a long reach. I don't know how long, but I wouldn't stay anywhere closer than Morro Bay, just in case I had a heart attack tonight."

Eleanor wrapped herself in my arms like a cat and whispered into my ear, "Kill it, Theo. Please. So they can rest."

TOM didn't say another word to me as he threw his two German leather bags into the back seat of his VW. There wasn't any pavement to leave rubber on, but he blew a cloud of dust over me that didn't settle until I went back into the house.

Laura dropped her single bag in the middle of the lobby and hugged Eleanor. I stepped up and she hugged me. "You guys take care of one another, okay? It was fun sleeping with you both."

Janice's eyebrows rose several inches. "Oh, shut up," I said. She laughed. Her bags were beside the door.

We escorted Laura to Eleanor's truck, threw her bags into

the back, and she climbed into the front seat, passenger side. I slipped behind the wheel. "A quick run down to San Luis Obispo so Laura can take the train, then I'll be back. Maybe ninety minutes, tops," I told Eleanor.

"I'll have our stuff packed," she replied.

"Keep Janice with you," I warned.

"And the gun," Laura said. She'd loaned Eleanor her father's .357 Magnum, given her a quick safety course, and showed her how to aim it and fire. I thought it was useless, but it gave Laura peace of mind and, I admit, me too.

Laura caught the ten-fifteen to Los Angeles. I was back at Monroe House in an hour and fifteen minutes. Eleanor and Janice were sitting on Janice's car hood, drinking coffee from travel mugs. We promised to stay in touch with Janice—she reminded us about the book she intended to write, with our assistance—and she drove north, toward the highway and San Francisco.

As for us, we got a room in Morro Bay.

I was sad to learn that a man died in Cambria that night. Cancer. I would liked to have gone to the local authorities and told them everything, but I knew the trip would be fruitless. They would never believe me. I took solace in the fact that the beast wouldn't have him for long.

Not long at all.

THE fumigation company came in on Thursday. They tented the house and started pumping poisons inside.

In the interim I'd had all the power to the place cut off. In fact, I insisted that PG&E disconnect the lines leading to the place. No electrical connection whatsoever. I'd be happy to pay for reconnection later, if necessary. I had the satellite dish removed. I even took out all the lightbulbs, flashlight batteries, anything that could hold a residual charge.

"Are you sure it won't . . . eat," Eleanor asked me. I knew what she meant.

I became the crazy man of Cambria. I hired men and women to circle the house with nets. Six people per shift, four shifts per day, twenty dollars an hour. They were to catch any animals attempting to get under the pegged canopy and into the house. They were to stop one another, for that matter. They thought I was crazy, but I got one of Eleanor's competitors, another property manager, to pay them in cash every day. I didn't want anything getting near Monroe House. I also surrounded the place with a temporary wire fence.

The first week the house was tented, I received a call from Tom at Occidental College. "The cuttings are all bad," he told me.

"Bad how?" I asked. How could cuttings be bad?

"Decomposed. Dust. There's nothing left to analyze. You've got to let me back in."

"The house is tented," I told him. "We're pumping poisons in at a prodigious rate, seven-point-two times the normal amount and the maximum the Environmental Protection Agency will allow for a building that size. Everything in it is dying."

"Theo, please—you don't know what you're doing!"

He called again, after we moved into a rented house in Los Osos near Montana De Oro, one of the most beautiful and small of the state parks, a bluff overlooking some of the most startling and gorgeous coastline in the world. It was kept separate from the Coast Highway by a forest of eucalyptus trees whose shadows probed like fingers across the road into the park. I must say one thing about Tom—he was persistent. "Theo," he said, "I can get guys with rebreathers to go in. Full suits, even. We'll just take a few cuttings."

"No," I said again and hung up on him. I didn't want that plant to survive in any form, if indeed the plant was the source of what was happening. I wanted everything dead, even the already dead.

Eleanor and I roamed the hills and estuaries south of Morro Bay and walked the strand north of it. We faced the brisk sea breeze and allowed it to tousle our hair as if we were living in a cosmetics commercial, snap our clothes, engage our minds. There is something truthful about the sea and its endless movement that gives solace. All things pass before the restless sea. No one thing can stand before it, certainly no horror. In its contantly redrawn facets are the DNA of existence, good and bad.

Janice called us regularly from San Francisco. She was having terrible, recurring dreams, haunted by her experience at the séance. Some of the things Laura experienced were now part of her memory, too, things she hadn't seen then but saw clearly now. Death. So much death. Janice was seeing a therapist, something I found startling as it never occurred to me a psychic would consult a psychiatrist. Still, she was in a good mood whenever she called and downplayed her personal response to the nightmares. She was coping, she said.

Then she swallowed the contents of a bottle of Seconal and left this world.

A neighbor found our number on a pad beside Janice's phone and called us. We in turn called Laura with the terrible news. She came up to accompany us to the funeral. The house we were renting had four bedrooms, more than enough room for guests. She brought a man, Dave Stewart, a carpenter. We heard them making love from three bedrooms away. "Wow," Eleanor whispered as Laura shouted out in sexual release. "She's really . . . getting it." But Dave left the next day and Laura said there was something about his work, an addition in Holmby Hills he was working on, and anyway, it wasn't as if they were an item.

It certainly sounded like they were an item the night before.

We drove up to San Francisco for Janice's funeral, whipping Laura's rented Ford Taurus around the cliffs and valleys of Big Sur to Monterey and then the final hundred miles to San Francisco. Janice had left instructions that her remains were to be cremated and the ashes spread at sea, so the wake was held at a bar down by the Embarcadero. The place was pretty well filled by the time we arrived, five minutes before noon. We knew no one, of course, and no one recognized us. We sat in a booth toward the rear of the bar with human backsides encroaching on our view.

A man named Dennis Crim marshaled the room by introducing himself. Dennis was tall and lean with a ponytail hanging from a balding head. He was one of Janice's friends, he said, and she had asked him to speak for her when the time came. Over the next half hour he recalled her life, the two marriages, the stillbirth of her only child, the disappointments and triumphs of her private life and career. I watched Laura as Crim talked. Her eyes were far away, boring so deeply into the naugahyde seat opposite her I thought it might melt through.

"The last months of her life were very difficult," Crim said, "as most of you know. Janice asked me to apologize to you, in particular those she asked extraordinary things from. The women she betrayed by deed or intention. The men from whom she asked . . . more than she should have. She told me that she acted out of desperation, that it wasn't really her who did those things."

Eleanor leaned over to me. "What things?" she whispered.

I shrugged that I didn't know.

Laura looked away before the question could be lobbed to her.

"Janice asks that you celebrate the good that was her life. Even though she ended her life herself, in her instructions left to me she wrote that her life was filled with good things. Remember the good things, she asked. And so we shall."

Crim asked for people to come forward and speak of the good times they'd shared with Janice. The three of us remained seated, and afterward, I approached Crim and asked him what he'd meant by saying Janice had betrayed women and asked too much of men. He looked me over for a moment before saying, "If it didn't happen to you, I guess it's none of your business, is it?" Funny. Crim had seemed much more accessible in a crowd.

During the trip back to the Central Coast, Eleanor asked Laura if she knew what Crim was talking about in his eulogy. "No," she replied, looking at the sea past her own reflected image in the glass.

LAURA left at the end of the week, having spent hours chatting with Eleanor while I worked at making myself scarce. Her final night in our temporary home was quiet. She seemed distant, particularly from Eleanor.

I drove into Cambria every now and again. People kidded me about my precautions regarding the Monroe House project. I was happy to be the eccentric, rich (so they thought) property owner who put some of the townfolk to work doing something silly.

My Monroe House Irregulars, as Eleanor liked to call them, caught dozens of squirrels, possum, quail, other birds of various kinds, several deer, and a cougar trying to get to the house. At first the animals were let go, but they would just come back, so we set up a kind of zoo with pens for holding the animals. There was an ordinance against this sort of thing, of course, so I hired an attorney to seek a variance, which was awarded temporarily pending a hearing. I hoped the hearing would be scheduled after the variance was no longer needed.

I kept putting off shutting down the fumigation. The truck came out every several days and pumped more poison in. Several of the neighbors complained, although about what I wasn't sure, because you certainly couldn't smell anything. Maybe it was the Irregulars camped out around Monroe House day and night. In any case, I offered each a settlement from my dwindling capital (I was still preparing a case against the Iron Granny, remember, a constant drain on my resources), and the neighbors accepted.

Was I crazy? Yes, I was crazy. Eleanor said, "It's got to be dead, Theo. It's been two months." Then, a month later, "Three months, Theo, it's got to be dead. Nothing could live for longer than that with so much poison being pumped in there."

I authorized a fourth month.

And then the Iron Granny's attorney showed up with a cease-and-desist order from a judge. The property had a lien against it—hers—and I was damaging the bed-and-breakfast, both physically and by reputation, although how a closed business can have "public good will" is beyond me. I called Abel and he advised me to shut the whole thing down—he thought I was crazy to be doing it anyway. Fumigation usually takes days, not months.

So I paid off the Irregulars one last time, had the wire fence removed, had the tent taken down, and Eleanor and I stood in front of Monroe House yet again, for the first time in nearly three and a half months.

"It looks the same," she said, marveling I suppose that the paint hadn't flaked away or the windows melted during the months of our poisoning the place.

"Yes," I said. "The same."

We released the animals. They darted for open spaces like inmates from a prison. The cougars and bobcat we turned over to the California Wildlife Department.

When it was completely safe to go inside, I took a claw hammer and climbed up into the attic. Eleanor insisted on accompanying me. I showed her where the vine had been. It was gone, not even a husk left. I used the claw hammer on other walls, in the attic, downstairs in the master suite and the family room, then down on the first floor, in the bedrooms, the pantry, in the kitchen and on one of the service porch walls. Nothing. No vines. Nothing.

Then Eleanor followed me down into the basement to the pit. The lime was still there, white-yellow, a circle. I walked to where the house was mounted on the foundation and dug, first with the claw hammer, and then with a shovel. Nothing. I crossed the basement and dug again. Nothing. I dug more holes, more, more, until Eleanor pulled me away from the shovel and told me to go upstairs.

Outside, leaning against Eleanor's pickup, I looked up at Monroe House. "It's dead," I admitted to Eleanor at last. "It's dead. It's finally dead."

"Yes, it's dead."

"So is Monroe House," I said. "From this point on, it's Lily's House. Is that okay with you?" I asked Eleanor. I don't know what I expected. I guess I expected her to go along with it re- signedly, to say all right, put the name of the dead woman whose place I took only when she was cremated, put her name on the place and be done with it. But Eleanor laughed, a small, joyful recognition that what had haunted our house, and us, was gone. "Yes," she said, "Lily's House. I like that."

Goddamn, I loved Eleanor ten times more than I ever had at that moment. I wished that I could quench her thirst, convince her that she was indeed beautiful, as beautiful as her sisters, as lovely as Laura, prettier even than Lily, the most beautiful woman I had ever known. But I knew it would never be. There is a hunger in each of us that can't be sated, or we'd all shrivel and die.

But goddamn, I loved her.

thirty-one

THE first time we had opened the front door of Monroe House after the fumigation, before we went inside and I took a claw hammer to the walls, we had found a small package that apparently had been left by FedEx sometime after we'd vacated the house and before the exterminators arrived. It was addressed to Eleanor Glacy. Inside was a photocopied book, a brief note from Eleanor's shorthand expert, and an invoice for seven hundred dollars.

Now, having checked the house, we retreated back into the sun while Eleanor read the cover letter.

"It's called Octavian Standard, Monroe's shorthand," she said before trilling the pages of the photocopied book. Its source was a reprint from the early 1930s, an English edition of an original book dating from the late 1880s. Eleanor's consultant had copied it from the Los Angeles Central Library where it was kept in the rare books section.

"Well, we can translate Monroe's journal now," I said with little enthusiasm. Monroe House stood in front of us with its uninvited guest dead—it was dead, wasn't it?—and translating Monroe's journal seemed to me at least like waking the dead. I wanted to go forward now, not back. I saw in Eleanor's expression that she thought the same.

"Yes," she said, "when we can get to it."

We were in Lily's House a week and making plans when Abel Gorman called me. "Finally got a court date?" I asked him.

The noise of carpenters and painters and tile people was almost deafening. Although I was technically broke, we were moving ahead with our plans to restore old Monroe House to what it once was, or at least to what we thought it had once been. It was to be Victorian, yes, but a lighter, freer Victorian with finer touches and more vibrant colors. Eleanor planned it all, every detail.

"There's news," Abel said. "Apparently Lillith collapsed at a concert last night. Cerebral hemorrhage. She died."

The report of Lillith's death came as a complete shock. I never really believed she was alive in the first place, merely a negative force in the world, an ill wind, but she had been an active ill wind. "So what does this mean, case-wise?" I heard myself ask, thinking in the crazy way of people whose loved ones remain with them in some intangible way even after they're dead, *How will I tell Lily?*

"Her heir is a cousin. She left much of her estate to various charities, the Lillith DeMay Foundation for the most part. I don't know what they do. Something with education for underprivileged women, something like that. Here's the funny part, strange I mean—I already got a call from the cousin. He wants to make a deal."

"What kind of deal?"

"He inherits, what? Several million dollars. My understanding is that the value of Lily's estate, yours now, is . . . one point seven billion dollars. But he's right, he can tie that money up for a decade with a good lawyer."

"What kind of deal?"

"Ten million, you get a check once probate has cleared."

"Hey, guys, cool it for a second, okay? Important call." The band saw next to the kitchen table was so loud I was shouting. The two carpenters operating it shrugged an "It's your money" gesture and stepped out to the porch for a break.

"You aren't going to let me take a deal like that."

"Right now, Theo, your legal fees are floating at around—" Abel checked some papers on his desk. I heard them rustle. "Ah, two-point-six million alone."

"Two-point-six million?!"

"I'm not cheap, Theo. I've had a bunch of associates working on this. We were preparing a major defense of your assets, so I don't think—"

"Okay, okay! What will this guy give up?"

"He thinks the money really should stay in the family."

"I am family. Closer family than he is."

"By marriage."

"A figure, Abel."

"Half."

Half. Half of 1.7 billion dollars. That's eight hundred million and change. Eight hundred million.

"Offer him five hundred million," I said cavalierly, as if I had any idea what five hundred million dollars looked like.

"Well, of course I'll offer him less. But he wants to retain the family businesses, particularly the publishing group. He's probably not going to want you to liquidate your portion, or place it on the market too quickly, which would drive the price down. You won't get a large cash sum, Theo." Abel said this as if I were about to go buy the Statue of Liberty and I needed cash-cash-cash.

"How much liquidity?"

"I don't know, maybe . . . twenty million."

I laughed. "Enough to pay off Abel Gorman in full."

Now it was Abel's turn to laugh. "Well, yeah."

"Okay. Let me know how it turns out."

I recalled the carpenters from the porch because time is money, and Lily's went forward.

I was able to procure a building permit that allowed us to push a new dining room out to the east, where a smaller but lovelier (we hoped) flower garden and gazebo would please patrons of the dinner house. Eleanor liked my idea of Lily's being a dinner house in competition with The Sow's Ear and The Brambles and The Hamlet at Moonstone Gardens. Eleanor wasn't sure she was up to competing against those houses as a chef, and she started looking for someone she could bring in. No matter, I knew Eleanor would prepare at least one dish a night, and probably more, because cooking was what she really loved to do.

And do I dare mention this? Well, Eleanor wasn't quite as lean as she had been. She was approaching her mid-twenties, still a kid, sure, but not a teenager anymore. Her hips were noticeably wider, her tummy, while still flat as a board, fuller—more lush, more womanly—and she was developing breasts that called for a bra, at least part of the time, in certain kinds of clothing. It was because she was eating her own food, I thought. Her legs remained long and lean, but her face was filling out, becoming more oval like her sisters'.

We planned to open in May, at the beginning of the tourist season, and marry a week before, in front of friends and family alike gathered at Lily's, the showplace of Cambria.

I didn't tell Eleanor about the offer, or Lillith's death, not immediately, anyway. Talk of the money made her crazy, like so much money would drive me mad and I would walk out on her. I planned to transfer Lily's over to her when probate and the deal with Lillith's cousin were done, but really, since California is a community property state, it would all be hers anyhow if something happened to me.

In the evenings, when the carpenters and paperhangers were gone, we settled into a near-married routine. I watched the Dodgers on the dish, or a first-run movie on pay-per-view. I bought a plasma high-definition TV, which Eleanor snorted at with disdain and soon was as addicted to as I, particularly to movies. I took her out to dinner almost every night, different restaurants, seeing what the competition had to offer. We danced in the new dining room to a CD playing on a bookshelf stereo, just she and I in semidarkness, her dress rustling as she moved, her new figure moving against me.

"You know, we haven't done it in here," I suggested playfully.

While our sex life hadn't died down too much, it was past the stage where every room, every dune, every situation had to be satisfied with shared romantic experience. "You'll muss my hair," she said in perfect imitation of Claudette Colbert from *Palm Beach Story*.

"Yeah," I replied, "and maybe your hairdo, too."

Could it get any better?

BUT there were times when we talked about it. The house. The . . . *thing* . . . in the house, around it, beneath it, whatever. And what it did, and could do before I killed it. Had it really captured all those souls, the life force of people who died in Monroe House, or near to Monroe House, or—goddamn it, for all we knew—blew past Monroe House on a breeze, having just died near Piedras Blancas lighthouse?

"What was it, Theo, do you think?"

"I don't know."

"Satan? A demon?"

"No . . . but I don't know."

"But it was evil. It killed some of those people. It—"

"I don't know what it was, Eleanor. I just know Lily asked me to kill it, so I killed it."

But had I set Lily free? Was there any way to know? With Janice gone, we didn't know anyone we could trust to let us know. I mean, it was dead, I'd killed it with months and months of poisons pumped inside the house, and disconnected electrical power, and food deprivation. Was there some other way this thing could live? Was it really a living thing?

The horror was too great to consider, that it might still live somehow.

Oh, I took precautions. I rented power equipment and we drilled down through the pit of corpses, not all of them animal (no, I didn't inform the authorities—this was Lily's now, and I wouldn't destroy Lily's reputation with Monroe House's horrors. I used a chipper to grind the bones into powder.) After twenty feet there was a cavern, and inside the cavern there was nothing. I found tunnels, two to three feet in diameter, that had once held roots. Gone. Dust. I had all this filled in with concrete, truckload after truckload of concrete pouring into the basement of Lily's, far more than would have been needed to fill a new basement. Afterward I put a thick slab where before there was only an earthen floor.

No, it was dead, whatever it was.

And Lily was free, with all the others. They had to be. She had to be.

Eleanor took to bringing Monroe's diary to bed and translating it. I don't know when she decided to do this, or that it was even necessary. I was surprised but didn't say anything. I lay on my side of the bed reading Tom Clancy's newest book, while Eleanor sat back-straight with the headboard, yellow tablet and pen on one side, the Octavian photocopy in her lap, Monroe's journal on the left.

"Anything interesting?" I asked finally, several nights into the new ritual.

"James Monroe has to be the most boring man in the world," she replied.

"You're starting from the beginning, right?" I could tell that she had. "Why not—" I reached over and flipped the pages to where Monroe's tight little letters ended and blank pages began. "Why not cut to the pass?"

Eleanor gave me a look that could wither stone. Even so, she began translating from the back of Monroe's journal, and I returned to Tom Clancy.

ONE night just before we went to bed we received a phone call. It was Laura. I noted a slight burr in her voice. She'd been drinking, but wasn't drunk. Not one of her words was slurred. She was at the Amtrak station in San Luis Obispo. "I thought you might want a guest. How is business, anyway?"

In my haste to restore Lily's, I'd lost track of Laura and was surprised to learn Eleanor had, too. "Sure. We'll give you a different room this time, how's that?" I asked.

"Doesn't matter," Laura replied with a laugh. "I'm still armed."

We drove in atypical silence to pick her up until I said, "Haven't heard from her for a while."

"No," Eleanor replied.

"I thought you guys were keeping in touch."

"We did . . . for a time."

"I know she's busy. Why anyone would want to be a lawyer, I don't know."

"Abel didn't tell you?" Eleanor asked.

"Tell me what?"

"He fired her."

"Fired her! Why?"

"She showed up for work drunk. Or drinking, at least. She was bitter about it at first, when she'd call, you know, and complain about Abel and . . . everything."

"When was the last time you talked to her?"

"I don't know, Theo. It's been months."

"Months?" I was astounded. These two women had bonded like sisters. "What, you let months go by and didn't call her?"

"Her phone was disconnected. I wrote her, but the letters came back—"

"Why didn't you tell me?" I asked.

"You were too busy."

"I was never that busy."

"She'd changed, okay?" Eleanor spat at me. "That's why I didn't go looking for her. She's become . . . dark."

"Dark how?"

"You'll see."

LAURA was sitting on a bench outside the train station, a single bag between her boots. She wore a corduroy jacket over a T-shirt and jeans. Her hair looked like it hadn't been washed in a while, and when she reached up to put her arms around me I smelled her armpits, a musky odor that I remembered from that first day, in her room, when she was wearing a teddy. I doubted she was wearing a teddy now.

"How are ya, kid?" I asked.

"Just 'top of the world, Ma, top of the world,'" she replied. I could smell the whiskey on her breath. Southern Comfort?

She kissed Eleanor, made a comment about her weight gain—hey, maybe they could share clothes now, huh?—and I grabbed her single bag and we walked for the truck.

I tossed the bag into the pickup. "When are you going to buy your own car, Theo?" she asked in mock disapproval.

"I'm inheriting this one," I said. "Community property."

"You guys are getting married! That's great."

"Next week," Eleanor said. "We sent an invitation, but—"

"Yeah, I went back to Wisconsin for a while. My mother died."

What can you do when an adult friend tells you her mother died? I hugged her again, muttered, "Sorry, kid," then Eleanor did the same.

"It's okay," Laura said. "She just dropped dead. Where can you stand in line for that, huh? I mean, when the time comes? Just die mid-sentence."

"Mid-sentence?"

"She was making a pie and dropped."

I opened the passenger door expecting Eleanor to take the hump seat, but Laura crawled in instead, meaning I would have to smell her the entire trip. Eleanor took the outside passenger seat while I circled the truck and climbed behind the wheel.

We were on Highway 1 again when Laura continued. "Abel fired me a couple weeks before it happened. But you know that." Actually, I hadn't known that, but it didn't matter. I knew it now. "So there was no hurry to come back. And I forgot to pay the rent, so they put my stuff in storage, ran up a bill . . . and sent my mail back. I didn't know."

"You can stay as long as you want," I said. I saw Eleanor's eyes flash. Wrong thing to say.

"Thanks, you guys. I knew you'd understand."

Three days almost six months ago. We'd known each other three days almost six months ago.

Eleanor said she was tired and went straight up to bed. I took Laura's bag to the room Tom had occupied, on the opposite side of the house from where Laura had stayed before. I dropped her bag on the bed, turned on the light in the bathroom, and was on my way out of the room when her hand touched my arm. "Theo," she said, "I've got this terrible headache."

"Brandy?" I asked, "or would you prefer something else?"

"Brandy doesn't quite do it for me anymore," she said. "Do you have any bourbon?"

"Be right back," I said.

When I returned the light in the room was out. There was only the bathroom light on. I thought she was in there, although the door was open and the fan whirring. "Laura?" I asked.

"Here." She was on the opposite side of the bed, in the shadows. She'd just stepped out of her jeans. The jacket and shirt were a pile on the bedspread. "Just a minute," she said. She slipped the bra off, pushed the panties down, then walked to the door where I stood with a bottle of bourbon and a glass in my hands. She saw me looking at her breasts, then down. I could smell her. She shook her finger at me. "Naughty-naughty, Theo," she said. "You can look all you want, but don't you touch."

I had no intention of touching. This body had not bathed in days, maybe longer. She took the bourbon and glass from me and walked back into the shadows, as if I were no longer there. She had what she needed and my importance to her had dropped through the floor.

Dark. She had become dark.

thirty-two

ALL her clothes were dirty. Everything. Eleanor retrieved them from Laura the next morning and went down into the new basement, where we'd installed the new industrial-size washers and dryers, and placed her clothes in a washer. She was still too big for Eleanor's clothes. Her bras were being washed and Eleanor's were certainly out of the question. As Eleanor told me later, you could see more of Laura with one of Eleanor's shirts on than off, so she loaned her one of my cowboy shirts with two breast pockets with arrows at each end (this is a story I won't tell) and an old, baggy pair of Eleanor's jeans, which were tight but fit.

Eleanor had to suggest that Laura take a shower and then brought her some shampoo to try, just to make sure that the golden girl washed her hair, too. The bottle of bourbon was half empty on Eleanor's first trip through the room, then three-quarters gone the second. Nothing to be done about this, I said, at least until she becomes a fall-down drunk.

I had told her about what happened the previous night and Eleanor's lips clenched just a little tighter. Something had passed between these two, something months before over the phone, or maybe after Janice's funeral when Laura and Eleanor had become cold and remote from one another. Whatever it was, Eleanor hadn't forgiven Laura for it. I knew better than to inquire—it was a girlfriend thing. It wasn't that we kept secrets from one another; rather, it was that we didn't bother to say everything. This is the truth of human relationships that work.

At breakfast Laura seemed her old self. She didn't smell, that was a good thing. Her hair looked as lovely and as blond as it was previously, still a little wet but snag-free. Even in my shirt her chest was a free-range sort of thing, but she otherwise looked presentable.

Eleanor shoved food in front of her like she was a lumberjack, pancakes, eggs, bacon, sausage. I had dry toast and decaf. Eleanor still thought I needed to lose some weight.

Eleanor was going to dance around this, I could see, so I asked, "Laura, dear, we love you. Now tell us what the hell happened to you."

Laura was startled that I'd come right out and asked it. "Ah, well—I have a little drinking problem," she said. "But not to worry, I'm going to AA."

"You can't drink and go to AA," I said.

"Well, I'm taking a little sabbatical from AA, but I'm going back."

"When?"

"After the next drink," she said firmly, with a smile that said she knew she was lying to herself. "Want me to leave?"

"No," I said. "Not yet." My look told her I knew something about drunks, and if necessary her bottom would skid across the new asphalt we'd just graded outside Lily's.

"Fair enough," she replied.

"Eat," Eleanor said. We all laughed at that one. Well, Laura and I did.

"No, she's right, eat. I'd like to talk with you before the afternoon glow sets in. Food will help."

"Well, aren't you the expert?" Laura said, eating.

"Dad taught me well." Still the reason I'm not much of a drinker, old Dad. "You were drinking when you were here the first time, but you had it under control."

"AA teaches you that you never have it under control."

"You know what I mean," I said.

"Since that night," Laura said, eyes rolling toward the ceiling, toward memories, "since that night I'm not sure I know what control is."

"I killed it," I said.

Laura made a mocking sound. "My, the great monster killer!" she said.

"He killed it!" Eleanor told her with just a little more emphasis than I liked. "He starved it to death! He murdered it!"

"Oh, good. Comforting. Old Soul Catcher is dead because a gimpy writer killed it. I don't know about you, but I'm relieved. Really, relieved. I don't have to worry about these nightmares anymore. Ping! Gone!"

We could say nothing for a moment. Laura scooped food into her mouth like an inmate who knows if she doesn't eat, someone will eat for her. She barely chewed.

"Talk to Tom lately?" she asked me.

"It's been a while."

"Tom's not gay," she said with a knowing smile. "He's not a pistol, either, but hey—he's not gay."

There was nothing to be said to that.

"While we were screwing each other, Tom asked me a question. Have you asked this question, Theo? It's a simple question."

"What is it?"

"If it's a living thing, do you think there's only one?"

WHEN she finished the bourbon, Laura asked for the key to the liquor cabinet. I opened it for her and she disappeared into her room with a fresh bottle, slamming the door behind her.

Eleanor and I went out onto the veranda—we called the porch a veranda now, and Monroe House Lily's, and changed all manner of names of things that themselves might not have changed at all. We sat in one of the two new swings. Wind rustled the trees. Mist danced at their tops. It was a glorious Cambria day.

"More of them," Eleanor said after a time.

"We don't know anything," I replied.

"You said you killed it."

"Tom said rare with a capital *R*."

"Meaning?"

"These events, these hauntings, are rare with a capital *R*," I told her. "If there are more, they're rare."

"What does he know?"

Ah, we'd stumbled across the truth. What did Tom know? Nothing. Tom knew nothing. I knew nothing. None of us knew anything. Not really.

"I'll find him."

"Okay."

"We'll hire professionals. We'll spend money. We'll find them, if they exist. We'll—"

"What money?"

I told her about the deal on the table, about the eight hundred million dollars in equity and twenty million in cash.

"When were you going to tell me about this?" Eleanor asked.

"It makes you crazy, honey," I said.

"I'm going to lose you," she said.

"See what I mean? Eleanor, you're not going to lose—"

"Theo, you look at every woman you see and imagine what it must be like to—You look at every woman you see, and with that kind of money and that kind of power you'll—"

"I love you. Sex makes guys a little crazy, yes, it's true, but with me it's just a dance, a joke. I'm not going to run out on you, or go out on you."

Eleanor turned to face me. Her eyes looked squarely into mine. "You want to know what came between Laura and me?

She asked me for permission to sleep with you, just for one night. She needed it, she said. She needed you, she said, just for one night. When I—I was stunned, Theo, I was stunned—when I said no, she suggested maybe we three could . . ."

I said nothing for a time. I knew, of course. I knew I could have Laura, and Laura knew I could have Laura, but the thing is, Laura knew she couldn't have me.

A billion dollars?

No, not that.

Or was it?

I WENT for a walk. I bought a magazine at the Cambria Drugs and a burger and corn fries at Linn's, then walked up to the Santa Rosa graveyard and looked at Eleanor's tree, the marble tree a man had had carved for a woman he loved. Had she been caught by the soul catcher when she died, I wondered, snatched from the sky like a butterfly and kept for god knows what purpose?

Had I released her when I killed that thing that once grew beneath Monroe House?

I wondered about Janice and her suicide. Why had she killed herself? Is that a question that can be answered about any suicide? I wondered. But it was the nightmares that . . . She told us about having the nightmares, I recalled, but not what they were about. Nightmares. Laura. Laura had nightmares.

I walked quickly back to Lily's, trotted up the steps, and walked directly to Laura's room. The door was locked, pushed me back like a stone wall. I was afraid of what I would find inside, so I called Eleanor, coward that I am, and asked her to bring the master key. At the last moment I took the key from her, unlocked the door and shoved it open.

Laura had pulled the drapes, so it was dark. She lay naked across the bed, the bottle empty beside her.

"You shouldn't see her like this," Eleanor said.

"Let's get her to her feet," I said. I pulled her to one side of the bed, then up with my wrists under her arms.

Eleanor brought a robe. "Let's get her into this," she said. We shoved her arms into the robe, cinched it closed and tied the sash into a knot. Eleanor took one side, I the other, and we walked her into the bathroom.

"Put her in the shower," I said.

We dropped her into the shower. I was going to take the robe off, but Eleanor said, "Leave it," then turned on the cold water. "Go on. I told you, she wouldn't want you looking at her like this."

So I went into Laura's room and sat on the bed. I heard her sputter as the cold water splashed into her face. I heard her throw up in the shower, twice, then a few minutes later a third time. "Damn it!" Eleanor said. I thought she might have said, "Damn you!" but there was so much noise, I couldn't tell.

I stood and started roaming around the room. I couldn't sit still. I read the wall calendar tags—"On this day in history, George Washington signed the . . ." and so on. I even went back a few months, playing the history game, did I know this, did I know that?

I saw Laura's single pathetic bag on the dresser top, not nearly as packed as it had been the first time she visited, when she was the lady lawyer and gunslinger and afraid of no one and nothing. The bag was open. There were letters inside. From Janice. But why would Janice write her letters? I got the distinct impression those two didn't like one another.

I began reading them.

I don't know, Janice wrote in one, *but I get the feeling it's been in this symbiotic relationship with us, with all the animals of the earth, since the beginning of time. We laughingly call ourselves the dominant species, but . . .*

From another: *I have that feeling, too, but I'm well past doing anything like that. I had my last period four years ago. I don't know what I would do if I was still fertile. I mean, if I believed. If I believed I suppose I would get myself pregnant. I'd choose a man whose looks I appreciated, or whose mind or personality I liked, and I'd just have him impregnate me.*

From a third: *Are our dreams our own? Writers talk about ideas just being "in the air," but are they really? I have dreams I know can't be mine, about real estate sales, for godsakes, or sexual dreams that have no connection to me whatsoever. And yet I dream them. Are they mine? Is that what's really happening?*

And so on.

"Please, god, don't!" Laura's voice gurgled from the bathroom.

"Stay in there, you bit—" but Eleanor stopped herself from becoming what we hate most about ourselves, that petty, selfish, furry creature of our evolutionary past. "Laura, you have to stay in there! You're in no condition to—"

"No!"

I heard a crash and rushed into the bathroom. Eleanor had shoved Laura back as the intoxicated woman stepped out of the shower, and she'd fallen into the wastebasket. Laura cowered now, knees to breast, arms wrapped around herself, looking up at me with the eyes of that tiny creature I mentioned a moment ago.

SHE puked for hours yet, dry heaves the final hour, and took some solid food around seven o'clock, which she promptly puked up on the rag rug in the parlor. She was working on her third robe, was still naked beneath it but whenever it flew open neither Eleanor nor I paid it any mind. She was our patient now, not our friend.

"I need something to drink," she said.

I went to get a bottle.

"Theo, you can't—"

"She'll go into shock unless she has a little," I said, and re-trieved the bottle. I poured her a small glass of whiskey, which she downed in a single gulp and extended the glass for a refill.

"Food, then booze."

"Oh fuck no," she cried.

Grilled cheese sandwiches. Hard to puke. She ate half of one in pinches. I poured her another drink and told her it would have to do for a while.

The first drink had had an effect on her by this time. She pulled her legs up on the love seat, tucked the robe between her legs in a ladylike fashion, and seemed almost tame.

"So, now we're all caught up with me, how are you two?" she asked.

Eleanor said nothing. Laura's desire for me had alienated her from her friend, probably forever. I said, "The Iron Granny died."

Laura clapped her hands, careful not to spill the drink on the love seat arm. "Good for you! Billions and billions of dollars for little Theo!"

"We're negotiating with her heirs. It won't be billions," I said.

"Well, let's put on mourning rags, then, and hell, we both could use a drink, couldn't we?"

"You and Janice were writing one another before she died," I said.

"Yes, we were. Kinda funny, in a way, because at first Janice and I didn't see eye-to-eye."

"But that changed."

"Oh yes-sir-ree-bob, it changed."

"Both of you having nightmares, right?"

"Could I have another drink?"

I looked at the grandfather clock, recently purchased and keeping excellent time in the corner. "In twenty minutes," I said.

"Then that's when I'll talk about it," Laura replied. She

turned to Eleanor, who sat beside me on the settee with her left hand on my knee, a habit of hers. *This is mine and don't you dare touch it.* "Oh, Eleanor, give it a rest, okay? I just think your husband's a nice guy, that's all. He probably couldn't do it either, but I was willing to try."

"Do what?" Eleanor asked.

"Plow a baby into my field," Laura laughed. "Didn't I mention it? I've decided to become a mom."

"What?!"

"Oh, don't let this little alcoholic thing mislead you. I'll be an excellent mom . . . as soon as I can find a man who can do the deed."

"Janice mentioned that she would try to get pregnant, too, if she was still capable," I said. "Why did she say that?"

"Drinky?"

"Seventeen minutes."

"Then that's when I'll start answering questions," Laura replied. Still, she was grinning, in surprise at herself maybe, or at the irony of it. "I took birth control pills for most of my almost adult life, you know. Popped one of those little babies every morning so I could sleep with whomever I wanted whenever I wanted and not worry about the mommy thing, or worse, the abortion thing. Turns out, not to worry. I've slept with— god, who haven't I slept with? Every adult male I know who can get it up, excluding Theo here. Cabbies. Bartenders. Two, three, four, once seven men in one night, and nothing. No little babies growing in Laura's tummy. I could use a refill," Laura finished, downing the drink, two fingers at least.

I looked at the clock. Twelve minutes. "No," I said.

"Then no answers," Laura replied.

"Did you see an OB-GYN?" Eleanor asked.

"Several. They all say I'm fertile. I should be manufacturing babies like a factory."

"Maybe it's the men," Eleanor said.

Laura laughed. "That's what we always say, don't we? It's the men. Goddamn them, they can't knock us up, or they do, or they get paid more than we do, or they think they can screw everything in sight, but we're supposed to remain faithful, 'cause everyone knows who his mother is, but it's a wise child that knows its father. Or some such shit as that."

"I just meant that—"

"Hundreds of men," Laura said. "I've slept with hundreds of men!" She was serious.

We listened to the clock tick, watched the pendulum swing back and forth.

"God, how much time, Theo? Please, how much time?"

Five minutes. I refilled her glass anyway.

"Thank-you-thank-you-thank-you," she said, downing the drink, four fingers deep, in a single gulp. Her head fell back and I was reminded of the night of the séance and Janice as she lapsed into a trance.

"Janice dreamed that it came for her, every night, and raped her, and made a baby," Laura said after a long while.

"That's what I dream too, every night."

thirty-three

You don't believe it?" Eleanor asked. "They're only dreams."

Laura took a deep breath, allowed it to stream out between her teeth. "Belief, belief, what do I believe? I believe for every drop of rain that falls, a flower grows. I believe that boys are made of snips and snails and puppy dogs' tails and—"

"I've had those dreams!" Eleanor said, leaning forward, challenging Laura. "I had those dreams when I came here and lived in this house alone—*alone*—for months before Theo came here. So what?"

I knew she'd had the rape dream. I knew she said she'd seen things, things she would never tell me about. But the full extension of that rape dream, conception and birth, no, she'd never mentioned that part.

"Oh, right, the virgin story. I remember," Laura said, dismissing it as somehow less than her own experience. "I don't know, maybe it isn't as vivid when you have nothing to compare it with."

"It's a nightmare!" Eleanor said. "You don't go sleeping with every man you can find—*you don't try to get pregnant*—just because of a nightmare!"

"Well, maybe you don't," Laura said. "Maybe you don't commit suicide either, because all of your eggs are gone and it still won't leave you alone. Maybe you're not woman enough, not *female* enough for it to really want you!"

Laura knew this button existed, and now she'd pushed it.

Eleanor leapt from the settee and slapped her, hard, across the face. I jumped to restrain her, but lost her hand in the arc of the second slap. I stopped the third. Eleanor shifted to her left hand and landed a third blow, cutting Laura's lip on her engagement ring. I pulled both hands behind her and she still spat at Laura. I pulled her back and sat her down on the settee, kneeling between them.

Laura was laughing. "If it were only so, sister," she said, and the way she said "sister" was meaningful, not toss-off. She loved Eleanor, deep down loved her like a sister, but none of that mattered now. It just didn't.

"It's the alcohol talking," I said to them both.

"The hell it is," Laura said, laughing. "But just suppose it is," she said, extending the glass, "the alcohol wants to talk."

She withdrew the glass after about a minute. Silence was a sewer that had opened up into the room. Finally Eleanor wriggled free of my grip. I tried to restrain her, but she stood and stepped away. "I'm just going to take a walk," she said. "Don't you touch her, Theo!" she barked, and I knew what she meant by "touch." We heard the screen door slam, but not the crunch of her shoe soles on the gravel that used to front the place. The new asphalt rendered her steps silent.

"Well," Laura said, "that went well, didn't it?"

"You should get psychiatric help," I told her.

"Janice tried that. She was institutionalized for a time, did you know that? Against her will, too." She wiped blood from her lip onto the left sleeve of the robe. "It got that bad. I mean, she was out trying to get men thirty years younger than her to—did you read that letter?"

"No."

"Maybe it's in my purse," Laura thought. "I burned some of them, the really bad ones when it became clear she was psychotic, she'd gone off the deep end. I mean, a fifty-seven-year-old woman who was well past menopause trying to get pregnant so some monster won't—" She stopped a moment and considered her words, what she was telling me. "I think because we were psychically linked together when I had those visions, when I saw all those dead people during the séance, it made her feel she could—"

"You need psychiatric help."

"No, really, I don't, Theo," Laura replied. She extended the glass. "What I need is a really stiff drink, or something else really stiff that will knock me up and make me unacceptable, like Eleanor."

"Eleanor's not pregnant."

"Didn't say that," Laura said, shaking the empty glass before my nose. "Just she's not acceptable. It doesn't want her, or it would have taken her already."

"I killed it, Laura."

"Oh you big, strong vampire killer," she said in a babykins voice, "why don't you pour me another drink, hm?"

I poured more whiskey into her glass, to the rim. She brought it to her lips and her tongue darted out across the surface like a prey animal at a watering hole, savoring the liquid before a tiger takes her life. "Oh, thank you, Theo."

"What can I do for you, Laura?"

She seemed to think about that for a time. She drank a sip, then another. Then she said, "You can let me stay here for a while. I don't have any money, Theo. I stopped making it and I spent a lot of it traveling around, so . . . I couldn't pay you. But if you could give me a room for a while, I'd be grateful."

"We could do that."

"No, you could do that. Eleanor's not going to want me around. Not anymore, and never again. And I don't blame her."

"You can stay."

"Okay. Good. Thanks." She sipped more whiskey. "And you

can let me have some whiskey, because it's the only thing, the *only thing,* Theo, that makes the dreams irrelevant. Doesn't stop them. Doesn't make them go away, but booze makes them irrelevant."

I gave her the bottle. "I'll get you more, when you ask for it."

"Good, good," she said, tucking the bottle between her knees, neck up.

"I'm sorry," I said after a time. "I'm sorry you're dying."

"We're all dying," Laura replied. "Dying's the easy part. It's afterward, now that's . . . that's what's tough."

I sat with her another ten minutes. Her eyes opened, then closed, feeling the alcohol spread through her body. Then she stood up, dropped the empty glass on the love seat and walked to the entrance to the room. She was a little drunk, not nearly as drunk as she would be in half an hour, but showing it in the imprecise gait of her walk. She turned and grinned.

"Say, cowboy," she said, uncinching the robe and allowing it to drop to the floor, "sure you don't want to see how long you can stay in the saddle?" For emphasis she stuck one hip out and slapped it. God, this is awful. I don't like to think about it, but Laura was still Laura. Her figure was still perfect. She was a natural blond with—I'm not going into detail. I felt myself get excited. "Who knows, maybe you're different from all those others. Maybe you can plow a baby into my field. How would that be, huh Theo, our baby? What would she look like? Would she look like me someday, but with some of her dad's brains, or would he be like you, but towheaded and funny to be with?" She shook herself drunkenly. Her breasts wiggled and her hips ground. It was everything I could do to remain sitting.

"No," I said.

She nodded after a moment, stood to her full height, bottle in one hand, door frame clutched in the other. "Doesn't matter," she said. "I'm fucked either way." She disappeared down the hall.

I WAS still sitting on the settee, thinking, when Eleanor came back an hour later. She saw the robe on the floor and realized what must have happened. "That bitch!" she hissed, and she started marching for Laura's bedroom.

"Don't bother," I said. "She's in a stupor by this time."

I heard Eleanor advance to Laura's door and knock. I heard the door squeak as Eleanor opened it. I heard silence. Then Eleanor was beside me again, raging but controling it.

We said nothing for a long time.

"Before she killed herself, Janice was . . . what? Barhopping, I guess. Hell, I don't know. Trying to get pregnant. Janice had already gone through menopause."

"That's crazy!"

Well, yeah.

More moments lost to eternity before Eleanor asked, "Theo, you didn't—?"

I merely looked at her and she turned her eyes away. "She's going to die," I said, "today, tomorrow, next month. Drunk, sober, somewhere in between, Laura's a dead woman."

"We should get her professional help."

"She doesn't want professional help, Eleanor."

"We could have her institutionalized," Eleanor said. It was a suggestion that came from pity, I think. I hoped so.

"Wouldn't do any good. Didn't help Janice. She was hospitalized for a while. Forced. Didn't help."

"She never mentioned it," Eleanor said, amazed. All the phone calls they'd had together, the hours of discussions of this and that, and never once had Janice told Eleanor that she was cruising bars for men to impregnate her when that was a rational impossibility. Or that she'd been placed in a hospital for the mentally insane. Or that she was going to kill herself because none of it made any sense.

"Laura's going to stay here as long as she likes," I said.

"No!"

"Yes, she is, Eleanor."

"She'll seduce the fucking gardener!"

"Not if we keep her drunk enough."

"Theo, giving someone like that alcohol is criminal."

"It's not a lot different from the Thorazine they'd pump into her if she were institutionalized, except here it's her hand on the syringe." I took Eleanor's hands in mine and drew her eyes to me. "I want you to go with me right now. We're going to get that gun of hers and hide it somewhere. Say yes."

"Yes, Theo," Eleanor replied.

"When she asks for a bottle, give it to her. Say yes."

"Yes."

"Okay then—"

"Theo?"

"Yeah?"

"You're going to marry me next week and we're going to Hawaii for our honeymoon, just like we planned. And when we return, I want that bitch out of here, I don't care where. Rent her a room, call her relatives back east, whatever—but I want her out of our lives, okay? This time you say yes."

I thought about it for a while. Unlike her treatment of Eleanor, Laura hadn't tried to take anything from me. She was adrift in a sea of madness. I would find her a place, a place far from my sweet, insecure wife. I said, "Yes."

She leaned forward and embraced me. For the first time in our lives together, in every kind of physical exertion, working, making love, exercising—for the first time I smelled an odor coming from her body. It was the smell of fear.

"I have something to show you," she said.

thirty-four

S HE led me upstairs to our bedroom and by the time we arrived I had what can only be described as a shit-eating grin
on my face. I expected romantic adventure. Why I should expect that from a woman who was anything but herself I don't
know. I just chalk it up to male vanity and sexual preoccupation.
Eleanor closed the door, saw the grin, sighed, then took me by
the hand and led me to our desk at the window, which overlooks the front entrance. She pushed me down, opened the desk
drawer, and withdrew Monroe's journal and her translation
tablet, which sat on top of it, placing them on the desktop.

"I've been making headway," she said softly. "It's good therapy with everything that's been going on."

"So, what did you find out?" I asked.

"After I translated the later entries," she said, strangely focused, strangely quiet, "I was able to backtrack and translate
where he made his initial discoveries. It's all in sequence now."

"Eleanor!"

"Go on," she said. "Read."

A moment later I heard the door close.

August 6, 1898

A tumult on deck. I go up. The sky is glowing red, the
huge trees along the riverbank in stark contrast against
smoke and fire. A deckhand plumbing the water depth
with line and sinker is not moving, glaring at the sky. I

wonder if the jungle is ablaze, if it might burn to the river and consume us in a fire storm.

I ask Captain Crétien if we are safe. He replies in heavily French-accented English that he thinks we are. His Portuguese, it's said, is even worse than his English. Crétien opines that it's not a wildfire we see. Then what? We shall soon know, Crétien says.

Our stern wheeler comes around the bend in the river and we see it. Several hundred Indians surround a tree, shouting, throwing wood at its smoldering trunk. The tree resists burning. Flames dance up its side, limbs catch fire, leaves burn away, then the fire dies out. Beyond the single tree bonfires provide kindling for the tree.

I ask Crétien what the Indians are doing. He suggests we push on to the next village. He gives the order. I ask Crétien why he is afraid. Crétien replies the Indians are dangerous. They are in a killing frenzy.

Over a tree?

I countermand the order.

We berth the paddlewheeler on the riverbank above where the fires are burning, then trek down to the site. Crétien brings six crewmen armed with carbines. He carries a .45 caliber automatic which hangs cowboy-style from a belt. Once among the Indians (who ignore us) we send our interpreter Julien to find someone to talk with. There are no volunteers among the Indians, but Julien finds a sailor standing nearby watching the events with a grim expression. He has been beached here almost four months, we learn, having fallen overboard from a ship heading upriver. He agrees to speak with us in exchange for a ride back to civilization.

Julien must still interpret. Luis Araulo speaks only
Portuguese.

Julien reports the Indians are killing . . . (These natives are Christian in name only, so this doesn't translate very well, Julien warns me) . . . "Devil Tree."

I ask why they kill the "Devil Tree"?

Julien begins translating before Luis is done speaking. The villagers believe the plant steals souls. Maybe
"souls" is not the right word. They have seen dead fa-
thers, mothers, dead children . . . walking.

I ask Julien, why this plant? He replies, it's old wisdom. Villagers don't know why. It's tradition. Find this
plant, kill it when the dead walk. The dead walk no
more.

I take a moment to study the plant. It's unknown to
me, like no other tree I've ever seen. It doesn't look like
any of the known Brazilian families, not Arecaceae,
not Apocynaceae, not Chrysobalanaceae. In truth it
doesn't look like a tree at all. Too bushy near the base
where the limbs are far from sunlight. The branches
look . . . I shouldn't say this, I shouldn't write this
down, but it looks strange and repulsive.

I tell Crétien I want a specimen of this species. I order Julien to negotiate with the chief. Both men look at
me like I'm mad. Crétien says the Indians are killing
their enemy. Do I want to side with their enemy? I assert that I must have a sample of this species. The
sailors look anxious. After a moment to consider, Crétien says no. I insist. My voice rises. Crétien pulls the
gun, orders the sailors to take me and return to the ship.

Back on the paddlewheeler as we prepare to make
way, Julien tells me Luis Araulo knows where there is

another plant. Upriver, he tells me, and small enough to dig up. Crétien has become almost affable now that we are safely onboard. He becomes even more concilatory once we are under way. Julien, Luis, and I join him in the wheelhouse. I tell him Luis knows where another plant is located. I see that it worries Crétien, stealing the plant from beneath the noses of the locals. Against this gamble is weighted the contract for a number of future expeditions paid for by the National Geographic Society, contracts I could negate with a single report.

Crétien agrees if we get in and out quickly.

Crétien lands the paddlewheeler five miles north of the great burning, flames we see even now over the wall of trees, the sky red with fire and smoke. Crétien, six crewmen, Julien, Luis, and I hack our way three-quarters of a mile inland to the site.

Luis was correct. He stumbled across the new species while walking. Even here, where all the plants are strange, this new species is stranger yet. The plant is four feet tall. It looks similar to its sibling now burning across the jungle, but here there has been no spurt of growth toward the jungle canopy above. The specimen doesn't look like a tree so much as a bush. Wide rather than tall and lush.

I order three sailors to bring shovels and start digging. I stand behind one, giving instructions. I tell them don't cut the roots, dig around them. The specimen is no good if it dies. Julien translates this as Crétien observes the glow on the horizon and turns grim.

The diggers expose the roots. I order the workers to stop, then I drop into the small basin and clear the dirt away by hand. The crewmen step away to smoke. I dig, probe with my fingers, push dirt out of hole, dig some more. Then I touch something . . . indescribable. Cold. Marble cold. Something terrible. Horrific. I brush the dirt away. I see it clearly now and back away, shout "Oh my God!" and fall out of the hole.

Crétien asks if I'm well from the ring of smokers thirty feet away.

I stare down into the hole. It's awful. I don't understand how it came to be here. It should not be here. It makes no sense.

Crétien asks again if I am well. Some of the men turn and take the first step to come to my aid. I know these men. Compared with the Indians they are civilized, but if they see what is entangled in the roots, they will bolt and leave the specimen behind.

I get to my feet. I lie. I tell Crétien I saw a centipede and it startled me.

Crétien laughs. The others laugh too.

I step back into the hole. I kneel beside the entanglement, so close to it that I smell it, rotting & lank. I dig fresh dirt from the banks of the hole and cover it up.

I recall the workmen. I tell them the roots are more extensive than we thought. Enlarge the dig area but keep the roots covered, I tell them. I send for more wood for a bigger crate.

They do not know. They must not know.

I stopped reading. Outside, Eleanor was playing fetch with George the dog. Down the street three boys on bikes were yelling at one another. There was a breeze that rustled the curtains. The sky was blue and cloudless. My heart continued to beat regularly. Everything was as it should be.

I turned over the finished sheet of yellow paper.

September 29, 1898.

Celia was surprised see me home months before the expedition was scheduled to end, but she was delighted with my return even though the house is not quite finished. There is the National Geographic Society to deal with, of course, but I'm certain once the new species is announced they will see things very differently.

Had the specimen taken down to the cellar. I uncrated it alone. Even though the cellar is unfinished—and won't be finished now until after this work is done—it provides a perfect workplace. The windows are located at ceiling level and provide more than enough sunlight to keep the plant happy. This place is very private.

November 4, 1898

I don't understand how it propagates. Yes, there is the symbiote issue, but the mechanism, the goddamn "how" of the thing is baffling. Most plants that depend on other species to propagate do so in a passive and mutually profitable way. Bees and flowers, as an example. This is very strange.

November 17, 1898

News! I took Celia and Lila to San Francisco for the week. When we returned I found that the plant had pushed its roots through the table and into the earthen floor. The table must have been rotting for some time, water leakage, obviously. Even so, this is extraordinary!

November 28, 1898

I have discovered that the plant's limbs are responsive to human proximity. Not much, mind you, but if one approaches a limb slowly, it retracts. I'm not able to spend as much time as I would like in the lab. Lila is sick with a cold and now Celia threatens the same.

December 10, 1898

Lila is very sick. Doctor out twice this week. Celia sick too, but not as much. I get down to the lab once a day for an hour or two. NOTE: Root system growing stronger every day. Extraordinary. The plant seems to adapt to its environment. In the Amazon it grew tall to compete with other trees for sunlight; here, it grows into the earth.

December 22, 1898

Lila buried today. I had to hold Celia up during the ride out Bridge Street. She is still numb and so young. Celia is . . . not herself. I pray that she recovers. She didn't want another child after Lila was born. Now . . . ?

December 30, 1898

The table collapsed sometime between yesterday morning & today. The plant rests on the earthen floor now, exposed roots twisted and crimped beneath it. Nothing of the horrific visage remains. I'm still no closer to understanding how its cycle of life works.

January 14, 1899

Celia sees ghosts. So she says. She has not yet recovered from Lila's death. Last week Mrs. Parsons died and Celia claims she saw her standing in our living room this morning. I will talk with Dr. Sorrenson about this situation at first opportunity.

January 23, 1899

Now it's Lila. Celia said she talked with Lila, who just wanted to run away and play as if alive. My wife has trouble sleeping now and has moved from our bedroom. ~~We do not~~ She is distant from me.

In the lab, the plant has settled into the new location as if it were always there. The root system is disappearing below ground level. The specimen is twice the size it was in the Amazon even though Cambria by contrast is cold and ill-suited to tropical species.

February 3, 1899

I awoke to a loud noise coming from somewhere in the house. I went out of the bedroom and found Celia standing at the top of the stairs. She was nude. I talked to her as if this were the most reasonable situation imaginable. I told her she would become cold without clothes. I am as dotty as she. She looked at me as if I were something else. Not human. Not her husband anymore. I led her back to her room and put her to bed.

February 19, 1899

Celia came to my room tonight long after I fell asleep. I have never seen her like this before. She was like an animal, impatient, gutteral, abrupt, and unclean. Decency forbids me chronicling what has happened to her and to us.

March 15, 1899

I found Celia in the lab tonight. The circumstances are horrendous, unspeakable. I cannot bring myself to record them. I returned her to her room. I now know

this species, this thing . . . I brought back from the
Amazon is the source of all the strange events that
have occurred since my return. I must kill it. But there
is a dilemma. I can't burn it like the villagers did. The
house might go up. If necessary, let the house go up,
but tonight I start with simple poison.

    It has to eat.

  It was the last entry.

  I found Eleanor sitting on the front porch swing, one knee
drawn up and reading a recipe book. I sat down beside her.

  "I guess we don't know, do we?" I said.

  "Start here," she replied, burying her face in my chest. "I'm
afraid everywhere, Theo, so start here in Cambria."

thirty-five

"WE don't know shit," Tom said. I'd flown down that afternoon, chartering a Beechcraft to take me into Long
Beach Airport. We were in a bar two miles from the campus,
the sort of place with linoleum flooring and faux wood panel-
ing. There were neon beer signs on all the walls.

"Yeah," I replied. "You said that before."

"We don't know how it reproduces, we don't know its cli-
matic requirements, we don't know if it flowers and bees polli-
nate it or it reproduces asexually or—"

"Okay!" I said. The beer was poured from a pitcher, ordered
to his taste, and it was awful.

"We could have had all that!" Tom asserted, pushing his right
forefinger into my shoulder. "We could've had everything! Except for you. You had to kill it!"

"Well, it's your lucky day, Tom," I said. I opened the case I'd
brought from Cambria. Inside were Monroe's partially translated
journal and the photograph negatives retrieved from Monroe's
effects, which might contain images of the plant. Tom read the
journal while I ordered a soda and bought a bar hot dog to absorb
what I'd already swallowed.

"Shit," he said at last.

"There may be more."

"I remember telling you that."

"Okay," I said, "I fucked up. My dead wife asked me to kill it,
so I killed it, and I made sure it was dead. I killed it five times

over, just to make sure it was dead. And you know what, Tom? I'd do it again! I'd do it again and again and again, because this species has got to be exterminated."

"I guess we've lost that opportunity, now haven't we?"

"You've tried the government?"

"I've been laughed out of every agency in Washington," he said, releasing the pent-up energy with a sigh. "I've lost any credibility I ever had. I wish I'd had this," and he shook Monroe's journal at me, "when I first went in. I'm going to have real trouble getting a second meeting with anyone now. Nobody's going to fund a search for a plant that's the source of the ghost mythos, that captures souls like fireflies, that—"

"How much would it cost?" I asked.

"How much would what cost?"

"Find 'em, tag 'em, exterminate 'em."

"Millions."

"How much to get started?"

"Millions."

"Will you take a check?"

"I DON'T want to leave her here alone," Eleanor said.

"She'll be okay."

We were dressing for the wedding shower, which, to my surprise, now includes men. How did we ever get roped into this? Sitting around opening gifts while women say "Ooh" and "Ahh" and guys wish they could kill some small furry animal? Well, I was the groom, so I had to be there, but my money was on a very small male contingent. Two guys, I thought. Maybe one of them gay and married to a moustache.

"She could burn the place down," Eleanor said.

"She doesn't smoke, Eleanor. That's how places get burned down, not by opening bottles of cheap whiskey, but by smoking."

"Good stock is wasted on her," Eleanor said defensively. Oh

yes, this was the other point of contention this evening. Eleanor had ordered a case of the cheapest bourbon available, all for Laura now. It didn't make a difference as she was just using it as a sedative anyhow, Eleanor explained. I tried to spell out to Eleanor that it would make a difference. The cheap booze would make her sick quicker, more often, and with more explosive results. I gave Laura a bottle of our best Kentucky bourbon just before I came into the bedroom. I moved the case of booze Eleanor had bought to the bottom of the locker.

"You like her," Eleanor said, by which she meant, *You want her, so you're treating her better than she deserves.* I would never admit to Eleanor that when I saw Laura, which invariably these days was naked, she aroused me. But my concern for her wasn't because of sexual arousal. She was a lost soul. Like Lily until I freed her (god, please, I freed her, yes?), like Eleanor when she found me sitting on the steps of this house with a cane braced across my knees. A lost soul.

"We could get someone to sit with her."

"No, she'll be fine."

"She might try to commit suicide."

"Laura? The only way Laura's going to die is with both guns blazing."

"Theo?" Pleading.

"No."

thirty-six

WHEN Laura awoke, Monroe House was dark and quiet. For her it would always be Monroe House, not Lily's, even though it looked very little like when she first saw it. It was the place where the horror began, Monroe House.

Laura had always felt trapped by her gender. It wasn't that she envied boys, really, or wanted to be like them. She just knew that it was women who paid the bills for whatever the boys bought. Her body was a baby factory, her breasts milk machines, her loins the loading dock. Women were baby factories. Men weren't like this. They had this one little organ that made them crazy sometimes, yes, but for them, a quick jerk-off in a field or a night of mad lovemaking were equal in consequences, at least as far as their bodies were concerned. The field would see the liquid evaporate with the morning sun; the girl nine months of morning sickness and a twenty-year commitment to raise a contentious human being.

No, not fair.

But she enjoyed the power of her gender, too, because where there were liabilities, there was also always power. Boys would far more prefer coming inside her than on some godforsaken field. Yes, she had power over them, and learned early how to use it.

But now that power was turned against her, because all she could think of was copulation. All she could think of was conceiving. She tingled with it. It made her ache. Now she was like the boy masturbating into the field to relieve the yearning. Now she was—

In heat. Like being in heat. It wasn't that, of course. Because even though she had slept with any man who would have her for months, it was really the creature that she yearned for, that she needed, the creature Theo had killed.

That night she'd emptied her .357 Magnum into it because it was going to rape her. But since then she'd become enlightened. By the truth. Oh, the awful, yearning, aching truth—she needed it! She needed it, and it made her hate herself. Yes, it was rape, because the rapist made her want to be raped. Madness!

The house was quiet and dark. Theo and Eleanor must be asleep, she thought. No, they were going somewhere. Theo had even asked her if she wanted to go. Yes, to a wedding shower. In Eleanor's hometown. She had laughed, because she was naked when Theo asked, and she hadn't bathed since . . . well, what did it matter anymore if she bathed? Yes, she would be the talk of the shower, she thought, the naked, filthy woman with the naturally blond hair!

Laura rolled from the bed and ran into the bathroom where she sat and relieved herself. She didn't bother to clean herself afterward. She didn't want to be attractive. She didn't care, really, but had she cared, she would have wiped feces all over her body. She sensed it was coming and would do anything not to attract it.

Yes, she would kill it, because it was the worst kind of rapist, it made her want it. It made her yearn for it.

This was not how she was. This was not how Laura had ever been, except maybe a little, for a while, when she was a teenager. But not to this degree. She wanted to rub herself against something. *Oh god, maybe I should die,* she thought. I've become an animal.

But she would get her revenge. When it came, she would blow it away, like she had the first time.

And then she would rub herself on something.

At three o'clock in the morning the hive began to make the honey. It was neither a hive, nor was what it made honey. Ecto-plasm is far more difficult to make than honey, and far more precious. The hive knew it would take everything it possessed just to make the man, but make him it would, for it too was suf-fering from a sexual imperative.

The sibling was dead, but before it died, it had transferred most of its knowledge and trinkets to this creature. The farmer was here, the beheaded mother and her children and husband from the wreck on the Coast Highway, the poor man who died of cancer that Theo thought he might release, hoped he would release, to the light or wherever it was souls went when the sib-ling was killed. And thousands, tens of thousands more. The process of transferring was long and tedious, and toward the end some trinkets were lost, and some knowledge. But not all. Not nearly all.

And time was growing short. The hive was fully grown and could grow no more. There were natural barriers to additional growth—location, access to water, food—but there were genetic barriers as well. Size brought with it increased probability of disclosure, and disclosure could mean death, as with the sibling. It was time to make the honey.

The form was a man who had lived in the late nineteenth cen-tury. His was a soul that was part of the hive, singular and in tor-ment, yes, but allied and cooperative, too. He was a brute, six feet, seven inches tall. He was allowed the taking, to take the woman, but would die in the process to be reacquired by the hive.

Had there been a living thing nearby other than trees and

bushes and weeds, the sound of the hive's humming as it made the ectoplasm would have been heard. But no, there was nothing. Animals that survived shunned this place.

After an hour the man was made. He appeared to be wearing clothes, but it was appearance only, merely part of the ectoplasmic construct. He was in fact energy, pure energy, and began to dissipate immediately.

But not too fast.

LAURA sat ashamed in the wing chair beside her bed. She had straddled the empty bottle of bourbon and rubbed herself against it to relieve the need, the unrelenting ache. It helped. For a minute, perhaps two, she was free of it, but now it had returned and she sat in the wing chair and cried and considered repeating the act again.

Maybe she could kill herself, she thought. Janice did it. But with pills she'd saved up over months, and Laura didn't have any pills, all she had was bourbon and she would pass out before she could drink herself to death. She had passed out many times before.

There was the gun, her father's gift to her, the .357 Magnum. It was hidden at the bottom of her bag, itself unused these past weeks as she'd had no need for clothes. She found the bag in the closet and shoved her hands in among the clothes, but there was nothing. The gun was gone.

Theo! Goddamn him! He'd deprived her of not only release now, from this terrible, awful need to fornicate, but of any means of self-defense, too.

There were knives in the kitchen! She slammed through her room door and down the hall to the kitchen where she retrieved the biggest, sharpest knife she could find. Yes, this would do, this would do.

It was then she heard the sound. It was a popping sound, and the tinkling of glass, so strange and distant, but approaching. Laura ran to the front door and pushed the window curtain aside. It was slightly foggy out, streetlamps looking a little like Q-tips, but not completely fogged in.

She heard the sound, then saw one Q-tip extinguish, heard it again, saw another lamp go dark. She was actually hearing the previous lamp extinguish, she realized, light traveling far faster than sound, first one, then the other. What could be mak-ing . . . ?

And then she saw him. It was the brute. It was the same brute she had killed months ago. He was back and the ache be-tween her legs told her what it was he was coming for.

"No!" she screamed. In Laura there remained the vestige of the attorney gunslinger, the woman who was proud of her fam-ily and proud of herself. There remained the unconscious, un-spoken knowledge that she was the embodiment of her mother and father's love for one another, that she had been constructed by their desire, one for the other, eyes and smile inherited from this one, hair and build from the other. And here she was, want-ing, needing—dear god, please forgive me!—yearning to couple with this thing, this unspeakable, inhuman thing.

The knife in her hand caught some distant light, for the life-time of a spark glistened with the promise of its capability. She could just run it across her wrists, first this one, then that one, and then she would be dead before he—it—got here.

She placed the blade against her left wrist, but a popping noise distracted her. She looked outside. The creature was closer now, and she understood that as it passed, it stole power from the light. It was saving its energy. Saving it for her. Saving it to . . .

Her gaze returned to the knife. It was going to kill her any-way, right? She was already a dead woman. But what if . . . what if her soul, the electrical energy generated by her body and her mind, were to be captured by this thing after it killed her? Like Lily.

Damn Theo! she thought. Damn him to hell. He'd taken her gun.

But there was the knife. She would need the right moment. Just the right moment. The moment when its lust would distract it.

Laura retreated to her bedroom.

She lay down on her bed. The sheets were clean. Theo had insisted that she get clean sheets every day, even though she refused to bathe. She pulled a crisp pillow behind her head and to one side and slipped the knife beneath it. When its lust brought it to her, she would kill it! She would castrate it, if she could, but if not she could drive the blade deep into its heart, again and again. She recalled the blood splatter on the walls of the other room the night she'd killed it before. It was a real man for a time, with real blood, and a real heart.

The front door opened. She didn't hear it, but felt a cool breeze waft across her sweaty body. She knew he was inside the house and moving toward her. At the same time, at this exact moment, she was going crazy with herself. She needed to rub herself against something again. Needed the release it would bring. She tried to masturbate herself, but she was too wet, the bottle misplaced, and the thing's approach distracted her, so she stopped and tried to control her need.

The sound of footsteps on creaking hardwood floor approached. The door was open this time, not closed, so she saw first his head, then his shoulders, then his torso come into view above her chest. He didn't stop at the threshold but came forward, eyes glowing as they had before. Laura's hand tightened on the knife. She wasn't going down without a fight!

Oh, but the need burned in her. *Dear god why am I like this?* she wondered. She wanted him. She really, really wanted him.

He would satisfy her, take away the ache, release her from the pain and yearning and humiliation of what she'd become. She saw that he was erect. It was a massive thing, bigger than she'd ever seen before, and it excited her.

Her hand tightened on the knife. She could do this! Yes, she could do this! And then run from this place! Run! Because it would kill her anyway, and then that other awful thing would happen, the thing that had happened to Lily and all those others over decades, over centuries of protracted life, passed from one dying monster to another, younger creature, and passed again. Life unending, humanity trapped and debased within the grasp of an alien species. She couldn't stand the thought of that. Anything, almost anything but that!

The creature didn't take her by the shoulders. He didn't try to kiss her. He whispered nothing in her ear, didn't make jokes, or tell her that she was beautiful. No, his hands took her knees and spun her around. For an instant Laura lost the knife, but she found it again quickly.

The thing's hands slid up her thighs and gripped her, forefinger and thumb on each thigh, and pulled her open. That's going to bruise, she thought crazily, as if tomorrow afternoon she'd wear shorts to the grocery store and everyone would know that her lover had split her wide with his hands and made these bruises. Some men made them intentionally, she knew, as if leaving flags on mountaintops. *I was here!* He pressed her wide, as wide as her legs could go.

She smelled him. He didn't smell like a man. He smelled like a fungus, like mushrooms, dank and neutral. His skin was uneven, not a man's skin at all, but a poor imitation. But that thing, it was hard and it was huge and Laura thought, *If he'd just rub it against me, just rub it so I could . . .*

She thrust with the knife then, missing his groin entirely but striking him in the abdomen. He staggered back, surprised that she would attack him. She saw the back of his hand fly toward her. It struck with devastating accuracy across her cheek and she flew up the bed, the knife flung off somewhere in the darkness. She was stunned, lost moments when light reeled in her mind, and then became aware that he was inside her.

She came instantly.

This was not lovemaking. This was not sex in the normal sense of the word. This was something far more primal, without social niceties. She suffered (no other word for it) another orgasm before he came the first time. She struck out at her attacker anyway, slapping him with her open palms, a torrent of movement that had no effect on him at all.

She felt the power of his ejaculation inside her, like a blow. He didn't stop, was not diminished by the explosion of whatever it was he had put inside her, but continued thrusting.

There was a sound after a while, heard distantly and from deep within herself, far from the animal she had become and near Laura Karczek, attorney-at-law, daughter and friend, lover and thinker. She realized it was her own voice screaming, "Yes! Yes! Again! Yes!" She was ashamed. Of herself. Of her species. Of her short, pathetic life, which she knew would shortly come to an end.

The event went on for what seemed like hours. She continued to be excited, released, reexcited, rereleased, again and again until she noticed that he was weakening. She expected him to go soft, but he didn't. He merely collapsed to the floor.

She lay on the bed for some minutes, amazed that the ache was gone, the nagging, unrelenting yearning between her legs and behind her brow. After a time she reached down there to feel what it was he had put into her. It felt like sap, tree sap.

She was not dead.

But he was. He was in fact no longer present, merely a kind

of outline of a man with little hills of substance, white and gelatinous, on the carpet.

Laura fell back. What had just happened? She was changed. She was no longer mad. She didn't think of men or sex constantly anymore, in fact, wondered why she ever had. They were unimportant. They were all her yesterdays.

After a time she stood. The sap ran out of her, but more slowly than semen. She walked into the bathroom and turned on the light. She looked at herself in the mirror and what she saw made her gasp. She was filthy with days, perhaps weeks of accumulated sweat and dirt. Her hair was a hive. Her thighs were bruised, as she'd expected, two finger bruises each leg, but otherwise she seemed fine.

She cleaned herself, then stepped into the shower.

In an hour she'd straightened the room, changed the sheets, cleaned the bathroom, gathered all the towels and other linens and placed them in the hamper in the service closet.

Her clothes were all clean, thanks to Eleanor. She chose panties, a bra, jeans, and a blouse, and her leather bomber jacket, which was her favorite. She borrowed Eleanor's hair dryer to blow her hair out. The perm was weakening but still effective, stringlets of blond hair that bounced when she shook her head. She had long since thrown all her perfumes away, but took some of Eleanor's, which were gifts that went unused due to her allergies.

She called a cab in Morro Bay, convinced him that he would be appropriately compensated for the trip up to Cambria, then took all the money out of the cash box behind the desk. She left a note that said,

> *Thanks for nursing me along through a tough time. I'm okay now. I've seen what was wrong and I'm fixing it. I'm*

stealing this money, six hundred dollars, but be assured I'll pay you back.

Eleanor, forgive me, I was crazy.

Theo, thanks for respecting this cowgirl even when she didn't respect herself.

Love,

Laura

Eleanor never heard from her again.

thirty-seven

THE taxi labored up the steep, craggy hill. It was hardly a road, and it was hardly a taxi. In back, Laura sat uncomfortably with her immense belly sticking out over her bent legs. She wore a full skirt and a blouse big enough to accommodate her enlarged breasts, together with the bomber jacket, which she couldn't close now, but which fit over her shoulders and arms just fine.

She tapped on the driver's shoulder when the taxi reached the crest. "Here," she said.

"Aqui?"

"Yes, aqui." She fumbled through a wad of money, trying to count out the agreed-upon fare, but finally thrust her hands forward and allowed him to take what he wanted.

"There is nothing here, señora," the driver said in heavily accented English.

"I'm going to meet my husband here," she replied in Spanish.

"But, but—" He shook his hands with a gesture that said, *How can this be?* "There is nothing here!"

Laura pushed her body out of the taxi. It was a struggle. Then she gestured for the driver to return to town. "Go! Go! I'll be fine."

The driver shrugged, rolled the bills that made up his fare—twice what they had agreed upon, but what did she know?—and shoved them into his breast pocket. He ground the gears a little placing the taxi into reverse, backed across his own path, and was soon braking to keep the car from rushing grill first down the hillside.

Laura watched him go. When the taxi crossed the next rise and disappeared down into the next valley, she looked around. There was nothing but desolation everywhere around her, but she was confident. Her baby kicked her and she laughed, caressing her stomach. "Quiet," she said soothingly. "Soon."

Laura began to walk up the crest. Somewhere up there was a cave, she had been told, where people caught out in the elements sometimes took refuge. Toward the back of the cave there was a hole, no more than three feet deep. The hole was a good place. She could rest there.

The gestation had been four months. Somehow she knew this, that it wouldn't take long. She'd made plans, borrowed money from Theo, arranged for a passport, dreamed dreams. Then, a week ago she flew to Chile. She arranged to travel far into the interior, where the people were as backward as they used to be in America, innocent, naïve, and lacking technology. In such a place she would thrive, she knew.

The climb was hard, her belly catching the wind and almost toppling her several times. Nightfall was upon her when she found the cave and collapsed at its rim with a grunt. She was hungry, but she had brought food, protein, hot dogs that she ate right from the package. She fell asleep.

Sometime during the night her water broke. This was meaningless except as an indicator, a vestige of the human birth process. The warm water rolling down her legs woke her. Time was growing short. She crawled into the cave, whose mouth was large enough for a tall man to stand in, and then farther back where the ceiling diminished to five feet, then four, then three, and then widened again. She felt the rim of the hole with her fingertips, breaking a polished nail on a sharp crag.

The pain was intense now, the birth moments or at most minutes from occurring. Laura lowered herself into the hole.

The pain became excruciating. She pulled the long dress up and pushed it behind her, not knowing what to expect, but it was not necessary. Her breathing became pronounced, she sucked for air, and blew it out in a method she'd learned with a friend while taking a Lamaze class some years before, but of course that too was unnecessary.

Before dawn she gave birth. She was overjoyed. She laughed with happiness.

She was still alive when the stalk flowered. "Oh my baby," she cooed, dying even then. Behind her, roots were fingering their way through her spine and into the fertile soil below, but that would take days yet to complete.

By week's end the physical part of Laura was dead. Her off-spring ate her, consumed her body for its nutrients. There was very little left of the woman who had once turned men's heads and stood up to judges and other attorneys without fear. The head remained, the skull, yes, but the brain was too great a morsel to leave uneaten. Her feet dangled. Her hands. Their bones.

THEREAFTER there were tales about a gringa ghost, a mysterious woman wearing a World War II–style American bomber jacket, flyer's pants and a silk blouse, with blond hair arrayed in ringlets that bounced as she walked, wandering the hills around the village, particularly when the mists swam the highlands. She was beautiful, they said. Sometimes she said nothing, but sometimes, rarely, she opened her lovely mouth and a terrible wail came from it, the bone-chilling, pitiable lament of a lost soul that rose with the winds of the highlands and was gone, whipped against the stone crags of the high country.

Children who told tales about her saw her later when they were old, and she had not changed.

Later, many said, the old ones joined her.

Sometimes the young ones joined her, too.

Laura was the hive. The hive was Laura.

And many others.

thirty-eight

THE wedding shower was just as bad as I expected. I oohed and ahhed a little at first, but then I poured myself a drink and sat back and studied the women, particularly Eleanor's sisters. I have come to reevaluate them. Oh, they're pretty in a lederhosen kind of way—you know, dimples and ample chests and cute little leather shorts. What I mean is, they're adorable, but would you want to spend more than, say, an hour with them?

Eleanor had grown quiet over the preceding few days, more like her old self, but at the shower she was wonderful, beautiful and radiant. I wanted to walk right over, pick her up off the couch where she was inundated with torn wrapping paper, and plant a wet one right on her lips. Which I did as her sisters and friends tittered and made lousy jokes about our getting a room and maybe Eleanor had better things to do than open presents. Well, we did, but hell—

Billy, Eleanor's dad and now my pal, had been roped into this affair, too, so we retired to the back of the house where he had screened in a kind of porch, no permit required. He had beer in a little refrigerator and offered me one—a light beer, of course—but I declined, knocking back straight whiskeys, a temporary departure from my old habits, it's true.

"Women," he said. "Can't live with 'em—"

"Yeah, yeah," I said.

He sat down on a yellow couch (yellowish green, actually,

and stylish back in the *Starsky and Hutch* days), propped his feet up, and unbuttoned the top of his pants. "The shit we go through," he said.

"Uh-huh."

"You've made all the difference, you know."

"Have I?" Here came the speech, prospective father-in-law to prospective son-in-law.

"You made a woman out of her. I never thought—"

Yeah, one day they're skinny and homely and gawky and the next day they're Cindy Crawford.

"I never thought she would turn out beautiful," Billy said, and that was quite a compliment, too, because not only was she not the product of Billy's loins, she was the daughter of his wife's affair with another man. He had every reason to hate Eleanor, and somehow he'd brought himself to raise her as decently as he could, maybe even love her, even if she was always the ugly duckling of the family.

"Late to bloom," I said. My mind was really on Laura, wondering if maybe Eleanor was right, we shouldn't have left her alone. She had fallen through the net each of us believes separates us from hell, dropped through it like a limb through a woodchipper. Gnawed her up. What had happened to the gunslinger, the tough woman who could face down the devil if she had to?

"You know, we really did think Eleanor was a lesbian," Billy said.

"We're not getting into that, are we?"

"No, no, I got a point," Billy said. "We just didn't communicate with her. She wasn't close to anybody, none of us, face always hidden behind a book. We took her to a doctor when her tits didn't develop—No! Don't laugh! We did! I thought maybe she was a hermaphrodite or something, but the doctor said she was normal physically, some girls just don't got much."

I was about to down my drink and go look for the pisser when he said, "She didn't say a word to me after that, not for six weeks. She didn't talk to anybody."

"You told her the truth before she could take it, Billy," I said, hoping my statement wasn't equally true with him. "She didn't need to know her mother had an affair and she doesn't have the same daddy as the rest of her sisters and brother."

"Yeah, we were pretty dumb to do that."

"It didn't help that her sisters all had tits that could feed half of Asia—"

"Hey!"

"—while she could strip to the waist and pass for a boy."

"She's starting to look—"

"Yeah, she's put on a little weight lately. Look, Billy, I've got to go take a leak."

"Oh, sure, right."

"You did the best you could. Who can do better than that?"

"You did," Billy said as I paused at the door to hear his final remark. "You opened her up. You made her feel confident. You're a better-looking man than any of her sisters ever dated. You've got more character, too, more weight. I mean, she must have had something all along and we never saw it."

"That's the way it is, sometimes," I said. "Most things in life are hidden."

THE wedding was, well, pretty. There were a lot of flowers I can't name and Eleanor and her sisters decorated Lily's to the nines. I had Tom be my best man because he was available and all the guys I used to know still lived in LA, two hundred and fifty miles south of Cambria, our home now.

Tom and I had become friendly again. I guess a grant of ten million dollars will do that. He said he was on to another situation, maybe another plant in the area. There was no way to track them, no way to identify them from the air, he said, so he was using local legends to help identify likely spots. He got this idea from Eleanor, who mentioned that it was generally believed by people in Cambria that Monroe House was evil, bad, a place to avoid if possible. Tom had found a place with a similar reputation south of town, an old farm that kept turning over to new owners every few years. He obtained the rights to dig, and if he found a plant, he would be able to take samples, flash freeze them to prevent precipitous decay, and then maybe come up with a way to track them from the air.

"How many you figure there are?" I asked him.

"They're rare, probably, but hell, how would we know? Ghost legends are everywhere, physical manifestations less common but not exactly rare either. But it's human nature to make these things up—ooh, ooh, spooky, you know?—so the answer to your question is, there could be tens of thousands of them, millions, billions—"

"Whoa, I don't think I'll be able to fund an operation that big," I told him.

"Doesn't matter, Theo, if I can document a species that lives parasitically off the human race, even after death, I'll have more funding than I can deal with. And the Nobel Prize!"

Tom started to dig at the farm as Eleanor and I left on our honeymoon.

WE spent a week in Kauai, on an isolated beach where we ran naked in the surf and Eleanor asked me to father her baby. She wanted to have a family, and while I never really saw the purpose of children—they're ornamental, I suppose, but progressively expensive—I said sure. She stopped taking her birth control pills and made demands of me that reminded me of our first days and weeks together. We made love in the sand, in the surf, here, there, everywhere. I'd never seen her so happy.

We went swimming one moonlit night, she a lean, lithe beautiful thing whose running gait was the leap of a gazelle, me a wounded, limping lion trying to catch her from behind. But in the ocean we were one, just two human beings, frail, yes, as momentary as a lit match within the scheme of time, but there we made the magic. Every ancestor I had ever had, from the first vertebrate to crawl from the ocean onto land to my dear sweet mother—whose grave I've only visited once but whose love will ever be a part of me—met every ancestor of hers. She conceived a hundred yards from shore, her legs and arms wrapped around me. "Yes, Theo!" she gasped when we were done, laying her head on my shoulder. "I conceived! We've made a child!" Some women know these things. Don't ask me how. We floated on the waves, bobbing like two corks tossed into the sea, with destiny our companion.

I DIDN'T tell Eleanor about Laura's call. She sounded sane for the first time since the séance. But she needed money to get on her feet. I wired her twenty thousand dollars and told her to keep it as a get-well present. She laughed and told me she was well, but thanks for the sentiment.

By the time we returned to Lily's, Tom had found the second plant beneath the farmhouse. He gathered enough data to prove that it was a new species, but proving the rest to a skeptical scientific community was going to take time. In the interim I insisted that he kill it, which he did.

There are times when I think I see Lily here at the bed-and-breakfast, and now restaurant, that bears her name. In a doorway. Walking away. Turning down a hall. I know it's my imagination.

Lily's dead.

Everywhere but in my heart.

ML

6/0